Beautifully DECEIVED

Thomas Jewell

Beautifully Deceived
by Thomas Jewell

For information, contact
BDI Publishers, Atlanta, Georgia
bdipublishers@gmail.com

Layout Design: Tudor Maier
BDI Publishers

Atlanta, Georgia

ISBN: 978-0-9836709-5-7

Preface

Author Thomas Jewell, has given us a compelling story that is sexy and spiritual. He takes us on a wild ride filled with love, sex, family, disgrace, and betrayal. We follow the life of DJ Murphy II, his relationship and marriage, his five kids, and the meteoric rise in his business and career. But someone is lurking in the envious shadows, eagerly willing to orchestrate DJ's downfall. DJ survives a dark valley of deception as a spiritual warrior, and it is his faith that ultimately leads to his redemption.

Knock, Knock!

The most annoying sound on the bathroom door was for a dad with five kids trying to get some time in the bathroom before one of the kids needed to come in. It was especially bad for me because I had a wife and four daughters with only one bathroom. You can't just tell your daughters to pee outside!

Knock Knock!

I would usually ignore the first few knocks. I would think, *Do you need a hair tie? That can wait until I'm done in here, or do you need to use the restroom?*

They knew I liked my privacy in the bathroom. Every man I know thinks of the bathroom as a place to clean up and unwind. In general, parenthood is not as easy on a father's patience as a mother's. After the first few knocks, the kids usually skedaddled unless it was urgent. Kids have no patience, so unless they had to pee, and say, "DAD, I HAVE TO GO REALLY BAD!" Then they would continue being a kid running around doing kid stuff.

My wife, May, and I didn't allow family time for TV or electronics. We raised our kids the old-fashioned way. We'd often say, "Go outside and play!" Or "Go be a kid!" We (May and I) refused to have our kids sitting inside staring at a screen all day and night. We considered that the lazy way out of real parenting.

It is 2017; it seems so many years ago now since I met May. We had our 5th and what would be our last child. We had three girls, then a boy, then one more girl. Poor fella! I tried for all boys, my son! Sorry! I always imagined having all boys and one girl. I didn't grow up with sisters or any type of Barbie doll environment. It was all boy stuff for me. I guess I broke too many girls' hearts in my teenage years, so I probably deserved four girls! I needed to learn one way or another how to be a tender-hearted man. These girls did it! Starting in 2008, we had a kid every two years. Yep, you read that right! Every two years, over a span of eight years, we had five children! Were May and I crazy? Yep! Crazy in love to say the least, and boy, do I have a story for you!

Knock, Knock!

I was exhausted this particular morning. The second knock was irritating! I ignored it again, thinking,

Please just go be a kid and come back later to bother dad.

Knock, Knock!

A third knock. Only this time, it was our babysitter, Raven. Raven had a deep voice, like a man. To be honest, I couldn't stand her voice. She started babysitting for us a little over a year ago at age fourteen. She was now fifteen, turning sixteen in a few months. She did an excellent job with the kids. Lousy with household duties. Never folded laundry. Rarely did dishes. I don't believe I ever saw her sweep the floors. You get the picture, great with kids, terrible with everything else. May and I didn't care much about the household chores. We wanted our kids to be safe and with someone they liked. We would take care of the rest. Raven started just on the weekend so that we could get date nights in. Surprisingly,

Raven would act like she didn't want to leave. I would think, *Haven't you had enough of these kids yet?*

All our babysitters before her would jump up and be ready to go with a look of, *GET ME OUT OF HERE!*

Not Raven; she would sit and chill even after we got back. That always threw me off. For the longest time, I just thought she loved our kids. That may have been true, but that was only part of the reason she wanted to stick around.

7

NICE TO MEET YOU

I am Durand Joseph Murphy II. People call me *D.J.*. My dad, Durand, named me after himself. Everyone called him Durand, but he wanted me to have my unique moniker. He had always wanted to name his first-born son after himself. My mom agreed if everyone called me *D.J.* My mother, Lucy Murphy, insisted on this! She would often correct people and say, "D.J.!, not Durand. His father is Durand!"

I always loved it! D.J. was different from everyone else and unique. It sounded cool too! My wife, May, liked it too. She especially liked the last name, Murphy. It flowed with her name.

May Maria Murphy! May loved the triple M sound. After I asked her to marry me in 2008, I would sometimes hear her whisper to herself, "May Maria Murphy," And then she would get the biggest smile. May and I were the definition of *crazy in love*. After our first kiss, we both knew, *This is the one!*

Any couple having five children within eight years in today's world is the definition of crazy. We also had the love part, to say the least! If it is possible to love someone *too much*, we did. When you fall so madly in love, it is a challenge to stay sexually abstinent. If not impossible.

May and I started the relationship by putting the cart before the horse. Our oldest, Demi, came a little early. My sperm sure did love her eggs. If I touched May, she would become pregnant. And I touched her as often as she would let me! Our children at this time were ages nine, seven, six, three, and one. Four girls and one boy. Oldest to youngest... Demi Grace, Scarlette Blake, Camryn Kate, Abraham William, and Blaire Anna. Our children are all amazing kiddos with tons of personality, and all are healthy. May and I have been very blessed. They are all beautiful inside and out. There is a lot of emotion running through our home with the four girls and May.

Woo wee, there is a lot! Abraham and I are outnumbered! Before Abraham arrived, I would tell May, "We are not stopping until we have a boy!"

After three girls, I remember praying, "God, please give me a son; he can even look just like his mommy. I just need a boy!"

Our boy came, and I thought for sure he was going to be a little turd to his three older sisters. However, Abraham was born a naturally sweet boy. He is kind to everyone. They all have completely different personalities. It is amazing how different our kids all turned out, coming from the same mom and dad.

GROCERY STORE

We met one day when May worked at a grocery store as a cashier. I was a rookie career firefighter. Each day the veterans would make a grocery list.

They would send me all over to get groceries for the

day. One day in 2008, I was sent to a grocery store on the opposite side of town. I'm quite sure they would do this just to piss off a rookie. This store was not the cheapest; it made no sense to drive across town. Anything vets could do to mess with a rookie, they would do. I got our grocery shopping done and started heading to the checkout. As I approached the checkout, I saw the most beautiful girl my eyes had ever seen. I'm a sucker for long dark hair and big brown eyes, but this girl was so much more than that. I felt my heart start to beat fast, and that rarely happened to me. I got a little closer, and she was stunning; big, pretty smile. long dark hair and big brown Mexican-looking eyes that seemed to glisten. You can guess which line I chose that day!

As I got next in line, I noticed she was not shying away from looking back at me. It was almost like she knew me. I was hoping she didn't know me too well. I had a reputation for being a player. I honestly was not a player; I just liked women and had not met *the one* yet. You could say I broke a lot of hearts before May. I was not a cheater; I would just date and dump. I always knew that when I met *the one*, I would never look at other females, even sideways, again. You could say I was fastidious and refused to settle for the next best. Petty things with women in the past would bother me. I had been engaged a few years before meeting May and wouldn't repeat that mistake.

An old wise man once told me, "D.J., let me tell you something. My only advice is do not settle!"

It stuck with me. I was not going to settle! On my wedding day, there would be no regrets.

It was now my turn in line, and I was face-to-face with this girl. Her beauty blew me away. I was speechless. Though I was known as a *player*, I was always bashful when I met a girl I was attracted to. This situation was no exception. I was standing face-to-face with the most beautiful female I had ever seen. She smiled and said, "Are you D.J. Murphy?"

Oh no! She knows me, I thought, still hoping she didn't know me too well. I had to take this girl on a date!

I could be something of a smart-ass. Almost every firefighter you ever meet has this trait. I'm unsure if I was a smart ass before the fire department. If I were, that personality characteristic would get much worse around all those guys. I was standing in line in full firefighter uniform, with my name badge on my shirt, *D.J. Murphy.* When she asked who I was, I pointed at my name on my shirt like a jackass and said, "Yes, I am."

I responded to her, "What's your name?"

She replied in the most confident and sweetest voice, "May Williams!"

Oh, buddy! I thought. This woman comes with a high price tag. We lived in a small town. Everyone knew everyone. I knew her family, and I asked, "Louis Williams's daughter?"

Louis was quite possibly the best-known businessperson in our town. I considered him an architect, but he had his hands on everything---real estate, commercial buildings, design, and many other things that made his money. She responded, "No, that's my uncle; he is like a dad to me, though!"

Oh great, I thought. I was staring at the most stunning female I have ever seen; I would love to ask her on a date, and she's a Williams daughter. I thought, *Do I even make enough money for this type of girl?*

She looked younger than me. I asked, "How do you know me?"

She replied, "Everyone knows you; you are D.J. Murphy. We went to school together. I was a freshman when you were a senior."

May seemed mesmerized that I was standing in front of her in a firefighter uniform. She also had to sense I was attracted to her.

Here we were, staring at each other like we had met our soulmate. Meanwhile, nothing was getting done with my groceries. I looked behind in line, and another person was watching us with a look saying, "Come on, you two love birds, I have groceries too!"

May saw me look behind in line, and she realized she had not started scanning any of my groceries.

She looked back at me again and smiled so big before scanning my items. My heart was beating very fast. Both of our faces were flushed. As she started scanning items, I started counting and organizing the cash.

Each morning all ten of the firefighters would pitch in nine dollars each. Nine dollars times ten guys is ninety dollars, which is what I had. However, it was in ones, fives, tens, and a couple of twenties. I probably had fifteen or more one-dollar bills. Most of the time, it was easy for a cashier. That is their job. Not for May. She was nervous around me and embarrassed because she had asked my name. I would find out later math was not her best subject.

SHORTCHANGE

She finished scanning the items. The total came to eighty or so dollars total. I was good at math.

Before she handed me the money back, I knew exactly what the change should be. May gave me the wrong amount, short a few dollars. I handed her all the money back and said, "Sorry, but this is not the correct change."

She grabbed the money, now in complete embarrassment. She counted it, or at least tried. She looked at me and asked, "How much do I owe you?"

I said, "You are four dollars short."

Any cashier would have double-checked, re-counted, and given the correct change. Not May. She didn't even care. She was standing in front of a man who before now was only a dream date. May still had that feeling of a freshman staring at a senior in high school. She grabbed four dollars extra, added it to the change I had already handed back and said, "Here you go!"

The butterflies in her stomach were overwhelming her judgment. Before walking away, I couldn't help but think again how gorgeous this girl was, and now how cute her personality was. We both gazed into each other's eyes while I grabbed all the bags of groceries. Stupid me, I walked out of the store and never asked her out. My bashfulness was on full display as well. As I walked out of the first sliding doors, I turned around and looked at her one last time. She didn't see me doing that. She was helping the next customer in line. I thought, *This wouldn't be my last conversation with May Williams.*

CYRA

At this stage in my life, I was convinced that I was going to meet the woman I would marry. Years prior, I was in a relationship for almost three years with a girl named Cyra. Cyra and I spent all our time together with other people. Cyra's stepdad and mom were the ideal in-laws. Her stepdad and I became close. So close that I ended up asking him for his daughter's hand in marriage-- not knowing I was doing it for all the wrong reasons. Cyra was in college to be a schoolteacher. She was great with kids. Cyra was beautiful as well. It was not until she and I moved in together and got away from group settings that I realized she had odd personality traits I couldn't live with for the rest of my life. One of the hardest things I ever had to do was break off that engagement. Her parents were devastated. Cyra was heartbroken, but she saw it coming. Cyra would have clothes lying all over the house in piles yet would need to adjust the salt and pepper shakers so the letters were facing one another precisely. It drove me crazy, and she knew it. The day I told her stepdad that I was breaking off the engagement, we cried, we knew that meant he and I wouldn't be together every day anymore.

I was in college at the time studying business management. I never felt sure that this was my calling as a career. As a kid and into adulthood, I had targeted one of two careers--pilot or priest. However, I always wanted kids, so the priest idea was not as strong as wanting to become a pilot someday. At my first meeting with a college counselor, she asked, "What would you like to study?"

I said, "I want to become a pilot and go to aviation school." The counselor next asked, "How is your eyesight?"

I responded, "My eyesight is good, but I'm color blind"

This college counselor didn't know that her next words would crush my dreams. She said, "I'm sorry, you need to pick another career. Pilots can't be color blind."

LAY DIRECTOR

After I broke off this engagement, I felt terrible for everyone involved. I had made the Dean's list in college studying business management, but it still didn't feel like my path in life. I told myself after crushing Cyra's entire family, I would practice sexual abstinence for one year and not date anyone. That same month a few good churchmen hit me up about attending a retreat weekend at the Catholic church. They said, "D.J., you have to come!"

I didn't hesitate. Halfway through the retreat weekend, I had 20 other men praying over me. It felt like they wanted me to enroll in Seminarian school to become a priest. I didn't take this route. Instead, I was nominated to become the Lay Director. The Lay Director led a group of men each week until the next retreat weekend. I agreed to this role. Each week I would organize a meeting on Sundays before or after church. We would read scripture and discuss numerous other topics. I told myself that by the end of the year, I would know if I wanted to become a priest. The year was concluding. We scheduled the next retreat weekend for another group of men. By the time the retreat was over, I had made up my mind

-- I wanted kids. I had also survived a full year of no dating and no sex from 22-23. Shortly after this year ended, I started to feel like I was about to meet my future wife. No less than a month later, I was hired into the fire department, withdrew from college, and now stood in a grocery store line staring at this amazing girl! Words were repeating in my mind after meeting May, *She is the one!*

I was fresh from leading an excellent group of men for a year. I had the feeling I was about to meet my future wife. And now I had just met this girl I wanted to make mine. At this time in my life, I worked a lot on my days off from the fire department. I never got a chance to return to the grocery store when I thought she would be working while I was off shift. However, when I was on shift, it didn't matter what grocery store the veterans told me to go to. I was going to where I met May. I would secretly drive across town, way out of the way, hoping to see this girl again. But I never saw her. It was towards the end of the summer of 2007. I assumed she was a college student. By the end of August, I gave up trying to find this girl named May.

THE MESSAGE

September was approaching. I remember the day like it was yesterday. I reported to the downtown fire station and was directed to go to Station 9 because a guy there had called in sick. This fire station was like a day off. Station 9 was slow, relaxing, and fun. Guys would play cards and cut up the entire day. I was the rookie and was messed with constantly, but I loved it. I vividly remember all the guys shacking up to take their afternoon naps after lunch. This routine is standard at any fire station--especially the stations where guys had 20-plus years or more in the department. These fire stations didn't have many calls during the day. Station 9 was in what firefighters call a *slow district*. Getting a permanent position at these stations usually requires 20-plus years of seniority.

I was still a "rookie bitch", as they would say. So, I didn't dare take a nap in bed. I was bored when everyone else shacked up. I entered the computer lounge and thought, *I'll check out my Facebook.*

At that time, Facebook still required a college email to register. I was not a huge fan of the platform. I only checked my account every few weeks. But when I eventually went online, there was a message from that pretty girl named May that I've never forgotten, "Hey D.J.! It's May! It was nice to meet you! If you ever come through my line again at the grocery store, I will count your change correctly!"

She had sent this message weeks before I saw it. I was so pissed I didn't check my Facebook earlier. My heart started beating so fast I couldn't even type correctly. I can't remember the exact words in my reply, but I also made sure she knew I was highly interested in her. I had never been this excited to take a girl on a date, ever in my life. Little did I know that day wouldn't come for months.

She soon responded...

"Hey, DJ! So nice to hear from you. I was wondering if I would ever get a reply! I'm so sorry I didn't give you the correct change at the grocery store. I was hoping for another chance, but I don't think we will have that opportunity. I leave to study abroad in Germany for college soon. I only work one more day before I leave. I look forward to hearing from you again!"

My heart sank. Here I was never so excited to take a girl on a date, and she was leaving for Germany?! I had so many questions now. I replied, "Germany?! What field are you studying in college? What made you decide to go to Germany? What semester are you in? How old are you?"

I had so many questions.

Neither of us knew yet, but the relationship had begun. May informed me she was studying for her Bachelor of Science in nursing. She loved helping people. She was studying abroad to help pad her resume for after graduation. She was nineteen years old. She went on to say that studying abroad was only one semester and that she would be back in the States at the end of the semester. After answering me, she asked, "Maybe we could see each other after I get back?"

At this point, I knew this girl was the one. I don't know how I knew, but I knew. Something just told me I was someday going to marry her. That said, I immediately tested a theory. I have always been an upfront, blunt, and honest person. So, I asked her key questions that would be decisive in pursuing a meaningful relationship with this amazing woman. She felt like a dream. I had to test my theory. When she received my second set of questions, she probably thought I was crazy! I didn't care. I dove right in! So how many kids do you want because I want six or seven? What religion are you? I was raised cradle Catholic, and religion is critical for me. I continued these litmus test questions. I knew this girl was special. I knew I would fall for her so fast if her responses showed she was similar-minded. I already had butterflies in my stomach and hummingbirds in my head when I thought of this girl named May for months before this Facebook message. I had never experienced a feeling like this before.

She responded immediately and told me she wanted seven kids. Her grandmother had seven kids, and she always wanted to have a lot of kids. That was the reason I felt the same way. My grandmother had six kids. Do you know how rare it is to find someone in today's world who wants so many kids? This response alone blew my mind. She went on to say she was baptized in the Catholic Church as a baby, but her mom started taking them to a Protestant church in her early teens because they loved to praise and worship and so on. She said she was not against raising a family in the Catholic Church. All her answers lined up perfectly. This girl could be the one!

Our conversations continued for a few weeks. We never met before she left for Germany.

However, before leaving, she was falling for me as much as I was falling for her. She asked in a message, "Have you ever used Skype before? If we both get Skype, we can talk internationally while I am gone!"

That message was when I knew, *May Williams feels as strongly about me as I do her.*

She wanted to communicate with me while she was in a whole other country. Before we knew it, she was studying abroad, and we were Skyping twice every single day. Germany was a seven-hour time difference. We both adjusted our schedules to Skype twice a day. We were both so hyper-focused on each other that it was a marriage in the making. We talked about everything--our family, friends, childhood, goals in life, etc. You name it, we talked about it. Our friendship was turning into a relationship. It was the highlight of both our days, hearing each other's voices, hearing everything about each other. We had to start coming up with new topics every day because, after about a month, it felt like we knew everything about each other. And the best part? We agreed on almost everything.

EXCLUSIVE

One night, I was at the downtown fire station. We had finished dinner, and each night, we would go down to wash all the fire trucks after everyone was done eating. I was the rookie still, so I would be the last to get my plate of food. I had to be the first to get done eating. That way, I could start washing the dishes before anyone else finished their food. Once I finished dishes, I would slide down the pole and get buckets of soap ready to begin washing the trucks. While May was in Germany, I would go as fast as I could through all my station duties/chores so I could finish before she called me. I was ecstatic to speak to May. She was my first thought when I woke up, my last thought when I fell asleep, and all times in between. I think she would say the same thing. We were both starting to feel that word love.

I finished all my station duties that same night. I went so fast that I had water all over my shirt. I was soaked just trying to get it done in time before she woke up and called. May had said she was going to Skype at 9:00 p.m. my time. I finished all my duties right before 9:00. My phone rang. If you have ever used Skype before, the ringtone is different than any other ringtone. That sound, to this day, still fills my stomach with butterflies and my heart with joy. I rarely hear it nowadays with all the other ways people can video call, but when I do, it is like the sound of heaven. I answered the Skype call to hear the voice of an angel. "Hey, sweetie! Watcha doing?"

I said, "Good morning, baby. How is your day going?" She would always fill me in about her day. It uplifted my spirit to hear her and everything she was doing in Germany. We talked for about 10 minutes, and she said, "Hey, I have a question, and I don't want you to take it the wrong way." There was nothing she could say at this point that I would take the wrong way.

She said, "Before I say this, I just want to tell you that I have feelings for you that I have never experienced in a relationship. I'm in Germany and should be having the time of my life, and all I can think

about is calling you. There was a pause. "Are you ready?" She said.

At this point, I was a little nervous. I thought, *Please don't ask me something about a girl in the past or something irrelevant.*

I responded, "Yes! I'm ready!"

The words she was about to say would stick with me forever! She continued and said, "Okay! Here it goes! Are we exclusive?"

Long pause on my end. I needed to process the word exclusive. I felt like an idiot. It was a long day; I was tired, and for whatever reason, the word exclusive was throwing me for a loop. *Exclude?* I thought in my mind. *Why would she want to exclude herself from me?*

My pause was so long. She was anxiously waiting to hear my response. I said, "What do you mean?" I still, to this day, I'm not sure why I didn't understand exactly what she meant. She said, "Exclusive!

You know! Like, we are not dating or talking to anyone else?"

Those words, still to this day, are the most heart-filling words any female has ever said to me. I was filled with bliss. Without hesitation, I responded, "YES! I would love to be exclusive with you!

"Do you want to be exclusive with me?" I could tell she was still pondering my initial pause.

"Are you sure?" She asked. I replied quickly, I could tell I had messed everything up by not responding quickly enough the first time.

"Yes! I'm sure! I'm sorry that I didn't understand the question initially."

She was still a little hesitant. May could have been thinking I had side chicks. Or that I was dating other women behind her back. I was not. The entire time she was in Germany, my life was all about this girl in another country. At this time, I was already exclusive. After I explained that I had already committed myself to her, she said, "Sooo yes?"

I replied, "Yes, May! Can I tell you something?"

"Please do because your initial pause has me nervous!" She replied in an almost sad voice. I continued, "Not only do I want to be exclusive with you. I can't wait to look you in the eyes, kiss you, hold your hand, and hug you!"

May said in reply, something I have now heard her say a million times, "Me too, baby!"

From this point on, we were exclusive! *Exclusively in Love!* I thought this would last forever! We hung up, and I walked outside. The biggest shooting star flew across the sky! I looked up to the heavens and said, "God, thank you for this girl named May! I know she is the one!"

Time passed. We Skyped twice a day every single day. The conversations became personal after we agreed we were exclusive. We started talking about our childhood and how we both came from broken homes with divorced parents. We discussed how we never wanted to put our children through a divorce. May talked about how her dad was an alcoholic and would disappear for days, if not weeks.

Sometimes he would show up after a few days. Other times, they would go looking for him. Her dad had gone to rehab multiple times for alcoholism, but he never quit. Her dad's alcoholism affected her deeply. She made me promise I would never become an alcoholic. I promised her without worry. My family struggled with alcohol as well. It caused family fights during holidays. It was a major cause of my own parents' divorce. Becoming an alcoholic was the last concern I had about myself. I was more worried about my temper that I developed in early childhood. To me, May was so perfect at this time I thought she would be my saving grace in keeping me calm. Little did I know we both had short fuses that had yet to surface through Skype. Our childhood memories were both scarred. The two causes were alcoholism and divorce.

FIRST KISS

The time was approaching for her to come home back home. Both of us were so excited we couldn't stand it. Imagine never going on a first date, never having a first kiss, never holding hands, never physically touching someone, and yet you were falling madly in love. We knew everything about our pasts. And everything we wanted for our future: the number of kids we wanted; what religion to raise our children; even how we wanted our first kiss to be. Anything we thought of, we talked about.

Emotional attachment is more impactful than physical attachment. Physical attachment is of the flesh. Emotional attachment is from the heart. The key to any marriage is keeping yourself physically and emotionally attached, no matter what! In any marriage, if you betray your spouse by becoming emotionally or physically attached to someone of the opposite sex, marriages crumble! May and I were emotionally attached. We had yet to experience physical attachment. However, we both knew that if our emotional attachment was that strong, there was a good chance our physical attachment would be just as powerful! I think we both would have been crushed if the physical part of our relationship was not everything we had expected. Good news for us! It was!

The day had finally come! May was on her way home. She gave me details of her flight schedule. She mentioned times, layovers, etc. She wanted to make sure I understood time changes and jetlag.

She promised as soon as she got home that coming to see me was her number one priority. She landed safely. It was late evening. She went home to visit her family first after they picked her up from the airport. Within an hour, she informed her stepdad and mom that she was going to go meet this guy. Can you imagine your daughter being gone for months, and shortly after getting home, she is on her way to meet a guy they had never met? I can only imagine the look on her parents' faces. They had to say, "Wait a minute? You just got home after months of studying abroad, and you are going to see a boy?"

They tried to stop her, but nothing was going to stop her from seeing the man she had spent all her spare time speaking with for the last three months. It wouldn't take me long to learn that no one could tell May 'no' to anything. If May wanted to do something or buy something, she was going to do it. She left the house and called me. "Hi baby, I'm on my way!"

I was so nervous. The way she said the word *baby* always got to me. I loved it!

I lived out in the country. A little farmhouse. The crazy part was I lived on the same road as her parents, only another four miles out farther into the country. This farmhouse, built in 1896, was my second house. As a kid, I always knew I wanted to live in the country someday. The house was nothing special, but it was in the country. It sat on a busy state highway. It was a white farmhouse, a story and a half, sitting close to the road. The house had an acre of land and had been added onto multiple times. It was all divided up: a one-car attached garage and a two-car detached garage, a gravel driveway with a huge tree sitting in the middle of the driveway. All the property was back behind the house. I was spending all my spare time and money slowly remodeling the property. I started on the land. I cleared out trees, planted fresh seed for the grass, cleaned out the old garages, replaced all the windows in the house, etc. The place was exactly what I wanted at the time, giving me privacy in a country setting. An old white farmhouse nestled in the country, with a cute little porch on the side of the driveway. The house needed a lot of work, and I was going to teach myself how to do it all on my own. I had little experience with construction; however, I knew this house would motivate me to learn so much more. This house would be where May and my first memories would begin.

May was on her way! I had a pair of brown Jesus sandals that had a strap going across the top. I found out later she didn't like those sandals. She later said, "I almost canceled the entire relationship because of those sandals!"

They were somewhat in style, though! Cut-off T-shirts were also the thing back then, and I was wearing that type of shirt. I had been lifting weights to buff up for months before she got home. I had a pair of cargo khaki shorts on and again, 'ugly Jesus sandals'. My clothing selection and sandals were awful. Good thing she was already addicted to me, so it didn't matter. She got out of the car, and I was standing on the front porch. I had never been this nervous before in my life. I was blind to all my surroundings. All I could see was this beautiful woman walking towards me. I'm still not sure why I didn't go meet her at her car. All I can think of is I was so nervous that I was paralyzed. She walked toward me. We both had to have a million thoughts going through our minds. Are we going to kiss? Are we going to hug? How are we going to say hi? The thoughts raced. She had on this cute summer dress. May was conscious of her weight and felt like that dress hid her belly. I couldn't have cared less. The dress was beautiful. It was flowing with the wind. She had on flip-flops. Her hair was long and down past her shoulders. May didn't have large breasts. I could tell she had no bra on.

I was never a big-boob kind of guy, but I liked all the other curves. Small boobs were my preference. No bra with that dress still appeared modest. This was my first time seeing her knowing how emotionally attached we were. I glanced at everything. Her feet and hands were sexy. The cheeks of her face were adorable. Her teeth were big and beautiful. Her nose and ears were so cute. And best of all, her thighs and calves were exactly what I liked. I already knew what her butt looked like from the pictures we exchanged back and forth. I'm a butt guy; I knew her butt was big and curvy. Every man has preferences in their taste in women. May looked like she was made for me. In my mind, she was perfect!

She approached, walking across the gravel driveway with a fond smile on her face. She was jet-lagged, yet she was never this excited to meet anyone in her entire life. We had both waited for this moment for so long. May walked up a couple of concrete steps, and now our eyes were locked on each other. It was our second moment of love at first sight. Most people get this experience once, if ever.

May and I got this moment twice due to the gap in time. Initially, we said nothing. That only lasted a few seconds, though it felt like minutes. It was like we were living in a movie. Only this movie was real. The moment had finally come. We knew everything about each other. We were both filled with so much happiness--we both were holding back tears of joy. I gently touched her cheeks with both hands. And said, "Can I kiss you?"

She smiled and shook her head yes without saying a word. As slowly as you can imagine, my face approached her face. We stared into each other's eyes until that very last moment before our lips touched. There was no awkwardness. It was the perfect kiss. It was like heaven came down and joined our lips to synchronize perfectly. We kissed, just lips only for ten or so seconds. I could smell her skin and

feel her warmth. The clouds separated, and the sun shined on us. The birds began chirping. Nothing had ever felt this perfect in my life. Our lips opened, and our tongues began to gently massage each other. I felt the wetness of the bottom of her tongue and the heat of the top of her tongue. Then our lips separated perfectly at the same time, ever so slowly. We pulled our heads back slowly. Her eyes were big, deep brown, radiating. Her entire face was glowing. She was looking up at me, I was looking down at her. We both knew. This is my forever person. I then wanted to hold her. So softly, I took hold of the back of her head. I brought her close to my heart. I smelled her hair and felt her body. Our bodies fit perfectly together. We held each other holding very tightly. We had waited for what felt like forever for this moment. I wanted to kiss her again. So softly, I pulled away. We connected eyes and began kissing again. This time we kissed for minutes. We had met our soul mates; this was real.

FIRST DATE

I pulled back, anxious to see if she needed anything. I said, "Are you hungry? Have you eaten?"

Some of my first words were about wanting to take care of her in any way possible. She said, "I'm so tired from the flights, but I could eat something. "

It was 8:30 p.m. She said, "I want something simple and quick; I'm too tired to sit down for anything fancy."

There was no way I was going to take her to a fast-food restaurant for our first date. The closest restaurant, not fast food, was a Chinese Restaurant. I said, "Do you like Chinese?"

She said, "Sure, anything will be fine at this moment."

We hopped in my Black Ford F150 and went to eat Chinese. Neither of us ate much. We just stared at each other with very few words. It was not the typical date. We had already been talking nonstop for months. We already knew everything about each other. We both said, "What?" multiple times. You can imagine sitting next to someone for the first time, a first date that was so far removed from a typical first date. We had that feeling of "Is this real?" Over and over! It was real! We were together! And it felt like nothing in this world would ever separate us.

As we drove home, I asked her, "Where are you going to stay tonight?"

The craziest question to ask on a first date. Without hesitation, she said, "I want to stay with you, but I'm not sure what my parents are going to say about all this."

I reassured her that I was completely okay with her staying at her parents' house but that I, of course, wanted her to stay with me. I would find out later that when May had her mind made up on something, no one could change her mind except herself. Though I thought there was no way she would be coming to stay with me on the first night, I was wrong. We waited too long for this day. Our hearts couldn't take being separated. That hour or so she was gone felt so long. I wanted to kiss her again. She called a little over an hour later. She broke the news to her parents that she was leaving the house and heading over to stay the night with some guy they had never met. It was an intense argument; I could tell by her tone. Her parents had to be so pissed. May didn't care. I was her man. I was her soul mate. I was her protector. She was going to sleep next to me for the rest of her life if she had it her way. Before she got back to the house, she said, "Something in my heart tells me you are worth it."

SATISFACTION

She got back to my house, overly exhausted. It was late, She said, "Can we go to bed?"

I said absolutely. I was a bachelor. I had a mattress on the floor in the bedroom on the second floor of the house. May was not used to seeing anything other than fancy living. Her family had money; she had never slept on a mattress on the floor. We went upstairs. Lying next to each other, we started making out. I was kissing her body; my big hands were massaging every inch of her skin. We both knew we had to refrain from having sex, especially on the first night. We knew it was inevitable, but this was the right thing to do that night.

I started kissing her skin. Her cheek, down her neck. She leaned up and took her dress off. I noticed May's only flaw on her entire body: she had inverted nipples. I was not bothered one bit by her breasts. I was surprised she even took her dress off. I knew that was her expressing how comfortable she already felt with me. As we continued making out, my hand was touching her entire body. I slowly massaged her breasts and down her belly. I ran my hand down her leg to her calf. I grabbed her feet and started to massage them. She let out a gasp. This was when I knew she loved her feet to be massaged. She grabbed my hand and placed it in over her underwear and simultaneously gripped my erection. When she grabbed me, she said softly, "Mmmmh, okay."

She must have been happy with her first touch. I started massaging her midsection. All around, including her inner thighs. Our bodies were heating up. Our mouths were locked again. She started sucking my neck. May wanted to leave her mark on me, and she did. I was now her property, and she wanted everyone to know at the fire station. No way was any other woman at a grocery store going to steal her man. I worked my hand back up to her belly and up to her breasts. I massaged them both. She arched her back, and this was my signal. I worked my hand back down, slowly. I got to her underwear and grasped her vagina. She wanted me as much as I wanted her. She knew if I continued, she wouldn't be able to stop herself. She grabbed my hand and said, "Not yet."

She sat up and slowly pushed my body down. She straddled me. No woman had ever felt this good on top of me. She started kissing my neck. Licking my body. Her head was slowly working her way down, kissing every inch she could. She kept her hands up high. She rubbed my chest. Stroked her hands across my shoulders. Her hands went down to my biceps. She squeezed my biceps and let out another satisfying noise. I had never been this erect. She continued until her face was below my mid-section and in between my legs. She stripped my briefs off. She was left-handed and so grabbed me with that hand while her face was hovering over the top of my manhood. It was her first look at what had been wandering through her imagination for months. She looked up and smiled with a sense of no regret.

Her tongue touched me. She licked from the bottom up to the top and looked up again with her eyes gazing into mine. She seemed surprised and started sucking. I arched my back. I could feel my spine tingling up to my brain. May had met her forever man, and she was going to take care of his needs the very first night together. Initially, she sucked gently as she was taking in her self-enjoyment. After a few minutes, her lips suctioned to the top, and she went down farther. The sound of pleasure as her lips came back up and disconnected. She grasped me with her left hand and started to slowly stroke up and down. Her tongue caressed the tip of my cock over and over. She started stroking harder and faster. I couldn't hold it in. I said with a gentle voice, "I'm cumming."

To my surprise, she started sucking harder at these words. She wanted all of me. I knew she was already addicted to me as I was to her. She was not going to just satisfy me. She was going to make sure I

knew that she wanted all of me. My body started to shake. She finished with no mess. She took a few seconds and looked up. The look on her face was like she wanted to say, *I love you, baby.*

It was too early to speak those words. She asked for a drink of water. I jumped up naked and ran downstairs. I got her the perfect ice-cold water. I brought it back up to her.

She took the drink and said, "Thank you."

"No, thank you!" I replied. She handed the glass back to me, and I placed the cup on the ground. We cuddled as tight as you can imagine. Embracing what felt like real love for the first time, I began to stroke her hair from her head downwards. May fell asleep in seconds. She felt safe with me. She felt secure with me. She fell in love with me. I watched her sleep and massaged her hair for over an hour. I was in love for the first time.

BREAKFAST IN BED

The next morning, I woke up before her. I'm a good cook. I knew from our conversations she was not a breakfast person, but she had not experienced my food. It was time for me to serve her.

I made my special biscuits and gravy. Breakfast in bed for the woman I just knew I was going to marry someday who had satisfied me the night before. Every time a cook makes breakfast in bed for someone, the number one goal is to finish the breakfast before they are out of bed. I rushed the breakfast. May loved to sleep in. I didn't know this yet. I walked back up to the bedside. She looked up, smelling breakfast, and gazed at her new man. May's smile was like nothing I had ever seen before. Big cheeks, big white teeth. The most beautiful smile. I'm guessing her smile was as big on this morning as it had ever been. She had fallen for me more deeply than she had ever fallen for any man. She looked so happy to wake up to me. I bent over and gently kissed her lips. It was the first time I had smelled her morning breath, and it didn't bother me. May grabbed the plate and said, "Yum!"

With her left hand, she started to eat. I was so attracted to her being left-handed. It was sexy. She finished her plate. She didn't eat her biscuits and gravy (B's & G's) like I did. She loved the gravy but only wanted a little. I wanted each bite slathered in gravy. She wanted just a little gravy for each bite. Her plate was finished with a good amount of gravy still on the plate. I was learning tiny details about her that I didn't know.

Next time, I'll give her just a little gravy.

I wanted to be perfect in every way for her. I was the first man who ever made her breakfast in bed. I was the first man who was already prioritizing her over himself. She was sure I was going to be her first and her last! I knew this was going to be the first of many experiences for her with me.

We spent the entire day together. It was too early for me to meet the parents, so she went home while they were both at work and grabbed extra clothes, girl stuff, etc. She called her mom and informed her she was going to be staying at my house again. Her mother, Jane, was displeased, to say the least. Displeased and dissatisfied with her daughter's decisions. Jane couldn't fathom her daughter moving in with a man. Jane would say, "You need to go back to your university and finish your degree!"

Jane was scared for her daughter. Her first husband was an alcoholic. She gave him chance after chance to stop drinking. I knew her mother had to be a forgiving person if she put up with an alcoholic for that long. I assumed, *like mother like daughter*, in the sense of being forgiving. I was not worried about extra chances with May. I knew May would always be my first priority. No way would I ever put

another woman over her from this point forward. But Jane struggled with believing that for quite some time.

Our first day together was one of the best days of our lives. I had never held a hand for that many consecutive hours in a row. Her hand was mine. My hand was hers. We were attached. The day unfolded, and the night was approaching. She wanted to shower. It was a long shower. She was getting cleaned up, lathering her silky-smooth skin, and ready for the night. She stepped out of the bathroom. Long dark wet hair. Curved body. The sexiest feet I had ever seen. Towel around her midsection. As she passed by me, she came up and kissed me on the cheek and said, "I really like you, D.J. Murphy!"

"I like you more May Maria Williams," I replied. She went upstairs and got dressed. I cooked dinner, and we sat together, praying before dinner, and ate. May couldn't cook. It was like she was in disbelief she had found a religious man who could cook and who also thought she was the most beautiful thing walking the face of the earth. I made a simple dinner: baked chicken smothered in cream of chicken and cream of mushroom soup. When she ate, she would hold her fork in her right hand and cut the chicken with her left. So sexy! I was overly attracted to that left hand. We finished dinner. I loved cooking, May loved to eat; we were made for each other. As we finished dinner, she cleaned the kitchen. She said, "You cook, I'll clean!"

I didn't mind helping. I dried the dishes as she rinsed them. We tidied up the kitchen and went into the living room. She was full of ideas for remodeling the house. I told her I wanted to remodel the outside first and shared all my ideas. May then told me her ideas and why the inside needed to be done first. There was no way she was going to continue living in a home looking like this. The farmhouse had old plaster walls, and the wood floors were original but in bad shape. May finished the conversation with words I never forgot as she said, "We can't raise a family in a house like this."

We had talked about everything before, while she was in Germany. However, to hear her say that after a full day with me, I felt my entire soul light up. May and I knew after one full day together, we were going to have children. Did she prevail in deciding whether to remodel the inside or outside first? Yes, she won that disagreement and every disagreement after that. May got what May wanted. I had no regrets about May. I wanted to give her the world if I could. We watched some TV and were both ready for bed after some more casual conversation. After her comment about raising a family in our home, I had only one thing in mind, and she did too: Let us get started on trying to raise a family! And we did! She said, "You ready for bed?"

"Absolutely!" was my reply. I knew what that meant, and she did, too.

THE FIRST TIME

We walked up the stairs, both knowing where this would lead. Our first day together was nothing close to a first day together with anyone else in our lives. We had talked for months hoping this moment would come. Neither of us was uncomfortable. It was like we had known each other for years. We went up to bed and lay down. I second-guessed myself on whether she wanted sex or just to mess around. One thing I wanted to make sure of is if she was comfortable and ready for our first time. I started gently touching and kissing her face. She reached down and grabbed me; at this point, she already knew what she was going to grab. She wanted me as badly as I wanted her. It was like she was thinking about it all day. Things picked up quickly. I rolled her over and slid my hand down into her. If she can grasp me, I'm going to grasp her! She gasped. I started massaging her. She was wet and ready. I took my time. She stripped my shirt off. She grabbed my shoulders and pulled me in close. We kissed, breathing hard. I

stopped us for a second and asked, "Are you sure you are ready for this? Are you comfortable enough?"

"Yes, baby, I want you!" She replied. I went down on her. I didn't take my time. I started sucking her and licking in circles around her clit. She took both her hands and pulled my head closer to her. I could barely breathe but realized for the first time how good she tasted. I went until my jaw was pulsating. I grasped her breast with my right hand and pushed her right thigh up with my left hand. I looked up. She grabbed my face and pulled me up, she was ready. We didn't even discuss protection. No questions were asked; we both wanted to make love to the fullest. As she pulled my head up, she brought me in close and started kissing me. She grabbed me and placed me inside her. I slowly went in. I wanted to treasure the moment. Our lives would never be the same. I only gave her half; she knew I was being gentle. May wanted it all. She grabbed me under my armpits with both hands behind my shoulders. She pulled me in and let out a slight squeal, *aaaah*!

We were making love for the first time, and nothing had felt that good. I was thrusting gently but hard. Our lips locked, and saliva was all over each other's faces. She started to sit up and placed me down on my back. May wanted to be on top. She got on top and straddled me. I grabbed myself this time as she leaned up slightly to make room. She slowly dropped her body into place and had the biggest smile as our anatomy connected again. She started thrusting her hips up and down and arched her back. She started with a gentle *ah-hhh* that gradually got louder. The gentle ahhhh turned into a loud moan. She started moving faster. We discussed later how hard it was not to say the words, *I love you*, during this moment. I took my thumb upside down and started massaging her spot. She arched her back farther, this time with both her hands on the bed behind her. She was moving her body forward and backward while keeping me all the way in. I said, "Cum on me," with a gentle voice.

She said in a scratchy, high-pitched voice, "Mm-mmh, I am!" Her voice raised, "I'm cumming, I'm cumming on you, D.J.!"

With those words, I couldn't hold it in. We went together at the same time. Our first time making love, and it was the definition of quintessential sex. She fell back on top of my body. Our bodies were covered in sweat. She kept me inside her. She said, "Ohhh myyyy Goddd" in the softest voice. She squeezed my body. I could feel her breasts pressing against my chest. I could smell her sweat for the first time.

She started kissing my right shoulder. She whispered, "That's never happened to me before."

I had just made May cum for the first time in her life and could tell she was not lying. She refused to pull me out of her. She started gently rocking back and forth like she was wanting more. May had just fallen so far into love, and I was her man. As she continued rocking, she started kissing my entire face with little pecks all over. She was entranced with me. She slowed the rocking, pulled off me, and placed her ear on my heart. She wanted to hear my heartbeat. She looked up and said in a strong voice, "That was so good!"

I said, "Yes, yes, it was."

We had just made love for the first time. Our bodies fit perfectly together. Our souls were joining as one. Our lives felt perfect now. It was the closest thing either of us had felt to heaven on earth. We had no cares. It was May and I in this world, and no one else mattered. If I could have, I would have paused that moment for eternity. She sat up for a second, reaching her hand down onto herself, almost like cupping something coming out. May got up and said, "I'll be right back."

I was confused because she had a weird look on her face. It was not a normal look. Moments later, she came back. I said, "What's wrong?"

She said, "Nothing, it's okay."

I didn't accept that answer. "May, what is going on?", I repeated. She said, "I'm bleeding."

I was confused. She was so wet there was no way I cut her. I also knew she had been with men before, so the other option didn't seem credible. *Maybe she started her monthly cycle?* I thought.

She said, "I think you just cut my cherry."

I asked, "But you've been with men before?" She said, "Yes, but this has never happened."

I had popped her cherry. I was in shock. May had slept with men before, and somehow that moment was saved for me. I looked down, she was still naked. I could see a little blood on her skin. She looked at me and said, "Apparently, I was saving it for you."

I was in disbelief, but it was real. Though I didn't take her virginity, that was the feeling we both had. All our past sexual relationships were gone. It felt like I had never been with anyone else. Those memories were erased. Any thought of any person either of us had ever been with was gone. She later said the same thing. Both of us had just made real love, not just sex, for the first time. I was 23, she was 19. It felt like nothing could ever separate us. It was at that moment that I realized *the one* was beside me. Our sexual desires felt fulfilled for the first time in our lives. From that day forward, we made love multiple times a day, every single day for months. I was hers; she was mine. Did we have moments of feeling vulnerable? Absolutely! May would often say, "You will never, ever leave me, right?"

"No, May, never!" I would say.

She would always reply, "You promise, promise, promise you will never leave me?" I would say every time, "I promise May."

When May would say this, I always interpreted it as breaking up with her or cheating on her. Though she meant exactly that, there was something else about May I didn't truly realize for a long time. Her dad had left her mom multiple times and would disappear and come back. When May said, "Never leave?" She also meant, "Leave the house."

As in, if we got into an argument, I wouldn't be allowed to leave the house. This statement I never understood fully. I would have to learn the hard way.

CHOICES

Knock, Knock!

The second time that deep, almost manly voice had a question. In my boxers up against the

bathroom sink, trying to shave my head. I never felt like I had privacy in this small house. The first few knocks, I pretended I didn't hear it over the noise of the head clippers. However, with a second set of knocks, I thought *it must be important.* "Yes?" I called out, still thinking it might be one of the kids, before hearing her voice.

"I need something for the kids from the closet in the bathroom. Can I come in real quick?" Raven said. I pondered. The weeks/months leading up to this moment were not good with this girl. I should have known better, but I'm the type of person who would give anyone the benefit of the doubt over and over. And I so desperately wanted to still believe she was innocent even though others were saying the opposite. Why? Raven was now fifteen, only a few months from sixteen, and getting her driver's license. The thought of my wife and me having a reliable babysitter who could help with transportation was going to be life-changing. With five children, May and I struggled terribly with babysitters. They would come and go. One day show up; the next day, call in sick. Before Raven, we had been through close to twenty different babysitters over the years. For me to tell May that I wanted to get rid of Raven and get her out of the house was not going to be an argument. It was going to be a blow-up! I knew that I would never slip up, either. I was a loyal man. I didn't care what others were warning me about. I loved May, and cheating or even slipping up would never happen. May meant the world to me even after ten years. I placed my selfishness of "having a reliable babysitter" over issues that were starting to emerge with people on the outside, bringing cautionary examples to my attention.

It all started on a date night, one night with May. May said, "Hey babe!? What jeans do you want me to wear?"

Looking back now, without knowing it, this was one of the last things I can remember May saying to me with her pure and innocent voice filled with a passionate love that should never have been taken away from her. I responded, "The light-colored ones! You know, the almost white ones?" I had a thing for extremely light blue jeans, almost white. With holes in the knees. May had nice legs, a nice butt, and would wear heels that would always bring any outfit together.

"Which shoes, babe?" May asked.

After 10 years of our relationship, she still wanted to impress me. She wanted me to still think, *Damn she's sexy!* And I still did! May could wear sweatpants and a sweatshirt, and I would get aroused. She walked out of the bedroom and said, "How about these?"

My God, I thought. I married the sexiest woman alive. "Yes, my love, looks perfect!" I said.

"Where are we going?" She continued speaking as she was excited to have a date night with her hubby!

"How about we check out that new restaurant downtown?" I replied.

"Sounds good, babe," May finished speaking as we were off on another date night made possible by a reliable babysitter who never wanted to leave our house.

BABIES

Ten years had come and gone in our marriage. We had five kids in less than ten years. It was what we wanted, but it was hard. Every day was full of crazy schedules and crying kids, and we had changed diapers for ten straight years. Baby Blaire was still in diapers. It was stressful. Somehow, we managed it all. Everyone called us crazy. Were we crazy? Yes! Each birth, there were moments any parent would say, "The birth of my child was one of the best days of my life!"

May and I experienced this five times! Five kids came with five pregnancies. Five children May breastfed. Hormones that seemed to never stop. There were meltdown moments for both of us. She was full of hormones. And I was stressed, wondering how I could make enough money to raise five kids. So, those eight years of having babies were stressful, to say the least. We survived the stress because of the small moments that were God's glory of life coming into this world through her and me. We survived those years because we never questioned our love for each other. Each child was like bringing another version of ourselves into the world. There is nothing like bringing life into the world with another person. I will never forget the moments of holding May's hand and rubbing her hair for hours and hours during delivery. I would massage her back for hours and hours. Then she would say, "Okay, stop!"

I would also massage her feet. Then spontaneously, she'd say, "Stop now, please!" May would say, "Get me ice chips!"

Then, "Hold my hand!"

Then, "Where's that pillow I told you to take away?"

I tried everything to make her comfortable in those delivery rooms. May was a soldier! She delivered the last 4 kids with no epidural pain injection. May wanted natural births, and she did it! Eventually, it would lead to the moment May would squeeze my hand so tight I thought she was going to break it as she pushed life out of her and into the world!

My favorite part was always after she was done pushing. The babies would always cry as the nurses would clean them up quickly. What followed was my all-time favorite thing ever with May. The nurse would hand me the baby. I would kiss the baby as many times as I could before handing the baby over to Momma May. I would hand our precious little new life to the most beautiful woman.

May would get a look that I only saw in these moments. She would smile and cry at the same time. As she would take the baby, she would look up at me every time with eyes that said, "I love this baby, but I love you even more, D.J. Murphy, for giving me this baby!"

I knew exactly what she was thinking. As she would slide the baby down to start breastfeeding, I would kiss May's forehead over and over, close to 100 times. When I was done kissing her forehead, May would say the same thing after each child. She would look at me and say, "I love you, baby!"

My response was the same each time, "I love you more May Maria Murphy!" We would often say, "I love you more,"

"No, I love you more!" Etc. Etc. After our children were born was the only time she was too tired to say it back.

"I love you more May Maria Murphy!" I would say each time. While still in so much pain, she would smile and look back down at the new life we brought into this world together!

We truly were never sure when we were going to stop having babies. May and I went into the relationship saying six. Or maybe seven. It was not until the final pregnancy that we started talking about calling it quits. Baby Blaire gave May a run for her money. Blaire had multiple markers for Down syndrome. As we continued through the pregnancy, each test would come back negative, but it was extremely stressful for May. It led to a final test where the doctors would draw blood from the baby. We decided against this. No way were we going to put our baby through that before delivery. So, though all the tests came back negative, there was still a chance of Down syndrome. May was terrified, and it stressed her out badly during the pregnancy. She ended up getting shingles on her back from the stress. Besides a miscarriage we had in between the birth of our first and second child, I had never felt so horrible for May. But Baby Blaire came out perfectly healthy. However, the stress of that pregnancy for May led us to decide to stop bringing new life into this world.

The easy decision was for me to get a vasectomy. I knew it was just the easier and cheaper way to go for May and me to stop having children. Having a vasectomy was against our religion. Afterward, I secretly had terrible regrets about it. I would say to May, lying, "I don't mind getting a vasectomy."

Deep down, though, I knew it was against everything I believed in religiously. After five successful pregnancies, we were both exhausted and ready to call it quits. We also both knew we had a long road ahead of us financially; and just raising our kids. May was coming off an incredibly stressful pregnancy. We had tried throughout the pregnancies to try by natural means to avoid getting pregnant, but that didn't work. It was not a joke; if I touched May, she got pregnant. Everyone said it. God loved us together. So much so that He blessed us over and over and over again. We knew it was a blessing as many couples struggle for years to have one child, let alone five. God wanted May and I to have children. The creation of life was the easiest part of it for us. We made love, May got pregnant. Six times total in eight years. Knowing what I know now, I would have never stopped having children with May until God stopped us. When I got that vasectomy, I felt that I was acting like God by thinking, "I'm going to decide if I'm going to have more children."

I should have let God decide that. From the moment I had that vasectomy, everything in my life CRUMBLED! And it crumbled dramatically.

TEN YEAR MARK

After our last child was born and we knew we were done poppin' out babies, I started pursuing an officer's position at the fire department. I was a multi-generational firefighter. I wanted to make the generations before me proud! Throughout my entire career, the fire department had been on a hiring freeze for almost ten years. Guys were not replaced. We had a mayor who couldn't stand fire-fighters. He hated us. Not a single firefighter that I ever talked to fully understood this. All of us thought, *Why does this man hate us so much?*

I was not just pursuing an officer's position. Simultaneously on my days off, I was growing a contracting business. Most firefighters worked side jobs unless their wives were making a lot of money. We only made a little over $50,000 per year. It was decent money but not enough to raise five kids. Could I get by? Sure. But I knew I had four daughters I wanted to someday send off to college and pay for their weddings.

Without recognizing it, I was becoming prideful. Though I was proud of my accomplishments. it was more than that. I wanted everyone else around me to be proud of me, especially May's and my family. May's Uncle Louis was the most successful businessperson in the city. His success resulted in the entire family becoming spoiled, especially May. May was what you would call the golden girl of the family, beautiful, respected, and smart. Her parents both had great jobs her entire life. Her Uncle was rich. Her

grandmother spoiled her beyond imagination. And May was my wife. I was now in charge of spoiling her. A lot of my pride came from trying to keep her happy and satisfied. It was not an easy task living up to her family's expectations and making them proud of me as well. May loved to spend money. She loved nice things. I wanted to give her everything. I hated telling her no. Keeping things simple was not a possibility. Simplicity was nowhere in my life at this time. I was nonstop busy and striving to make enough money for my wife and five children.

The business I was growing started when I was young. I partnered up with my dad (Durand Sr.) in his construction-type business. As I got older, I wanted to become more independent. I wanted my wife to say, "D.J. has his own business, and he's very successful."

I wanted to someday make enough money so that I could give her all the things she wanted from this world. As the saying goes, "Money is the root of all evil."

I am here to tell you. It is. Raising five kids, you naturally go broke. Especially in America, where social media triggers many women to constantly seek self-gratification by buying things. Between fortune and fame, I sought fortune. I wanted to create a fortune and give it all to May, with enough for my kids to have an inheritance someday. May was the center of my world. I wanted to keep her happy and satisfied. I knew she liked material things. May was a bargain shopper, but she bargain shopped a lot!

PRIDE

In 2012, May and I brought our third child into this world. I stopped doing business with my dad, as I no longer felt good about our working together. By then, Dad and I didn't agree on anything. My dad and I were best friends. He was also a career firefighter. We were together every single day. My vision was to expand the business, while Dad's vision was set on retirement, leading us to go separate ways. Looking back, I would never have decided to separate from him. Pride was creeping in and getting stronger.

Meanwhile, Dad and I were getting into heated arguments. Pride eventually led to destruction. I needed to be humbled. The destruction didn't just slowly happen, it came like a damn Category Five Hurricane! Everything was lost.

From 2012 through 2016, I had some success. Nothing great, but success. I was managing my own construction company, and it became my primary focus. I lost track of what is so tremendously important in life--FAMILY! May was feeling lonely. She started to tell me this. She asked me to start coming home at 4 p.m. each day. She missed me. She wanted me home. All points were valid. The strongest fact was, as she would say. "You're the boss, you have workers, let them work, come home to your family." I listened and tried every day to be home by four. But most successful business owners will all tell you the same thing: *When I'm not there, I'm not making money, and things go bad.*

My workers were all great guys. They all had families and followed good family values in their lives. One of the biggest mistakes I made in my business was getting too close to them. I had a big heart. They had families that needed to eat. They had bills to pay. I prioritized them over my own family when it came to money. Often, I would be waiting to get paid myself. This would cause my bills to be late. The extra stress of this impacted my family, especially my marriage. I would tell May, "Can we wait until next week before going to the grocery or pay for this or that?"

"May, I had to pay the guys, and the company won't get paid until the job is finished," I would often say.

These moments in life led me to pray for specific outcomes. I would pray, "God, please help me make enough money to someday work from home!"

I wanted to see my family more. I wanted a real change in my life. To put it simply, I wanted a simpler life, and I wanted God to rescue me, yet I wanted to have all the money. God knew I was an extreme personality type. I do everything all in. He knew to slow me down, it would take a life-altering extreme circumstance to stop me in my tracks and save me from PRIDE! I had to lose everything to be slowed down. Not just material things. I had to lose my reputation. So how was God going to do this?

NAÏVE

KNOCK! KNOCK! I responded to Raven. "Yes, you can come in and get something for the kids out of the closet."

Again, it was our only bathroom. I stayed up against the bathroom sink. I didn't even look at her. I continued shaving my head as if she were not even in the bathroom. Raven grabbed something out of the closet. I have no idea what she grabbed. She left the bathroom and closed the door. It was quick. I thought, *Maybe everyone telling me to be cautious with her is wrong!*

That thought didn't last long. My mind started to race. Thoughts rushed in of every situation that had happened in the previous month with this babysitter.

Moments later... Knock! Knock!

I thought, *Surely this is a kid this time.* It was Raven. She asked, "Hey! Can I come in again? I need something else for the kids out of the closet."

I can still remember her voice. It was not a normal voice for a standard request. Most everyone can relate to when someone said something in a sweet tone, but it felt evil. It was like she was acting sweet and innocent, but it was far from it. My mind raced again, reviewing all the situations leading up to this moment. My mind exploded instantly with this second set of knocks and hearing her deceitful tone.

It started with the light-colored jeans I requested May to wear. May and I shared similar birthdays. Both were in April. It was in April of 2017 when I told May to wear those sexy jeans. Less than a week after Raven heard me request those jeans, Raven decided she needed a pair. Raven had never worn light-colored blue jeans before hearing me say that to May. The first week of May that year, she bought a light-colored pair of blue jeans. She wore these jeans often. The difference between May's jeans and Raven's? Raven's jeans were the same color but with large holes in the thighs and knees. Her first time wearing them, she asked me, "Hey, D.J. do you like my new jeans?"

Every time I saw her in those jeans, I started to feel uncomfortable with this 15-year-old babysitter who had become so close to our family. Not to mention she was living with us 50% of the time. I convinced myself that it was just a coincidence. But was it? It didn't stop with the jeans. The coincidences continued and they escalated quickly. But I had a big heart and continued to give this person the benefit of the doubt. That was a mistake.

I would describe myself at this time in my life as optimistic and naïve. I always tried to find the best in people. I refused to believe that someone could have negative or evil intentions. I tried to have a good relationship with everyone in my life. If I couldn't establish a positive relationship, at the minimum, I tried to get along. I just loved people. I loved the camaraderie in group settings.

I enjoyed having parties and hosting friends or family. I even liked hanging out with people who didn't like me. I would make it a goal to get them to know me better so they might think, *This guy is not all that bad after all*. I was not afraid of any conversation with anyone. Today I'm very guarded with any conversation.

THE CREW

The following incidents with Raven involved the guys in my construction business.

My construction company had landed a big job. We specialize in polished concrete. Polished concrete requires machinery that carries more value than my truck. I felt as if I had finally made it when I got this $100,000 commercial remodeling project. All the arduous work I had done felt like it was finally going to pay off. My employees were excited as well. Together we had grown the company to a level that everyone was satisfied with. The workers were on full payroll. They were paying into unemployment, federal tax, and state tax. It felt like, as a team, we had accomplished our first primary goal together: a legit operating, profitable business.

Over the years, I had many diverse types of men who worked for me. I then had four main men. I will start with Todd. Todd was the goofball. One might say he was not the sharpest tool in the box. We called him "Big Goober". He was the least effective worker. Over time he became skilled at specific job duties, but he remained the least useful worker. At times we would run out of work for him to do that we needed to be done professionally, so he would often clean the trailer. He wore thick glasses and couldn't brush a straight line while painting. He was clumsy and would make messes and spill stuff. He was tall, so we would often have him do work that the rest of us needed a ladder for. Over time he got better at certain things, and we knew we didn't have to go back and double-check all his work. He would hold his temper in. I never saw him express anger. Todd was like a Big Teddy Bear; He was a sweet man with a big heart. Like all the other guys, he loved his cigarettes. I never smoked cigarettes, but I often saw him bum cigarettes off the other guys. We relied on him, but he was unreliable. He would show up every day, then disappear for weeks. He would often express his gratitude to me. Of all the guys who worked for me, he thanked me for employing him the most.

Next was Tim. We called him Uncle Timmy. We brought Tim on to work with us when we landed this big job. In the months leading up to it, he started coming around a little, knowing we were going to need more labor for the big project. Tim was older than all of us. He was skilled in drywall installation and fit that description. Tim looked like he lived a rough life. He was of average height and lanky with a wrinkled face, stained teeth, and a red face. He didn't speak a whole lot, but we listened when he did. In his short stint working for us, he showed up every day. If the guys were working, I would often let them free-lance. Tim liked the work atmosphere. I assume he thought he was underpaid. To be honest, we all were. Tim was also a nice guy. I never got to know him like the rest of the guys.

Then there was good ole Ezra. We called him Arthur. He hated his first name, which was Arthur. So, needless to say, that's what we called him. Ezra was a little, stocky guy. He couldn't stay out of jail. He was the more than three-strikes guy. He would get out of jail and stay sober while on probation. But when stressed after getting off probation, he did drugs. When Ezra was off drugs, he was one of the nicest guys. Drugs clouded that huge heart of his. Ezra loved me. He had a big smile every time I saw him. He had a clean-shaven head that glistened. He was like Popeye the Sailor Man, but instead of spinach, it was amphetamines.

I wrote letters to Ezra in jail. I also wrote letters to his probation officer, trying to get him off probation. I always had hope for him. I would make him wear jeans because he had a probationary ankle bracelet that tracked him. Customers hated guys with ankle bracelets. But he was a good, skilled employee who worked hard. The short little fella needed a ladder for everything. He loved Jesus and would talk about his faith. But as soon as he got that ankle bracelet off, it was less than six months later that every time he was back in jail. It is hard to tell what he's up to today. Last I heard, he was back in jail. I miss his big smile.

Finally, Wyatt. Before I employed him, Wyatt worked for an irrigation company installing sprinkler systems. Once, I was working for a dentist in a nice neighborhood on a golf course. Every day I saw this guy working down the street who looked like Jesus (Wyatt). He was on this job digging holes, installing an irrigation system every single day, and was arriving at his job site before I arrived at my job. I was like, "Wow, this guy works his ass off!"

One day I stopped and got out of my truck. As I approached, I noticed he carried a pistol on his side. My thought was, *Nice, he protects himself at all times.* The sun was rising over the horizon. It was a clear, sunny day. He was already sweating. He liked to get to the job early before the sun blistered him, so he could get done early. He looked up and probably thought, *What does this guy want?*

I immediately noticed his blue eyes. I'm not gay, but this guy's eyes were beautiful. Brown hair, a big beard, average height, average weight, and carrying a confident demeanor. His standard words were, "What up, BUDDY!" And that is exactly what he said to me that day.

I could tell he was a gentle soul. I responded, "Hey man, you like digging holes?" Wyatt replied, "Well, buddy, it pays the bills."

"Right on, man," I replied.

I continued. "How much do you make, if you don't mind me asking?"

"Not as much as I think I should be, buddy." He said this knowing he deserved more money. Wyatt said *buddy* more than Ronnie Coleman.

"Yeahhh buddyyy!"

I ended the conversation by saying, "Well, listen, man, I have a little construction business and would love to have you come to work for me."

And, of course, he said, "Okay, buddy, I'll have to think about it."

I shook his hand and told him my name was D.J.. I gave him my number, and we went our separate ways. I think we both left that conversation knowing we would be working as a team someday. Our personalities just clicked. I quickly learned before Wyatt ever came to work for me that he was a loyal employee. He refused to leave his irrigation boss hanging. I would text him often and ask, "Are you ready to come to work with me yet?"

Wyatt would always say, "I'm keeping you in mind, buddy."

Wyatt wanted to work for me. However, he struggled, leaving his current boss with no replacement. Eventually, irrigation work got slow, and Wyatt came on board to work for me. I started him off at twelve dollars an hour, he was only making ten an hour with the irrigation company. At the time when Wyatt started working for us, my job site supervisor was a Mexican man, Gonzalo, and that is what we called him.

Gonzalo was bilingual, fluent in both English and Spanish. He called it Spanglish. Gonzalo was a stocky Hispanic man. He was free-spirited. Loved people. Laughed all the time. His personality was like mine. He would cut up and mess with people in a fun way. He was always late to work but never missed a day. Gonzalo was single; loved his player status. Partied on the weekends and worked his ass off during the week. I loved Gonzalo's famed saying, "Oh yah yah yah."

His accent was Hispanic with an American twist. His English was well-spoken. If he took a phone call, it was straight up-to-speed Mexican Spanish. I would always laugh when I heard him on the phone. I tried to get him to teach me some Spanish, but I never caught on. I would always joke with the crew and say, "Rapido!" Meaning, let us get this work done quickly! Gonzalo ate healthily and worked out every night after work. He had a great soul, a great personality, and like Wyatt, was very loyal. And anytime you said something he liked, it never failed, that he would say, "Oh yah yah yah!"

Gonzalo and Wyatt were by far the best combination of workers I ever had. They worked hard and efficiently and completed jobs professionally. Customers would praise those two guys. I could leave and do estimates, get material, or whatever, and I never worried about the job getting done correctly. For about a year, everything went perfectly. May and I were busy having kids and raising babies while these two great men ran the business by themselves. I don't think I ever had a single complaint during their stint together. Winters are typically slow for any construction company; otherwise, I kept these guys busy. But as the saying goes, all good things come to an end.

Gonzalo started to become lackadaisical, knowing he could rely on Wyatt. Wyatt became irritated, feeling like he was carrying more responsibility than Gonzalo. Eventually, these two great men couldn't stand each other. They were complaining about the other behind each other's backs, frustrated with the other's work, and both wanting a raise. My first thought was, *I'll separate them*. However, I just didn't have enough work to keep them separated all the time. They both were good enough to start and finish a job themselves. I needed to decide how to resolve this problem.

Unfortunately, there wasn't a clear decision that was going to work out the best for both. Wyatt was the first to arrive and the last to leave every single day. He also needed the extra hours because he was a new dad. Gonzalo was still a single man. He was getting to work an hour late every day and leaving early every day. It led to a tough conversation I had to have with Gonzalo, who, at the time, was one of my closest friends. To keep working for me, Gonzalo was going to have to take a step back and let Wyatt take the job site lead. Eventually, that led Gonzalo to take a job in another state with warmer weather. I was bummed, to say the least, when Gonzalo left. Occasionally he and I still talk to this day.

INSOMNIA

Knock! Knock!

Raven knocked the second time. *What could she possibly need that is so important to have to come in the bathroom again?* I thought. It sounded credible as she said, "I need something else for the kids out of the closet,"

In that evil yet trying-to-sound sweet voice. By then, I was done shaving my face and was almost done shaving my head, working on the back, which is always hard to do. Only this day, shaving the back of my head was especially difficult. I was going on for four days with no rest. When I say four days with no rest, I am not exaggerating.

A little over a month or so before this bathroom moment, I was referred to a doctor by a coworker at the fire station for Attention Deficit Disorder, or A.D.D. This coworker, Cole, was not exactly everyone's favorite around the firehouse. He was short and liked to stay in the whispers around the fire department. He worked his way to captain, then chief quickly. He was in the middle of everything, meaning gossip. He knew the mayor. He knew the city council members. He talked to everyone. However, many called him a snake behind his back. He had never done anything directly against me. So, I didn't judge him. Cole liked my dad, who had just retired from the fire department, a lot. I never really understood why he liked my dad so much. Cole would just say, "Your dad is a great dude!"

Cole and I were two of the hardest workers around the fire station. I was always around him because we were constantly getting shit done while most of the other guys were lazy. We liked things clean and neat. We liked the firetrucks detailed and organized. Cole took to me because he loved my dad.

As my career developed and I started to pursue a captain's position, Cole was in the shadows trying to help me. We spent a lot of time together. The fire department schedule is 24-hour shifts, so you naturally become close to a lot of guys. Cole eventually felt comfortable enough with me to tell me how he was able to, in a lot of ways, outwork me. Which was no easy task. I worked hard. Cole had a little help to outwork me, medicine! I will never forget the day he asked, "D.J., you know you're A.D.D., right?"

I replied, "Ya, I've been told that since I was six years old by my preschool teacher." He said, "Do you take anything for it?"

"No," I replied.

He continued, "Here, man, call this doctor. He's awesome and will help you out."

"Right on, man." Little did he know that calling this doctor would lead to the destruction of my life. After this conversation, I remember thinking, *I am overwhelmed with work, kids, wife, etc. Maybe I should try some medicine to help with my focus.*

So, I called the doctor's office. I set up an appointment. I will never forget my first appointment with the doctor. He asked a bunch of questions. I must have answered them as a perfect match to the prototypical A.D.D. personality. The doctor said, "God created science, and science created medicine, so God created medicine to help people just like you."

He continued, "You should not have gone this long feeling like you needed something to help you stay focused."

So, I had a prescription called into the local pharmacy, and I was on a trial run of Adderall. The doctor mentioned some people don't do well with Adderall, and if I struggled in any way with it, he would stop Adderall and let me try the other form of attention deficit medicine, Ritalin. I had no clue what this meant. I just said, "Okay, thank you for your time, Doc, I'll let you know."

My initial prescription was an extended-release low dose. I felt no change in my lack of focus. After a month, I went back to the same doctor. I explained my experience was only a minor increase in focus. Part of me at the time felt so ashamed of myself. Here I was in my mid-30s and getting help with this thing called A.D.D. for the first time. The doctor's solution was to increase the dose slightly and for me to take an immediate-release dose instead of an extended-release in the morning. Oh, how quickly my life crumbled after this.

Knock! Knock!

I was irritated. I was frustrated. I was on day four of the immediate-release Adderall, and it was exactly as they say in the streets; Adderall, for me, was my "poor man's cocaine". I had not slept in four straight days. I tried; I couldn't sleep. It felt like the devil was whispering in my ear, "D.J., you can keep going."

My spiritual consciousness with God was saying, "D.J. STOP TAKING THIS SO-CALLED MEDICINE."

I later googled what happens after three days of no sleep. After three days of no sleep, your ability to think is profoundly limited, especially with multitasking and focus. Your judgment is affected, memory is impaired, hand-eye coordination is altered, and your decision-making ability is, let me say, SCREWED! After four days of no sleep, they give it a name: "Sleep deprivation psychosis." One's perception and interpretation of reality are severely distorted. One also has an urge to sleep that becomes unbearable. Looking back, it made absolutely no sense at all that I was shaving my face and head that morning in the bathroom. That routine in my entire firefighting career began in the morning before my fire shift. That morning, I was getting off my fire shift and heading to a construction job site. Why was I even shaving? I hated shaving my head and face. Not once in my working career had I shaved before going to a construction job site. Instead of heading to a job site, I should have been heading to bed.

On day four of the immediate-release Adderall, I remember the drive home from work. I swerved off the road a few times, slapping my face and rolling down the window. I knew I needed sleep. However, May and my house were not set up for me to go sleep in the summer while the kids were out of school. We lived in a 2-bedroom 1 bath single story house. Sounds crazy right? May and I had just sold what we initially thought was our dream home. We had a 5,300 SF house in the neighborhood. The house was enormous. When we purchased this big house, I remember thinking, *I am giving May our dream home.*

We liked the house and thought we would stay there for a long time while we raised all our kids. Our third, fourth, and fifth children were all born during our time in this big house. Our mindset was we could have ten kids in this house! As time passed, May and I started discussing moving out to the country. Initially, we looked for land. But land was expensive, and then we would have to build a house.

That idea was shot down quickly. We almost gave up on the idea of moving to the country until, one day, I saw a tiny little house on ten acres close to town. The property was beautiful, with rolling hills, two huge barns, a stream that ran across the entire property, trees, wildlife, seven acres of hay, and three acres of grass. It was amazing. Every person who saw the property was in awe. In awe of it, but not the house. Nestled in the countryside of Eastern Illinois. This property had great potential. We just knew that small of a home would come with sacrifices. Privacy was the big one.

The house was tiny, with only two bedrooms and one bath, and the entire thing needed remodeling. The only way May would agree to buy the property is if I promised her to remodel the entire main part of the house before moving in and later add on to the house. The problem was that we purchased the house at the same time my construction company was starting the $100,000 project. I was going to have

to be Superman. I wanted to impress the love of my life and simultaneously make good money. I was taking on the largest project I had ever landed in my construction business, a full-blown house remodel, and I had just become captain at the fire station, which also came with extra responsibilities. I did it all somehow. I had help from my workers, family, and friends. Everyone pitched in. I can only imagine how many people behind my back thought, *What is he thinking?* They all made comments like, "D.J., you are going to kill yourself!"

The house remodel was almost done. The $100,000 construction project was close to completion.

I was doing well as a captain those first few months, though I was exhausted from overwork. When it was all almost done. I was the most exhausted person I would ever be. In a way, I was starting to feel relieved. May was happy with the house remodel. My customers were happy with the construction project. And I achieved my goal of becoming an officer in the fire department. That feeling of relief didn't fix the exhaustion or my scatterbrain. My solution? Try Adderall. And how convenient! I was referred to a doctor who encouraged scientific help from God, with a so-called medicine to help my focus.

During all these projects, my workers would often come back to the house after a day on the job.

We had two barns. One barn sat up close to the house. The second barn sat back a short distance away. You can visualize the typical farm-style house with a gravel road leading to the back barn. That back barn was where I kept all the equipment that we didn't keep in the mobile enclosed work trailer, which remained on the job sites. If the guys needed to drop something off after work or pick something up, that is where we would meet. I was remodeling the house most of my days away from the fire department during the day while the crew was taking care of the big project. Often, we would meet up in the back barn to exchange equipment or just to catch up on everything at the end of the day. Every night I told May, "I need to go organize the back barn. Baby, I know I'm absent from you and the kids. Once this back barn is cleaned up and organized, I will be able to breathe."

May tried to be understanding, but she knew I was working extreme hours. May couldn't stand a cluttered home; I couldn't stand my new workshop not being clean and organized. She tried so hard to be patient with me. This back barn was my first true workshop. I wanted it done. The only problem was it was huge! A simple project, it was not.

The barn was originally built for horses. There were five horse stalls sitting on the back side of the barn with horse mats resting on a dirt floor. The rest of the barn was concrete. The barn was big, 30' by 55', with a hay loft across the backside above the horse stalls. This barn had sat there for ten years with no TLC, and it needed tender loving care BADLY! It was disgusting when we purchased the house. The hayloft was the worst job I may have ever had. There was a wise old raccoon that lived in that loft for who knows how long. This raccoon shat, pissed, you name it. When up there, I wore a mask and went to work. I loaded and hauled out fifteen large trash bags of raccoon shit. It was the most awful job you can imagine. This alone took me multiple nights to finish. I purchased a dumpster, and week after week, I would load it up and haul everything out of the barn, including junk left behind by previous owners. I began pressure washing everything inside the barn after pushing everything out of the barn. When I say the experience was awful, it is an understatement. However, as each night passed, the barn started to look nice.

Sometime during the process, I mentioned to May that I would like her to bring me water occasionally out to the barn if she thought about it. Someone else heard me say this. May and I were in a rocky spot in marriage. Having five kids under the age of 10 was hard enough, but I was also working nonstop. It was a tough spot in life. I was gone often, thinking I was doing the right thing, trying to support my family of seven. Not only was I often gone at the fire station, but when I was home, there was no quality time. I could tell May was starting to resent me for making us move into this farmhouse. Did it end up looking beautiful? Yes! But it came with a price. Our marriage was crumbling. Wives need quality time with their husbands. Children need time as well. Their dad was absent for months. I was not just full of pride. I was impatient. I was prioritizing my interests first. I was failing as a husband and father. I became so consumed with all these projects I even stayed home instead of going on a family vacation. This was one of my many regrets during those months. I was failing not just my kids but the most important person in my life--my May.

MIXED FEELINGS

One day, my crew showed up after a long day of work. I was beaten down trying to get the barn organized and finished. As the sun set, out came Raven, walking towards my crew and me. I was still naïve about the developing situation I had on my hands with her. The guys had been casually mentioning things here and there about how I needed to be careful around her (Raven). I just blew it off. I would say, "Guys, she's like a daughter to me. She has been my babysitter for a year and a half, and she appreciates what my family does for her."

The guys would shake their heads. I was oblivious to this escalating problem. I would defend Raven and say to them, "Raven like being at her real home, and she feels comfortable with my family. Guys, I'm only trying to help her!"

When I would defend Raven, the guys would have this look on their faces, thinking, *D.J. has no clue what is at the back of this girl's mind.*

Here comes Raven right after I had just defended her to my crew. This was the moment I began to think, *The jeans, the overly nice expressions, and the odd comments. Maybe my workers are on to something...*

If you can imagine the typical female strutting, seeking attention, here it came. Raven walked straight up to me, handing me the water, and said, "Here you go, D.J.!"

She smiled at me while she gazed into my eyes. I looked back at her with a look of, "Ummm, thanks?" She turned to my workers standing to my right and asked, "You guys need water?"

Raven was not using her normal tone. She sounded like a wife taking care of her husband and his crew. My stomach felt sick with the thought, "These guys may be right!"

Ezra responded first and said, "Nope, I'm good, no water for me!"

With the most smart-ass tone of voice. Wyatt replied, "No, Ma'am, all good."

The others shook their head no. She responded, "Okay!" In an enthusiastic voice. As she turned around, her walk was ridiculous. If a female ever wanted attention with a walk, here it was. I saw it and knew the guys had already been saying stuff about her. I looked over at my crew. They were all staring at me with the look, *YOU SEE IT YET?* Tim's expression got to me. He was slowly shaking his head back and forth. His expression said it all. He had to be thinking, *What the fuckkk!*

Tim didn't need to say anything. Ezra spoke, "D.J., I am telling you that girl is up to no good."

I responded, "Bro, come on, really!?"

I still tried to play dumb. I genuinely wanted to believe this was not happening, though it was pretty clear. Wyatt didn't like my response. At the time, I considered him to be one of my closest friends. He always had my best interest at heart. Wyatt said, "Buddy! We have all been trying to tell you to watch yourself around that girl, she's up to no good."

For the first time, I acknowledged them. "Okay, guys, I get it."

Was I still in denial? I had mixed feelings, to say the least. I acknowledged what the guys were saying. However, I didn't want to believe this girl had feelings for me beyond a father figure. Raven and

I had become close, much like a father/daughter relationship. We had conversations like a father would have with his daughter. She had been our babysitter for almost two years. She and I becoming close in this manner seemed normal to me. However, now I had mixed feelings.

CLIPPERS

Knock! Knock!

"Sure, Raven, you can come in again and grab whatever it is you need for the kids." I was standing in my boxers and up against the sink. Raven came in. Initially, I didn't pay her any attention. As I struggled to shave the back of my head, apparently, Raven was struggling to find whatever she needed from the closet. Over a minute went by, which seemed a little long for "grabbing something real quick out of the closet". I was finishing shaving my head. Since I was a kid, one of the most bothersome things for me has always been hair stragglers. I hated it as a kid into adulthood when the barber would miss even just the smallest spot. I knew I was obsessive, tired, to say the least, and probably had missed a spot on the back.

Feeling this, I spoke without thinking, "Hey Raven, will you check the back of my head to see if I missed any spots?" I no longer finished saying this when I thought, *This girl, at this time, is the last person I want checking the back of my head.*

But it was too late to say never mind. She so quickly said, "SURE!"

It was like she was waiting there in the closet for me to ask her this exact question. I had already shaved most of it. All I needed was a quick and final glance. She got right next to me, leaned up on her tippy toes, and spoke. "Yep, you missed a spot," While she grabbed the clippers. I stayed up against the sink.

She got her face close to my head and said, "I need you to turn." "Turn?" I replied.

She continued, "Yes, turn, I can't see good!" I thought, *Why do I need to turn, May has never asked me to turn? My head is done, just hit the spot and be on your way.* I was already having regrets about even asking for her help. She was then standing on my back right shoulder. No way was I going to turn in my boxers to my right to where my front side would be facing her. I turned to my left. I had never been in a more awkward moment. *Why did I even ask for help?* I thought to myself again, almost disgusted with myself. She started shaving the back of my head. What felt like minutes was probably 30 seconds.

She finished and said, "There you go!" Again, in that deceivingly sweet voice.

"Thanks," I said in an almost smart-ass voice. I turned back towards the bathroom sink. Surely, she will leave the bathroom now. Nope! She had still not found whatever it was she was looking for in the closet. I was done at the sink, ready to get in the shower. I didn't want to move until she was done in the closet. I waited. A brief time passed, and she closed the closet door and left the bathroom. I never did see what it was she needed so badly out of the closet.

My crew said, "Watch yourself around her!" But now, I let her shave the back of my head. *This couldn't get any worse,* I thought. I was wrong, it would only get much worse. I was a loyal man. I not only saved all my sexual energy for my wife, but I also never once did anything close to encouraging any sort of temptation from another female. Now, I allowed a female, other than my wife, to be overly close in a privileged setting. I jumped in the shower. My exhaustion was overwhelming me. I felt dizzy. I put my head down as the shower head beaded the back of my head and neck. Thoughts of the weeks leading up to this moment circled in my head. My employees, my friends, my brother-- everyone was right. I had a problem; it was time to talk to May. I was still in the shower, and every scenario started popping into my mind again and again. It felt like a nightmare.

THE MOM

After about a year of Raven watching our kids, she started to open up to me about her home life. She hated her mom. Her mother's name was Karen, and she fit the description of a woman we today label as *a Karen*. Raven said her mom would scream and yell non-stop. Karen was a foster parent, a foster parent with no patience. Raven often said she didn't like being at home. She couldn't stand being around her mother. She would straight out say, "My mom is psycho."

I honestly felt bad for Raven. A daughter calling their mom psycho seemed extreme. Raven grew up with different foster kids as part of her family life. Raven was a bastard child, born with no dad around. Raven only mentioned her dad a few times. She said her real dad was in prison in Texas. The full story would surface later.

Karen was not just psycho at home. She was a registered nurse at the local hospital in Eastern Illinois. May was also a registered nurse at the same local hospital. May tolerated Karen because when May was a child, Karen occasionally babysat May. I can't remember the connection, but I want to say they attended the same Christian church or some other social organization. May didn't like Karen, but she tolerated her. May would come home from work and talk about how crazy Karen was. May rarely had to deal with her directly but would hear stories. The entire hospital avoided "Crazy Karen". When I say, "No one could stand her! NO ONE could stand her."

The first time I met Karen, she wanted an estimate on painting a room in her house. She lived in a small neighborhood on the edge of town. I showed up to do the estimate. Karen answered the door. "HEY, D.J.!" – Have you ever met a woman who, after speaking their first words, makes you think, *This bitch is crazy!*

Karen was the most ADHD (Attention Deficit Hyperactive Disorder) person I had ever met. I don't say that lightly. For the first twenty minutes, no exaggeration whatsoever, I stood in the family room entryway listening to her talk about all the crazy shit that came to her mind. I asked myself, *What the heck did I get myself into?* It was that moment when you meet someone, and they talk so much that you can't even get a word in. This was that moment. I tried multiple times just to get a word in, and it was damn near impossible. Karen told me all about her life. She had just given birth to twins with her husband. She wanted this project done, that project done, and another project done. She fostered kids and went into all the problems these kids had, but she needed the extra money. But then she justified herself by how she was not fostering kids for the money. This and that, and so on. My mind was blown. This woman was crazy. After about twenty minutes, I finally had to stop her from talking by way of interruption. I said, "Karen, do you want estimates on all these projects you want done?"

She replied, "Oh No! I just want an estimate on this bedroom back here."

"Can you show me the bedroom?" I started quickly before she got into her next rant. Karen proceeded down the hallway. The bedroom was at the back of the house on the left. Here came another ten minutes of Karen's rambling. Why did she think this or that color would be best? If she should remove the wallpaper bordering or keep the wallpaper? Paint the ceiling or leave it alone? I stared at her the entire time, thinking, *I'm never going to get out of this house.*

I interrupted her again, "Karen, I need to know what to estimate. If you do just the walls, it would cost about $200 in labor and 1 gallon of paint; maybe 2."

She responded, "Oh! $200 for just the walls? Well, I guess I thought it would be cheaper than that." A slight pause, her first paused moment in 30 minutes. The pause lasted two seconds, and she said,

"Okay, just do the walls!"

I responded, "Sounds good, I will be here Friday next week and get this knocked out for you. I have another appointment this morning, and I'm running a little late, I need to get going!"

I ran out the door as quickly as possible. I was not going to give her a chance to say anything else. Even the smallest project estimate took way too long. As I was driving away, I thought, *Maybe she will cancel!*

That next Friday came, and she didn't cancel. I decided to take one of my guys to help me so I could complete the job as fast as possible. Karen was gone that morning, so we knocked it all out as fast as possible. We were so close to getting out of the door before she came home. We didn't make it. Unbelievably she looked at the room and said, "Looks good, guys!"

I was so relieved; I could have sworn she was going to have some type of complaint. We had everything loaded back up in the truck. My workers would always walk back in with me to say thank you for the work. Karen started in again about everything in her life. Five minutes into listening to Crazy Karen, my worker taps me on the back and gives me that look saying, *Bro, I am out of here!* And heads out the door. I eventually found my break in her never-ending, long-winded diatribe. That is putting it nicely. "I have to get going," I said.

Karen responded, "Well, I have not paid you yet."

I had already made my mind up that with this woman who was May's family friend, the job was going to be free. I had just painted a bedroom for a foster kid, and a little charity towards that kid, not Karen, meant something to me. I said, "It's free, you owe me nothing."

Karen couldn't believe, "REALLY!? Thank you so much. You don't have to do that!"

"It's my pleasure. Have a nice night," I replied and ran out the door. This woman was nuts, and I couldn't wait to get home to my family.

BROTHERS

The beads of water continued down my body. My mind continued to race. I put my hand on the shower wall. Naked and now afraid. I now had to tell May I let the babysitter shave the back of my head. How was I going to tell her? When was I going to tell her without kids around? How was she going to react? While still standing there in the shower, I fell asleep. Out cold. A few seconds later, my hand slipped off the wall. Somehow, I caught myself without falling. It was not just my hand that was slipping. My mind, body, and now heart were all slipping. My mind was out of control. My body felt like I was put through a meat grinder. My heart, for the first time in my entire marriage, was saddened by a decision I made. After four days of no sleep because of one mistake, anger set in. I was mad at myself, and now, for the first time, I was mad at this babysitter. My workers, friends, brother, everyone was right. I needed to be careful. I needed to get this girl out of my house. And now I needed to talk to May. Talking to May was not going to be easy. May was not exactly the tender-hearted pushover.

May was the middle child. She grew up in between two brothers. She had an older brother Richard and a younger brother Jack. Richard liked everything to be his way. As a kid, he was particular with his stuff. He had matchbox cars and would have them in a specific order. May thought it was so funny to go mess them all up and put them out of order. Richard would lose his mind. May loved torturing Richard. Richard wanted his stuff left alone. No way would May let that happen. She was his little shithead sister. Richard had some type of slight educational impairment as a kid. He was embarrassed by it, and I think to this day, it is part of his drive to be successful. Richard hates wasting money. He's still, to this day, very particular. May's biggest memories of childhood with Richard are not good. Richard accidentally hit her once with a golf club and May had to get stitches. Another memory, which was the biggest memory May would recall with Richard, was him messing around with a lighter and, by accident, burned down their house. From what I understand, the house burned all the way down. In this part of Eastern Illinois, it was a volunteer fire service. They would say, "It took them forever to show up!"

Jack was the baby brother. Jack was the athlete. He played soccer, golf, and other sports. Jack was tall, lanky, and fast like their dad, Curt. You put those two next to each other, and it was like you were looking at the same person. Jack struggled his whole life with A.D.D. Everyone struggled to hold a conversation with him. Jack had a lot of personality. He loved having a fun time and taking risks. Jack loved our kids and would stop by often to see them. At one time, Jack and I were close. Right out of high school, Jack moved in with May and me for a brief period. I disagreed with it and expressed that to May. However, I lost. I rarely won any disagreements. Jack would pop in and out at all hours. It was not good for May and my new relationship, but May didn't care. She wanted to help her brother, so he moved in! May's entire life, she got whatever she wanted. That included our marriage. I would often disagree with her requests; I would always give in because arguing with May when she wanted something important to her was World War Three.

MAD LOVE

May got what May wanted. It was the biggest issue in our marriage. May might be the best person with words I have ever met. She should have been a lawyer. She could manipulate anyone to side with her. Eventually, people she was close to, that she was around the most, would just concede. May could never keep a *best girlfriend*. She had multiple girls that she would meet and be BFFs (best friends forever). Then, all of a sudden, they would stop talking to her. That is what May hated about our marriage. May had to answer to someone besides herself. I was a dominant male figure that she fell in love with. This led to May being aggressive in our marriage. She would ask me a question; it could be

anything! And if I said no, 99% of the time, watch out! She was short-tempered, to say the least. I was short-tempered, as well. I noticed May's short temper within just a couple of weeks of our relationship. May has a way of pushing people to their breaking points. Our marriage was no different. I was of no help to the situation either because I am also a very dominant personality.

My biggest flaw in our marriage was allowing myself to get mad when May flipped out. It always started when I disagreed with May for any reason. She was also good at influencing people to be on her side. In a way, pinning people against the person she was in an argument with. She's not just like that with me. She's like that with everyone. I didn't think it was fair play, especially with her husband! I grew to hate standing up for myself when I knew she was going to disagree. May started to realize our arguments were not healthy. She and I had everything else figured out! It was just these blow-up arguments, often over dumb shit. This is why they call it *crazy in love*! When May started to feel our disagreements were unhealthy, she began to request counseling.

We started going to counseling when she was pregnant with our first child. We wanted to learn how to communicate better during heated disagreements. After multiple months of counseling, this elder female counselor one day said, "May, do you mind stepping out for a minute?" May had to be thinking, *Oh she's going to give it to him.* To be honest, that is exactly what I thought the counselor was going to do. May steps out.

The counselor says, "Pull your chair a little closer." I did.

She continued, "D.J., you are with a very emotional and now pregnant woman. You chose to be in this relationship with her and to get her pregnant. She's not going to get any better any time soon. Try agreeing more and speaking less. This is not your fault, but unfortunately, she shows no signs of wanting to change herself. She just wants to change you."

I looked at this elder female counselor and said, "Okay. So, what do I say to May about our discussion?"

"Tell her I said to you she's pregnant and more hormonal than normal, and you need to give her more grace," She responded. I walked out thinking, *What in the fuck just happened?* The counselor had said that May was in counseling to change me and not herself! I thought, *That is kind of messed up, and that counselor has like 40 years' experience.* We never stopped going to counseling. May requested, and I would be forced to go throughout the years. That might be the thought of every man secretly, *My wife is forcing us to go seek counseling.* I was forced, but I went into counseling wanting to improve our communication skills. Little does May know that every single counselor we have ever seen in our entire relationship has said something similar to what our first counselor had said.

Our last counselor looked directly her and said, "May, when you back him into corners, that makes

D.J. feel threatened. Especially when you are grabbing his mouth, telling him to shut up." The counselor continued, "I highly recommend a "timeout," in these moments."

Every single counselor we ever saw has said something similar. During times of heated disagreements, it is incredibly wise and healthy to take a TIME OUT! May never listened. I could say, "Time out! And May would follow me all around the house relentlessly to get her point across. Unfortunately, I never blamed May.

Why could May not calm herself down? Childhood baggage bullshit. Her dad Curt was an alcoholic

who would go on speed and alcohol binges. When he did this, he would be gone for days, sometimes a week. This childhood memory of her dad leaving fucked May up in the head. May refused to let me leave or take a timeout. I had to either agree with everything, or it was a fight. Which eventually led to me being in a corner. Which eventually led to me feeling threatened. Which never ended well unless I gave in. After the very first counselor, I would be saying, "Time out, time out, time out."

May refused. She has never been able to control her rage in our marriage. The crazy part? I love this woman so much it would only bother me for a few hours, and I was over it. I saw May's flaws and thought, *I don't care as long as she never divorces me and stays loyal.* Unhealthy disagreements never stopped. The problem persisted over the years. Counselor after counselor. Nothing changed. Time-outs or safe spaces never existed. If I left, I would be the biggest piece of shit husband in the world. Though I never cheated, never watched porn, didn't masturbate, and stayed as loyal to her as I could. I was not allowed to leave or get a time-out, even if she knew where I was going. She always knew where I was, she tracked my phone. After years went by, I started to think. *Does May potentially have some type of "manic disorder?"*

She would get so mad over the smallest things if I disagreed with her. I can't tell you how many times I said, "May! Agree to disagree, babe!" Never worked. Our fights got worse. Her aggression towards me increased. She started to become handsy. This led to me leaving the house and saying things I didn't mean out of anger. I would leave the house and drive around and would come back after I thought she calmed down. May started counting how many times I left.

Now I had the biggest issue of my life on my hands. How do I approach May about this babysitter, knowing if she disagrees, it could end up being the biggest argument of our life? And now, I'm not just telling her that we need to get rid of Raven. Now I had to tell her she shaved the back of my head and all these other "devious circumstances." I had a problem. Now a bigger problem. How could this possibly get worse? Flashbacks with Raven continued. I had to have my stories lined up to tell May before approaching her. If not, all hell would break lose.

DISCOMFORT

A week prior, my brother, Matt, stopped by the house to give me a hand with a few things. Matt had been around Raven many times and never had a "good feeling" about her. We were in and out of the house while Raven was watching the kids. I asked Matt to stop by before I relieved the babysitter of her duties so we could get the few things I needed done without distraction from the kids. With five young kids running around, it was always a challenge to be productive around the house. Matt and I were walking in and out of the house. As I walked in, it seemed like every single time Raven was bending over as we walked by with tight spandex on that didn't seem appropriate. If she didn't have her special jeans on, it would be skintight spandex every other day. May would always tell me they were comfortable, and that is why women wore them. I always thought they were a little over the top, especially for women with curves. Raven had curves; the choice of clothing was not appropriate in my mind. It seemed to me a modest woman would bend over by going into a crouched position, not straight legs bent over at the waist. As we walked in, on three separate occasions, Raven bent over. It was not necessarily the bending over that was the problem. It was the timing of the bending over. It is not a coincidence to bend over like that multiple times in a row at just the right time when we walked past. I felt uncomfortable. I almost felt embarrassed by what my brother was witnessing. I already knew how he felt about her, and now I knew he was going to say something.

My brother had never once, in 30 years of brotherhood, said something about a female making him uncomfortable. After the third time in a row, as we walked back outside, Matt looked at me and said, "What is up with your babysitter?"

I knew what he was talking about, but I wanted to reaffirm that what I witnessed is what he witnessed. I responded, "What do you mean?"

Matt said, "Bro! She's obviously seeking attention as you walk through your house. She's bending over, and it is a little weird, man."

I blinked slowly, took a breath, and responded with concern, "I thought the same thing Matt, I honestly have been questioning a lot of situations with her lately. My crew is even saying stuff to me."

Matt continued, "I'm just telling you, man, something is up, and I don't like it."

I replied, "I agree, man. I am not messing with that girl. I would never do anything to hurt May."

Matt said, "Ya, I know, but don't get yourself in a bad situation." We continued with the work, and the subject was dropped. Both of us questioned Raven's motives.

SAY WHAT?

I finished in the shower after almost collapsing, grabbed a towel, and sat on the edge of the shower. I recalled a disturbing flashback from just a few days prior. It solidified what all the people who were concerned about the nightmare girl, Raven, had been saying. To this day, my biggest regret was not getting this female out of my house after that moment. Looking back, not having a clear mind was no excuse. My thoughts cycled repetitively, like a nightmare that wouldn't end.

Less than a week before the bathroom incident, I was finishing a job an hour away. The crew and I were restoring a concrete floor for a school. It was a workshop maintenance area pole barn where they would pull buses in and do bus maintenance. They wanted the floor to be a professional epoxy application, enabling them to clean up the floor easily. We were finishing the prep work and about to apply the epoxy. Epoxy jobs are finicky. Once you start applying the product, there is no turning back. You apply the first coat; then, you must recoat within a specific timeframe. The time limit for a recoat is different for all products. Our specific recoat window was between four to six hours after the initial coat was applied. We finished the prep work. We applied the first coat. The weather changed.

Humidity increased; temperatures dropped. Our second application time changed. Instead of a two to four-hour window, it was now six to eight hours later. We were all upset. This meant we had to go home and drive back at night. I bribed the guys with a bonus just to get them to show up. We finished at 10 p.m.. It was 11 p.m. before I walked back into the house. This was the end of day two, with no rest.

I got home and scavenged the refrigerator for food. I found some junk snack food. I did most of the cooking at home, May was not a cook and didn't like to cook. I didn't expect any leftover dinner. I was at the fire station the next day. May was at the hospital the next day, she was already in bed for the night. I was not a big drinker, but I did like a Miller Light or two after a long day of work. I sat down in the living room, kicked my feet up, and took a big breath. I noticed Raven had a friend over, and she said, "Hi, nice to meet you"

I responded, "Howdy, nice to meet you!" "I'm Raven's cousin, Betty."

I replied, "Hi, Betty, welcome to the house. Make yourself at home."

I could tell she was older than Raven. I continued, "How are you two cousins?" Betty gave me the whole story.

She explained how they were related and continued, "I live in California; my dad owns a construction company. We used to live here, but my dad had a dispute with a cousin, and we ended up in California. I'm on break from college, and every year, I visit Raven. We usually get ourselves in trouble." The two of them looked at each other and laughed. They seemed to have a good friendship.

I continued, "Well, make yourself at home, Betty. Welcome to my house. If you are old enough, grab yourself a beer, I know college students like to have a drink while on break. I only have a few, so I know you won't get carried away."

Betty replied, "I'm only nineteen, but thanks anyway!"

Betty continued, "How did you and May meet? Five kids? Y'all are crazy!"

I responded, "May was on a mission trip. No, sorry, let me correct myself. May was studying abroad in college. We met before she left and talked every single day until she got home. We had a baby within a year and married each other shortly after Demi was born. I knew she was the one before she came home from Germany."

"Ahhhh nice!" Betty said.

Simultaneously Raven jumped in and changed the subject, it was as if she didn't like to hear about May's and my love story. Raven jumped in the convo. "Speaking of a mission trip! I am going on one soon!" Raven had never mentioned this before.

"Where are you going, Raven?" I asked.

She continued, "I'm going to Haiti with a group from church, and I'm soooooo excited!"

I responded like any father figure would. "Raven, make sure you stay in your group while you are on the mission trip."

As any 15-year-old, oblivious teenager would respond, Raven responded. "I will be fine! Everyone says it is safe!"

I continued in father mode, knowing she was not thinking about safety. "Raven, sex trafficking does exist in other countries. Make sure you stay with your group. Men are stronger than women. No one wants to see something bad happen to you. If you stay in your group and don't get separated, you will be fine."

Betty spoke up, she could tell I was trying to give some fatherly advice. "D.J., Raven is pretty naïve.

She doesn't understand what other countries are like yet. She's still a..." There was a long pause.

I responded, "Still a what? I'm confused."

Betty answered quickly, "Never mind! Forget I said anything."

As with any conversation, when someone starts to say something and stops, the curiosity kills. I said, "No, no, still a what?"

Betty said, "Well, you know!"

While simultaneously looking over at Raven. I replied again, "No, I don't know."

Betty looks over at Raven again, and Raven whispers, "Shut up, Betty, you're embarrassing me!" Betty spoke again, "You know? A virrr,"

It was like she was messing with Raven, who got frustrated and finished the phrase. "I'm still a virgin, okay? Happy?"

I stepped in and said, "Good! That is good! Save yourself for marriage. Boys at your age only want one thing anyway. They will use you and get rid of you. May and I both wish we would have saved ourselves for each other." Raven was now giving Betty the big eyes. The look seemed different than normal. It was like before I walked into the room; they were having a similar conversation. However, Betty had already let the cat out of the bag.

Raven continued, "Well, that doesn't mean I don't have fantasies!" Immediately I thought to myself, *Say what?!* I must have had a look of shock on my face as I turned, looking at Raven as those words exited her mouth. Raven was looking at Betty as she began to speak, but then she turned her head and looked directly at me. By instinct, after hearing someone say something like that, I was now looking at her. It was the most awkward feeling I had ever experienced. I couldn't help but question why she said that and why she looked directly at me after saying it. *Did what I think happen, just happen?* I thought again to myself, *Was Raven caught off guard by her cousin and, in some type of passive-aggressive way, sliding me a hint?* My first thought was, *surely not!* I was the naïve one! I had been lectured multiple times within the last week by my brother and my crew. *Holy shit!* I thought. That just happened, and all the signs are saying this 15-year-old babysitter was speaking directly

97

to me. I looked over at Betty, her eyes showed she was as shocked as I was.

It was time for a subject change. I said, "Well, I'm going to go sit outside. The lightning bugs are out, and it is cool to see this time of year. There are hundreds of them out there in the field." I stood up and walked out of the room, heading outside. I started shaking my head in disbelief and thought, *What in the fuck is going on?* I already knew the answer to that question. Raven had some type of feelings for me, and I was not in a good place. I was in my own damn house and felt uncomfortable. My problems were piling up. May was unhappy with my work schedule. I was on this new medication, causing me to have sleep issues. I had stressful construction projects going on. I was remodeling my house and trying to finish the barn. I just got promoted, and that came with extra responsibilities. Our union was under contract negotiations. Having five kids under ten years old was stressful enough. And here is this girl I trusted who is now making me uncomfortable in my house. My mind was consumed, and to top it off, I was even more bothered by something else.

BABY BOY

Just a few weeks prior, I was on shift, and we were dispatched out to a medical call. Surely you have been close to a fire station at some point in your life and heard what we firefighters call "the tones." The dispatch tones. Some of those tones we never forget. The tones went off. "Medic 15 and Engine 9, Medic 15 and Engine 9 be en route to 1211 East Wind Street for an unconscious, unresponsive ninety-year-old male. Last known breathing three minutes ago." It was the sound of death due to the age of the male. However, three minutes is not that long. There was hope. We rushed out of the station. I was the officer in charge.

"Engine 9 clear dispatch," I said over the radio. On this day, I was the only Emergency Medical Technician (EMT) on the truck. The chauffeur (driver) and the back-end guy were both veterans who were grandfathered in and were never required to receive their EMT certification. Which meant I was the officer in charge and would be the primary caretaker for the patient until the medics arrived. The medics rarely arrived before us, if ever.

We arrived, and I went over the radio again, "Engine 9 on scene dispatch." The back-end guy grabbed the bags, I walked fast up to the door. Any time we heard the words "unconscious and unresponsive," it was a faster-than-normal walk up to the house. A lady comes running out saying, "HURRY, PLEASE HELP, PLEASE, DO SOMETHING, PLEASE!"

These words were common for us but not for a ninety-year-old male. The lady continued, "In the hallway on the right!"

I remember thinking, "She's frazzled. He's 90 years old, lady!" I get to the hallway, turn right, and on the ground is a nine-month-old baby lying on his back, unconscious and unresponsive, with a man attempting CPR (cardiopulmonary resuscitation). My heart had never sunk so fast in my life as, in a panic, I thought *How did dispatch get this wrong? Nine months? Ninety-year-old? Oh my God!*

"Sir, please stop CPR and take a step out into the hallway. I will do everything I can to help the child." The baby boy was unconscious, unresponsive, and without a pulse. I started chest compressions and looked up at the guys with me in that hallway. Their mouths dropped. We went to work. I was an EMT, not a paramedic. A paramedic has more schooling, experience, and privileges than an EMT. EMTs are limited in what they can do, especially with a 9-month-old.

For a medic, this was a nightmare call. Here we were with a nine-month-old child that was dispatched as a 90-year-old male.

The first thing any type of medic does is check the airway. Is the airway clear or obstructed in any way? I checked the airway, and it was clear. I asked the back-end man to get the Bag Valve Mask ready. We call it the BVM or Ambu bag. It attaches to oxygen, and you hold the device over the patient's mouth. Simultaneously you tilt the head and lift the chin to open the airway. When you squeeze the device, it pushes oxygen into the patient's lungs. If you see the chest rise, then you know you have a good airway. We established an airway and gently started giving 30 to 40 forced breaths per minute and 100-200 chest compressions per minute! All done simultaneously while asking as many questions as possible to the parents. The first question in these situations is always, "Did the child choke?"

We were taught to go through a list of questions that is an acronym, S.A.M.P.L.E.: which translates as signs/symptoms, allergies, medications, pertinent history, last oral intake, and events leading up to the crisis at hand. This acronym helped us to quickly ask questions. I asked all these questions to the parents, but they were not able to give any clues as to why this child was unconscious and unresponsive without a pulse. No signs or symptoms leading up to the baby collapsing. No allergies. No medications. No pertinent history. The last oral intake was a bottle of milk. No significant events led up to the current

emergency. We had a nightmare situation on our hands. I only had one child like this before this and wanted little Jacob to start breathing so badly!

I will never forget that first child. I was doing everything possible to bring that baby boy back to life. I knew what to do from a medical standpoint. However, I was secretly praying over and over in my head to Jesus to please intervene and rescue this beautiful baby boy. A medic always checks pupils for dilation. Dilation of the pupils can help with diagnosis. The nine-month-old little boy had the most beautiful blue eyes. He had light blonde hair. He was so gorgeous he looked like a girl. His skin was warm to the touch with a perfect, freckled little face. We worked him, I prayed, and up until the paramedic ambulance arrived, the baby boy was still unconscious, unresponsive, with no pulse. We informed dispatch that it was not a 90-year-old male but that it was a nine-month-old male. You could hear the sad response when dispatch responded with, "We are clear, Engine 9."

The paramedics finally arrived, and they assumed what was called command and control of the patient. They are of higher rank in the medical field. There is a lot that happens quickly when trying to save a patient. Often in these circumstances, the medics will ask if one of our guys can ride with them to continue chest compressions while they do everything else. The paramedics asked, "Can someone ride along?"

I responded, "Yes."

I carried Jacob into the ambulance. I was holding him with one arm, resuming chest compressions with my other hand. I placed him on the cot in the back of the ambulance and never stopped chest compressions. Think of chest compressions as keeping the heart beating and keeping blood flowing throughout the body. The medics started an IV and did everything they could to save the little guy's life. By the time we arrived at the hospital, baby boy Jacob with blonde hair, blue eyes, and a little freckled face, was still not breathing and had no pulse. I knew and thought, *He was not going to make it.* When you arrive at the hospital in situations like this, the doctors are ready to go.

The paramedics can help. However, there are also nurses standing by, ready to do their job. Little Jacob was wheeled in on the cot while I continued compressions until we reached the Emergency Room. A nurse looked at me and said, "You're drenched in sweat. Let me take over from here."

I looked down at my shirt. I was drenched in sweat without even realizing it. The entire medical call had worn me out. I accepted her relief. I took one last look at the little guy and walked away. I walked out of the hospital, and the crew was there to pick me up. I jumped in the fire truck, and we were all silent. We were back to the firehouse, and the back-end guy says, "That was FUCKED!"

"Yup!" I said, fighting back tears.

We pulled into the fire station. I jumped out and thought, I want to get this report done immediately. I needed to finish this call and do it now. When you're the officer, you're never really finished with an emergency call until your report is done. Officers must fill out a report online into the database after every call, no matter what. I filled out the report in detail, and I was done. The total time of the call from when I laid eyes on Jacob until the ambulance passed him over to the hospital was twenty minutes. It may not seem like a long time, but it is when you have no signs of life. Little Jacob had passed away. I was the first to touch him and the last person to hand him over to the doctors. I didn't need to call the hospital to find out if Jacob had survived. I knew the answer. He'd passed away, and it messed me up.

103

I went out to my truck. At the fire station, your vehicle in the parking lot is about the only private spot you can find. I sat down in my truck and just started crying. This little boy didn't make it, and I was blaming myself. I was going through every second of the medical call with questions for myself. *Could I have done anything differently? What did I do wrong? How could I have done something better? And where was Jesus when I needed Him?* I cried for about 5-10 minutes. Just then, the backend guy walked out of the building. He was a veteran. He had 28 years of service. His name was Daniel. We called him Danny.

DANNY

Danny's and my families were related. We were fifth cousins or something like that. He was like an uncle to me. I called him Uncle Danny. Danny was at the end of his career. He couldn't stand the job anymore. Before Danny got to my truck, I stepped out. Danny asked, "You okay, D.J.?"

"Ya, man," I replied.

He could hear the sadness in my voice. He continued, "It is not your fault, buddy. You did a good job.

There's nothing better we could have done."

"Thanks, Danny, that means a lot," I responded. He tapped me on my shoulder giving me an " I love you, man" moment. We said nothing else. He went home and to bed. When I returned home, I sat and looked at the tube, and nothing registered as happens when watching TV and your mind is completely messed up. And just a few days later, I was sitting in my living room listening to strange words come out of a babysitter's mouth. The problems were not going away. My life was rapidly falling apart.

SLEEPING BEAUTY

I started walking out to see the lightning bugs. As I walked, I had to pass our bedroom. We had a window next to our bedroom without a curtain or blind. If the front barn lights were on, I could see May's face while she was sleeping. The barn lights were on. I could see her face perfectly as it was facing my direction. I have always loved watching May sleep. Through all our arguments. Through all our problems. I adored her. She gave birth to five of our children. May was precious to me. I recently read that when a man says to his wife, "You are the most beautiful woman I have ever seen.", the man knows it is a lie, and he's just trying to "suck up."

But I told May every single day for over ten years that she was the most beautiful woman I had ever seen. The difference between other men and me? I meant it. May meant the world to me, and she was the most beautiful woman I had ever seen. I never said it with any doubt. I think May believed me. Maybe not at first, but as time passed, I said it every single day. I think she started to believe it. Looking back, it might have played a factor in her holding tight to our marriage. She had a man who thought she was the most beautiful walking woman that he had ever seen. She knew no man would ever truly feel that way about her again, so she stayed strong and avoided ever letting go. Our wedding vows meant something to her.

I will never forget our wedding vow rehearsal. Father James, the Priest who married us ended up baptizing all our children. Father James was always a "by the book" kind of guy. After I went to May's dad and received permission to marry May, I went straight to Father James. I was terrified because we already had a child out of wedlock. Father James knew me well. He knew I had been inspired to become a priest in the past. However, I refused not to have children of my own. I loved kids, there was no way I was going to live my life without my little rascals.

I asked Father James, "Can May and I get married in the Catholic Church even though we have a child out of wedlock?"

He responded, "D.Jayyyy, I knew this question was coming eventually." He paused. I looked him dead in the eye and said, "You know how much this means to me."

He responded, "I will marry you. However, I want you to take the premarital wedding classes, and I want you and May to practice abstinence starting now until the wedding."

My eyes got big as I thought to myself, *I can't have sex with May until our wedding?*

I quickly responded, "Deal!" It was more important to me to be married in the Catholic Church than it was to make love to May. May reluctantly agreed. We knew we had no other choice. We both had gone through classes and understood how important the Sacrament of Marriage was, not just to us but to God Himself.

WE SLIPPED AND FELL!

We took premarital classes, and we practiced abstinence. I can't remember the total period of abstinence; I do know it was over six months. It felt like years. March of that year, with our wedding scheduled for July, we slipped up. It was the only time we slipped up, but we failed. May was horny, I was always horny. We had made out so many times during this "time of abstinence," but somehow, we always stopped ourselves.

It felt like a suitable time to celebrate. We had just finished adding a master bathroom to our house and had remodeled most of the house by this point. We converted a family room into a master bedroom and added a nice master bathroom. Our bedroom was freshly painted, and our bathroom was done and nicely finished. We had May's sleigh bed frame from her mom's house. Our house was starting to feel like a cozy home, and May was incredibly pleased. I walked up to her while she was lying in bed reading a book at night as she always did. I kissed her forehead and said, "Thank you for all you do for our family. Breastfeeding our daughter. Keeping our house clean and organized. Working a part-time job to help our finances. Going to school to become a nurse. Thank you, May, you are amazing, and I can't wait to marry you."

She would always look at me with these big brown eyes full of love. I could always tell by the way she looked at me that she loved me. I would always think, *This woman truly loves me.* It made me feel so special to have a woman who genuinely loved me. She gave me more of a look than just love. She pulled me in. We had survived months without making love. We had resisted and stopped ourselves so many times. We were two horny humans, and the temptation this time wouldn't be overcome. I was still standing but bent over as she grabbed my face, pulled me in, and started kissing me. Our tongues met. She always liked her tongue on top. She was not going to stop herself, and I could tell I was not stopping us either. Our willpower was gone at this moment.

When she was very excited and eager for sex, I could tell. She would kiss with a larger mouth. Her saliva would be slathered on my cheeks. I was bent over, still standing on the ground. She took her left hand, grabbed me, and squeezed. I could feel my erection send a sensation up my spine. May whispered, "I want you." She started undoing my belt and unbuttoning my jeans. She spun her body up from her reading position and, with her left foot, pushed my jeans to the ground. She pushed me back and stepped off the bed, and got on her knees. Before she slid my briefs off, she grabbed me again with her left hand and my sack with her right hand.

She looked up at me with a look of, "I'm going to taste you!" She looked back down slowly and slid my boxers off. When she was horny like this, she would suck hard and slow. She would often say, "I love your dick."

I believed her because of how she would suck me. After about a minute, I couldn't take it anymore. I pulled her up. She was wearing my T-shirt. She loved wearing my T-shirts, especially my fire department shirts. I assumed this brought back her memory of when we met. "Are you D.J. Murphy?" She ripped my shirt off. I aggressively pushed her down onto the bed while I was still standing on the floor. She had black panties on. I ripped them off. She had wet hair, having just gotten out of the shower. She liked when I would suck her toes. I started licking her leg from her thigh up to her feet. Nothing grossed me out with May. Her feet were sexy to me, and she had just showered. I started licking the toes of her right foot.

As I sucked her big toe, she said in a high pitch but not a loud voice, "Lick me." She was not talking about her toes. She loved my big hands; she would call them "magical." I took my right hand and placed it on top of her vagina. I could feel her moist vagina steaming. We were caged animals breaking out. With my hand upside down, I spread her lips with my thumb and index finger. I started licking her in circles at the top. She arched her back and pushed my face into her.

After a moment, she also couldn't take it anymore and she said, "Make love to your future wife!" I stood up, grabbed her hips, and pulled her to the edge of the bed. I bent down one more time and licked slowly from the bottom to the top with a big tongue.

"Ahhhh," She squealed as she continued, "Make me cum."

I grabbed myself and started rubbing back and forth across her clit. I enjoyed making her wait long enough to almost beg for me. "Fuck me now," She said in an aggressive tone. I pulled her hips in and right away went inside her deep. This was something I would normally have to wait a few minutes for. But not this time, May was opened up, soaking wet, and ready for it all. I took my right thumb upside down and started rubbing her clit with a gentle force.

Seconds later, she screamed, "I'm cumming, I'm cumming!" I was surprised at how fast she was cumming. It hadn't crossed my mind that she was "extra horny" from ovulation. Her vagina made a sound. Like a gush of water being squeezed from inside her walls, pushing across my dick. I had to taste what just came out of her. I pulled out and immediately started sucking every inch of her vagina.

"I need to taste you," I said. Seconds later, she pulled my face up. She took her left hand and wiped my face off, covered in her cum.

"I want your dick again," She said.

She grabbed me and placed me back inside her. I started thrusting as she spread her hips up and out. She wanted all of it. She grabbed my right hand and placed it back onto her clit. I rubbed her until she came quickly two more times back-to-back. She screamed, "Oh my God, Oh My God, Oh My God."

After she exploded the third time, she pulled herself up. She turned around and said, "Come here." She wanted it from behind. She loved me to finish from behind.

"Come inside your future wife!" She said again.

I got behind her on my knees. I grabbed myself and went back inside her. She went down to her elbows. She knew this was game over for me. She had been fulfilled and wanted me to finish. I pulled her hips up into the air. I started thrusting again. She screamed, "Give it to me, D.J.!"

I took my time as her high-pitched noises continued, "Ahh, ahh, ahh." "Cum baby, cum!" She groaned.

I did. I finished. She fell onto her chest. I fell with her. "Stay inside me for a minute," May said. She wanted to soak in my cum and the moment. She would often say this. Our sex life was good and stayed great our entire marriage. At this moment, we knew it would be months before we would make love again.

She pulled herself off me as she flopped down, twirling face up, and said, "Come hold me."

We lay next to each other sweaty and sticky. May said, "I love you so much, I am the luckiest woman alive when I'm with you. You treat me so good; I am spoiled."

I replied, "I love you too, baby, I am a lucky man as well. I will never betray you; we are soul mates. I can't wait to marry you." She started to kiss my entire face. We were magically in love. Two alpha humans who passionately, with all their hearts, loved one another. We stared at each other almost as if we were thinking, *Is this real?*

She said, as she always did after sex at night, "I'm hungry Daddy. What are you going to make me?"

I responded, "How about one of your grandma's famous ham sandwiches? We have the baby sweet pickles and Lay's potato chips."

"Yaaaa, perfect!" She replied. Her grandma would make ham sandwiches with sweet baby pickles and then put crushed Lay's potato chips on them when May was a kid. I loved them, they were so good! No matter what I prepared, she loved it. She loved my food. I loved serving her food. We were matched for each other perfectly, and she loved to eat, which was important to me because I loved to cook.

A MOTHER'S NIGHTMARE

Love was trumping all other issues in our life. We were surviving on love. It was the definition of crazy in love. We both had childhood baggage before marriage. This came with stress we didn't foresee. It was not just May's hormones throughout and after the pregnancy and birth. At three months pregnant with our first child, May asked for relationship counseling. I was 23, she was 19. May deserves all the credit for recognizing that we didn't handle disagreements well. I was young and reluctant to agree to counseling. However, I loved May. I knew I wanted to be with her for the rest of my life. Eventually, I agreed to go. I knew we had both said things to each other out of anger; that this was unhealthy. What we didn't realize is counseling would make things worse before improvement; however, we needed to forgive and heal. Forgiveness and healing were something completely separate from counseling. We didn't just need relationship counseling. We needed individual counseling for effective forgiveness and healing, but we were too young to realize it.

We both said things we regretted. We never healed from those moments. Looking back at some of the things I said, I was not just in the wrong, I was not anywhere close to the man, future husband, and soon-to-be father I should have been. I could blame it on age, lack of wisdom, or whatever else. The truth is, I said things that hurt the person I cared the most about. To this day, I still have so many regrets. Words I spoke out of anger were not my true feelings. Comments I made in heated arguments such as, "I would never have married you if you didn't get pregnant with Demi."

Those words were evil. They were said out of anger. If May had never become pregnant with Demi, I can say with all my heart, mind, body, and soul I would have still married May without question. I didn't just love May. I adored her. I felt a connection only true soulmates experience. God led us to each other. If we had understood how to forgive and heal in the early stages of our relationship, it would have helped so much moving forward in life.

I grew up without any sisters. All I knew was how to be a man. I didn't understand how emotional and tender a woman's heart is. My biggest regret is not understanding that even if I disagreed with her, May was entitled to an opinion. I wish I would have respected and acknowledged her opinions. Instead, we both had the same mentality, "My way or the highway." All while in the back of our minds and our souls, we knew life without one another would never be fulfilling. We had met the "love of our life." Neither of us was ever taught how to handle disagreements and ultimately achieve a mature and healthy relationship. This was something we were going to learn the hard way.

One month after our oldest child was born, I was laid off from work. That came with financial challenges we didn't foresee. The fire department was supposed to be one of the most secure jobs. That was proven to be untrue.

Pre-marital sex comes with consequences. Anyone reading this who disagrees is in denial. This one slip-up during our "Practicing abstinence phase" caused a second pregnancy we were not ready for. May and I, having a pre-marital child, thrust a responsibility into our lives when we were still immature. We were so young and just simply not ready for this added responsibility. We loved our daughter. We raised her with love. We both wanted a lot of kids, so this came naturally to us. However, it took our attention off one another, which we needed at the time. Our attention and energy were spent on our baby girl. It put our relationship before marriage at risk. Somehow, we got through it, but we needed more time to understand each other and grow together in maturity first.

Father James knew we needed to practice abstinence. He had experience with other couples. May and I only had two requirements. Pre-marital classes and practice abstinence until the wedding day. May and I knew better than to give in to the temptation. We knew it would come with consequences, and it did. That March moment when we slipped up before our wedding day, you can guess what happened. May got pregnant a second time before marriage. Our temptation got the best of us. A hard lesson in life was coming our way. Having sex even once can cause pregnancy. That's saying the obvious, right?

Neither of us was ready for a second child. May and I both wanted to have a lot of kids. However, the rest of those children were supposed to come after the wedding. Every time May got pregnant, she would come to me with excitement and joy. This pregnancy was much different. May came to me with sadness and self-resentment. She informed me she was pregnant from our one-time slipping up. It was March when we slipped up. By April, she knew she was pregnant. Our wedding was not scheduled until July. May was going to be "belly showing" for her wedding pictures, and she was very bothered by this.

May always had a vision of her wedding day. She was going to be beautiful, skinny, happy, and admired by everyone attending. She knew this pregnancy was going to cancel all these "picture perfect"

wedding day moments. At the time my expressions and reactions would be best described as quietly in shock. My thoughts were, *How are we going to tell Father James? How are we going to tell our parents? How is May going to handle this? How were we going to handle this?*

I had a real-life fear of uncertainty that I had not experienced since I was a child when my parents went through an awful divorce. That feeling of fear was back in my life fifteen years later. I had extreme anxiety. I was an optimistic person who had never experienced anxiety like this before. May was experiencing all the same thoughts. This was when we should have gone to counseling. We didn't go seek help. We dealt with it on our own.

The month of May came, and we kept the secret of her pregnancy. We told no one. We didn't know how to tell anyone. We were busy planning a wedding, that was stressful enough. May woke up and said she didn't feel good. She was having sharp pains in her belly. Throughout the day, she was bleeding/spotting. Our nerves were a mess. Later that night, May contacted her OB doctor. Her doctor said if the bleeding became worse, to go to the Emergency room. Before the sun rose the next morning, I heard May crying in the bathroom. The OB had told her that if she miscarries, she will know. Can you imagine hearing those words from an OB? For every mother who has experienced this, it's horrific. May was on the toilet. I went in to check on her. She was bawling her eyes out. This situation became the worst experience of our lives until then. In a way, May resented me. I was supposed to be the leader of our home. I was supposed to be a man of God. I allowed temptation to get in the way, and now she was experiencing the worst situation of her life. I tried to hold her as she sat on the toilet. She said, "Go, I need space."

I was heartbroken. May was heartbroken. We were heartbroken. I respected her need for space. This was our first experience of what felt like the death of a child and a dagger to our hearts towards each other. Miscarriages are horrible. It was my first experience, and I just assumed the best thing to do was to give her space. It was not the best decision. I failed May. I failed as a father. I failed as a friend. I failed us. All because I allowed her to have space.

May again her OB again. By the end of the conversation, May knew she had just passed a child out of her body. It was the most horrific phone call. She was on the floor crying after that phone call. I tried again to hold her; she wanted space. I should have forced my support. I failed. I continued to give her space. She stood up and said, "I have to go to the Emergency room. I just had a miscarriage".

My mouth dropped. My stomach knotted up. I started to ask May questions. At no point was I trying to blame her. I just didn't understand how this was possible. I can't remember the questions I asked. However, the questions were not at the right time or place. May took my questions as if I was blaming her. I was not blaming her. I was living in a moment of life that neither of us had ever experienced. How was May to know what the cause was? She had no clue why this had just happened. Before we headed to the Emergency room, the worst possible situation happened. May was back on the toilet. We had always talked about having twins. My dad was a twin, her cousins were twins, and we wanted twins. We wanted May's first pregnancy after getting married to be twins. May was back on the toilet, passing a second child. She miscarried her second baby. May was devastated. I was devastated. We were devastated. Our life together felt like it was crumbling.

May passed the second child, two miscarriages in a short period. I never embraced her as I should have. I continued to tell myself, *She wants space.* She didn't need space, she needed to be embraced. To this day, my stomach drops at the recognition that I didn't do more. It was May 2009, and we were

heading to the Emergency Room. The worst part? It was Mother's Day. May and I were heading to the Emergency Room on Mother's Day. To say we were crushed is an understatement. To say May was crushed didn't even begin to describe how she was feeling. We were in the Emergency Room and spoke very few words to each other. We were in shock. We were heartbroken. The love of my life had just miscarried two children, and I had no idea what to say. I was silent for most of the time. May didn't even want me to hold her hand after the few questions I asked her to try to figure out why this had happened. I don't blame her. It was the most awful experience of our lives, and I had no idea how to embrace her. To put it simply. I failed in all aspects as a father, future husband, and friend.

May eventually looked at me in the late evening and said, "You need to go get Demi (our daughter) and take her back to our house." This surprised me. I wanted to stay by May's side. This was another moment I should have been more empathetic. I should have refused to leave her side. I should have embraced my future wife. Instead, I followed her orders. I left the hospital to get our daughter. I can't describe the guilt I had in the hours and days to come.

I texted May multiple times, "Do you want me to come back up there?" I just wanted her to say, "Yes, come back."

May never did. She said, "No, stay with Demi."

May was crushed, and she wanted to be alone, but she needed me. This was one of my biggest failures in our relationship. Eventually, she called and said, "Come get me."

I pulled up, and she was wheeled out to the car. I remember my heart dropping lower than ever before. I had no clue how serious a miscarriage was on a woman's body, physically and mentally. Typical man moment, I assumed she would walk out and be fine. Did I show up with flowers? Nope! Did I show up with a card? Nope! I showed up as a man who failed.

Every Mother's Day since then has never been what May deserved it to be. Mother's Day should be a joyful moment for a mom. A day of happiness and celebration. Mother's Day for May is sadness and sorrow. Many people say, "If you could go back and change anything, would you?" Yes, I would. I would. I would change what I said to May that wounded her soul. I would have written a letter. I would have brought her flowers. But most importantly, I would NEVER have left her side. I failed May way before we ever got married. May knew it.

BROKEN HEART WEIGHT LOSS

When I met May, she weighed around 170 or so pounds. I loved every inch of her body. She would say she was overweight, and I would reassure her that I thought she was perfect. I never once body-shamed her. I truly loved her natural body. I couldn't care less how much she weighed. She was the most beautiful woman I had ever laid eyes on. She was perfect to me. That was all that mattered. After the miscarriage, she didn't eat. She had a deep sadness in her that I had never seen before. She was on a mission to fit into a wedding dress, and now her sadness prevented her from eating regardless. A few weeks after the miscarriage, May and her mom went wedding dress shopping. They ended up at a resale shop. May found the most beautiful dress that she wanted to wear.

May was not driven by the best motives. The miscarriage changed her. No one was going to tell her she couldn't fit in this dress. When a woman is driven by sadness, it is almost impossible to change their mind on anything once that kind of decision is made. May was going to weigh 125 pounds on our wedding day. She was going to be the most beautiful bride. She was determined, as I had never seen her before. She worked out every day, and she ate hardly anything. The wedding was approaching, and May achieved her goal. She was fitting in her dress. I was not allowed to see her until the wedding day in her dress, but she did it. May was beautiful to me no matter what weight she carried -- 170 pounds or 125 pounds.

I felt the same about her. She could have weighed 200 pounds, and if she were all mine, I wouldn't have cared.

TEARS OF JOY

The wedding rehearsal came. May's personality is organized and structured. When things are out of place, May becomes a different person. May had the entire wedding organized perfectly. She planned the wedding rehearsal, and everything went perfectly. We were at the church rehearsing for the wedding before the rehearsal dinner. Father James and a lady who worked at the church went over everything. At the end, Father James called May and me up in front of everyone to rehearse our wedding vows. I was surprised. I thought I wouldn't recite the vows until the big day.

Father James started, "Since it is your intention to enter into the covenant of Holy Matrimony, join your hands, and declare before God and His Church. Do you, Durand Joseph Murphy, take May Maria Williams to be your wife?"

I responded, "I do."

Father James continued, "Do you promise to be faithful to her in good times and bad, in sickness and in health, to love her and to honor her all the days of your life until death do you part." I lost it. I started bawling my eyes out. In front of everyone at the rehearsal, the big strong manly man D.J. was showing how big of a baby he really is. I was revealing how vulnerable May made me. I loved this woman unconditionally.

I responded, full of tears, "I do!"

May looked at me. She squeezed my hands. She said, "D.J., it is okay." What she didn't know was that I was not just crying tears of joy because I was so excited to marry her. I knew without a doubt in my mind that God had placed in my life the most precious woman who I adored without measure or any doubt, I was so proud to marry this woman. May was my everything.

My tears caused May to tear up a little. It was now her turn. Father James smiled and continued, "Since it is your intention to enter into the covenant of Holy Matrimony, with your hands joined together, declare before God and His Church. Do you, May Maria Williams, take Durand Joseph Murphy to be your husband?"

May responded, "I do."

Father James continued, "Do you promise to be faithful to him in good times and in bad, in sickness and in health, to love him and to honor him all the days of your life until death do you part?"

May responded with the biggest smile, "I do."

We then pretended to place our rings on the other's ring finger. Father James saved the rest until the wedding day. He said, "I will save the rest until tomorrow, D.J. can't handle the rest today!" Everyone laughed. All the groomsmen came up behind me and started messing with me. May and I smiled at each other.

Everyone was hungry, and we had a rehearsal dinner to attend. I said, "Let's all go get some food!" Everyone smiled, and off we went. The rehearsal dinner was perfect. May had never been so beautiful. She wore a purple and white, flowy dress with heels. She was stunning. We had drinks. We ate. We danced. Everyone was having an exciting time. Tears of joy were everywhere. May's parents, my parents, all our close friends and family, everyone was having a fun time. May and I felt like the entire world revolved around us. We couldn't wait until it was official.

FINAL BACHELOR DAYS

As with any wedding day, the night before May and I went our separate ways. She went with her bridesmaids; I went with the groomsmen. For the groomsmen, it was time to party. I had planned a three-day groomsmen bachelor party fiasco. It was all clean and fun, but we lived it up for three days. The wedding was on a Saturday. We started on Wednesday night. We went to an indoor go-cart facility. I had never been before and heard the carts were fast. They were. One of the guys wrecked into the side of another one of my buddies, and the guy that got hit had a huge bruise on his side. That same night we went to a piano

124

bar. I loved piano bars. We requested all kinds of music. ACDC, 2 Pac, etc. We requested it, the piano guy played it. After the piano bar, nothing exciting happened. Like any bachelor party, the guys badgered me into going to a strip club against my wishes. No lie, we were in there for about five minutes, and the guys felt bad knowing I was uncomfortable, so they all said, "Okay, let's go." We stayed in a hotel, and the next morning, we made plans to go wakeboarding.

The first night put a hurting on a few guys. It was disappointing that before we could go wakeboarding, we had to go get fitted for our tuxes. Somehow, I got all the groomsmen to the tux shop. However, afterward, half of them were so hung over they dropped out of the wakeboarding day. The survivors of the first night headed to the wakeboarding day. We had an absolute blast. Wakeboarding takes a lot out of you; by the time we were done, everyone was exhausted. We played some card games and then hit the rack (bed). Though wakeboarding seemed like a great idea, it had a negative impact on me. That lake was known to be dirty. I had always struggled with my allergies after swimming in that lake. This was no exception, Friday morning before the rehearsal, my allergies were awful. As the saying goes, I felt like shit. What I didn't realize was the other effect wakeboarding had on me. Guys with hairy butts can relate. I was chafed. Not a little chafed, big time chafed from the wakeboarding. My butt was on fire by the time the rehearsal dinner came. I was still able to walk but knew I needed some butt powder or lotion, but it was nowhere to be found.

After the rehearsal dinner, I finished up three days of partying with the guys. We got back to my house and started the beer-drinking games. You can imagine what the guys were saying, "D.J. is getting married! LET'S GO!"

For a moment, I forgot about the growing problem on my butt, not my hand! Around 9 p.m., half drunk, it hit me. I had a serious chafing issue taking place and needed to get some lotion now. My wedding day was the next morning. How was I going to heal my butt cheeks? I quietly escaped the party room. I snuck into my bedroom. Unfortunately, my bedroom had no lock on the door. I snuck into the bedroom, closed the door, and found some lotion. My pants were down. I was rubbing lotion on my ass cheeks. I heard my childhood best friend Maximus (we called him Max) say, "Where's D.J.!"

Here I was in a crouched position, pants down and naked, rubbing lotion on my ass cheeks, and it sounded like a stampede of buffaloes coming to find me. I was the groom; no way was I going to go fall asleep, they thought. I can imagine what all the guys running into the room were thinking. I was secretly trying to go fall asleep. All of them rushed through the bedroom door. I was in so much pain from neglecting my butt cheeks I didn't even attempt to pull my pants up. I said, "Hey guys! I have a severe problem!" They all erupted laughing.

At this point, even I thought it was funny. I was laughing and crying in pain at the same time. They refused to let me lie down. I finished lathering my cheeks and went back to beer-drinking games. We had so much clean fun that night. No one vomited, to my knowledge. No one passed out early. At about 2 a.m. we all just looked at each other and said, "Let's go to bed!" BEST DAY EVER!

The next morning (the big day!) I woke up before everyone. I made breakfast and started getting all the guys up as I said, "Get up and get dressed! You dumbasses are not making me late for my wedding!"

I had another best friend, Ezekiel (we called him Zeke), who flew in from Florida. Zeke was notorious for straggling along and making everyone late. To this day, he has no concept of time. He's an attorney now and still has no concept of time. Zeke wouldn't get up. "Zeke, get up! Zeke, get dressed! Zeke, COME ON MAN!"

Max could tell I was getting pissed trying to get Zeke up. Max took over for me, Max was a big boy, and no one messed with him. Max got Zeke up finally, and we barely made it on time to the wedding.

I will never forget our wedding day. It was a calm summer day, but it was raining steadily that morning. We ate breakfast. Well, at least some of us did. We got to the church, and my ass cheeks had never felt so on fire my whole life. I was absolutely miserable. This was the most important day of my life, and I was so mad that I had the terrible discomfort of this chafing. We were inside the church, and I stepped outside for a minute to catch some fresh air. The rain had stopped, and for a moment, the sun started to shine as people started to arrive for the "Big Catholic Wedding." I was sitting on a ledge right outside the church. I had a look of misery. Not because I was getting married. Because my butt was on fire. People were walking in saying, "Hi." They all had to be thinking, *D.J. looks like he doesn't want to do this.*

Little did they know I wanted it so bad that I was walking like a cripple just to marry my May.

The wedding started. Everyone proceeded down the long aisle in front of the guests with no hiccups. After I walked down the aisle, I was to take a seat next to the altar and stay there until May came down the aisle. It was not long before here came May. To this day, I have never witnessed anything as beautiful as her walking down that aisle. It was like all the Angels in Heaven singing and rejoicing, and a light from Heaven was shining on her entire body. May was the star of the show. She was remarkable, extraordinary, and staggering, and my heart was full. This was my wife. May was mine forever. Her dress was amazing. Her makeup was amazing. She was amazing. She was perfect to me.

She proceeded up and sat next to me. I stood up and said, "You're so beautiful." She said, "Thank you! Are you excited?"

I said, "Yes!"

She then looked at me and said, "What's wrong?" I said, "Nothing, don't worry about it."

She said, "No, D.J., what's wrong? Do you not want to do this?"

I replied, "Yes, I want to do this. I paused. My butt is chafed bad!"

May had the biggest sigh of relief. I terrified her for a second. The wedding proceeded. We exchanged vows and said our "I do's!" The church had these big stained-glass windows, and right after Father James pronounced us husband and wife, the sun shined through the clouds, and the entire church lit up. God's glory was upon us! It was simply something out of a movie. The celebration was on!

When we got to the wedding reception, I had to go into the bathroom to lather more lotion on myself before I could walk in for the presentation. I may have stalled the presentation by a few minutes. The DJ said, "Ladies and gentlemen! I now present to you! Mr. and Mrs. D.J. and May Murphy!"

It took everything I had to smile. I was in so much pain. However, I had never been so happy in my life. I had just married the most amazing woman. May was mine, I was hers, and we were now bonded by a seemingly unbreakable marital covenant ordained through God Himself! It felt like nothing could ever separate us.

GULLIBLE

My brother was my best man. Matt was my little brother, and he was a jokester. He was always the life of any party. He had planned a best man speech for the ages. A few months before the wedding, a bunch of us early twenty-year-old guys organized a football game in my backyard. At the time, May and I were still in the country house that sat close to the road. We had one acre of grass behind the house. It was the perfect football field. A bunch of us guys randomly decided to go play some football. I'm sure it started with one of us saying, "You think you still got it?"

So here we were, half a dozen of us in our early twenties sprinting slower than we ever were in high school. During the game, I saw this critter pop out of the burn pile. I was a city boy growing up as a kid. I ran over to look at the animal as it scurried off into the cornfield. My comment was, "Guys, you see that? What was that?"

Without hesitation, one of the guys said, "It's a snipe, D.J.!" I responded, "A snipe?"

One thing about me is I have always been extremely gullible. The other guys immediately chimed in, "Ya! A snipe!"

The next thing I knew, the football game was over, and all five other guys were telling me all about this animal I had never heard of called a snipe. It blew my mind, and I believed them. You can imagine the description they filled me with. "Bro!

They are the rarest animal." "Dude, I can't believe there is a snipe in your yard." "Don't ever corner it. They are vicious." Etc. Etc.

I was gullibly tuned in. Did I ever google it? No, I didn't. I took their word for it. "Sounds good, guys, that is crazy. Let's finish the game,"

I spoke. I loved sports, loved competition, and it was rare at our age to get all those guys together.

My brother had this entire story up his sleeve for the wedding reception. Matt's best man speech had everyone rolling in their chairs laughing because up until the speech, I still believed in the little animal called a snipe. After he told everyone how I believed in snipes and had everyone laughing. He turned the direction of the speech to how he knew the love I had for May and had everyone crying. Matt and I were brothers, the love we had for each other was irreplaceable, and he knew his big brother was deeply in love with this woman. Matt thought May and I were perfect for each other. Matt finished the speech by saying, "I have never seen two people love each other as passionately as these two love birds."

The wedding reception was amazing. I was in pain, but I got through it. May had never looked so beautiful, and I was the luckiest man in the world. I will never forget when I looked over and saw her dancing with my grandfather. I had always looked up to my grandfather. He was a hard-nosed, mean-looking man with a big heart. When he was dancing with May, he looked so happy. My grandfather passed away not long after our wedding. It meant the world to me that he was able to enjoy my wedding, dance with my bride, and live to experience his oldest grandchild's wedding day.

SWEATY SEX

The wedding reception ended, and we were on our way to a hotel. May wanted to stay at a hotel instead of our house to enhance the romance of the day. When we got back to the room, we were both exhausted. No matter how exhausted we were, we had not made love since March, and August was approaching. May said, "Hey, hubby, are you going to help your wife take this wedding dress off?"

We were both gross and sweaty. We stunk, and I had a bunch of damn lotion on my ass. It didn't matter. She was as ready to go as I was. I walked up to her. I will never forget this moment. My dream girl, who means more to me than anything I have ever touched, is now my wife! I didn't doubt that I wanted to be married to May for the rest of my life. She was the key to making my heart flutter and, of course, excited me in other noticeable ways. I got close to her face. I said, "You are so beautiful, I am the luckiest man in the world, and YOU'RE MY WIFE!"

She responded, "You're quite handsome, too, my husband, and I feel like the luckiest woman in the world."

All our anxieties about the miscarriage and having a baby before getting married were gone. It was her and me in this big world, and we both knew that as long as we had each other, it was enough to last a lifetime. No one and nothing else mattered if we had each other. She looked up at me with those big brown eyes, gazing into my soul and filling my life with love with just a look. May passionately loved me. We started to kiss. We were about to make passionate love for the first time with zero guilt, and we had not touched each other in months. She turned around and said, "Take my dress off, Daddy!"

Over the years, I have taken every single type of dress off of May. The wedding dress was the hardest to get off. Pins here and there, zippers, etc. It was no easy task. By the time I was done, my erection felt like it had a heartbeat. She felt it brush up along her butt cheek when I was so close to taking the dress completely off. She softly moaned, "Mmmmm!"

She reached her left hand behind her and grabbed me. She took the tips of her fingers and started to massage me. It was like not having a piece of your favorite candy in six months, and then someone hands you your favorite-colored starburst. You don't just devour it. You slowly take small bites and chew slowly. That is how May was massaging me. Up and down gently. I could feel her fingernails, and she could tell I was ready. May was never shy about how much she liked my shape and size, she had missed it, and I could tell. I finally finished removing the wedding dress. She had never felt so skinny. I kept her in place with her back to me. I hugged her from behind as I gripped both her breasts. I slightly bit her ear and whispered, "I love you so much, my wife."

I slowly worked both my hands down to her sweet spot. My body was slightly to her right side. She rotated her head around and started kissing, sucking, and licking my neck. I took my left hand and grabbed the top of her hair. I engaged my right hand and started massaging her clit up and down, side to side. I reached down lower and pulled her natural lube up from inside her. I started massaging faster. She closed her eyes and rested her head on my left shoulder as she moaned, "Ahhhhh ahhhh ahhhh."

Each moan got louder and higher pitched. "Ahhhh ahhhhh"

And louder. Then a high-pitched, long squeal came out. "Ahhhhhhhhhhhhhhhhhhh."

She almost collapsed. I grabbed her. I turned her around. She looked up at me and said, "I have missed your magic hands." I lifted her up into the air while I was still standing. She straddled me. Neither of us had to do anything. She landed perfectly, and I was inside her. She started screaming. She placed her breasts in my face as she gripped the back of my head. We could feel the sweat dripping off our bodies. We could feel the clammy skin on each other from the longest day of our lives. She started thrusting up and down.

May was not ever quiet during sex. She got louder and louder. I went as long as I could but needed to make her cum again. Our thoughts mirrored one another. She whispered in my ear, "Make me cum again my husband." I softly laid her down in the center of the bed. I kissed her thigh and her calf.

She said, "Come here and make love to your wife." I kissed her belly button, up her rib cage, the side of her right breast, and up to her neck. She took her left hand and placed me inside her. It was our wedding night, and I was going to passionately take my time and make love to my wife. I gently made love to her. I smelled her hair and her sweat. I loved the smell of May's sweat. I licked her neck and tasted the salt of her sweat radiating from her body. The heat from our bodies was elevated. I started to thrust a little harder. Hard in, slow out. I fell to my left side. She took her left leg and put it around my body. I gripped her clit with my index and middle finger. I could always tell by the way she felt if she was going to cum, and I could tell she had been craving me for many months. It felt like forever since we had made love.

She came quickly a second time and screamed, "Yes, yes, yes, don't stop, YESSSS!" She finished. I could feel her cum rush across the skin of my dick. Right after she finished, she started queefing.

She queefed multiple times. She said, "I'm sorry."

As she smiled with embarrassment, I loved every sound her vagina made. I always wanted to make her as comfortable as possible. I responded, "Nothing to be embarrassed about. Let that trapped air come out."

She said, "I'm done, hubby. I can't cum again, I am exhausted. It is time for you to cum inside your wife, for the first time as WIFE!" She pulled out and started to turn over, thinking I wanted to enter her from behind. But I didn't. Though I love every sexual position, this was our wedding night.

I said, "No, stay right here." I placed myself back inside her. I was always good at holding off until she was done. Not once in our entire marriage did I ever prioritize myself over her. When she was finished, then I would finish. I hugged her as she licked my ear and neck. I was getting close. I started to kiss her, and right before I came, she said, "Give it all to me." I arched my back while looking at my newly wedded wife. I exploded inside her. Months of abstinence released. My entire body went into chills. I fell on top of her.

She whispered, "Was that worth the wait?" "Yesssss," I replied.

She continued, "Was that everything you were hoping for on your wedding night?" "Yes, I love you Mrs. May Maria Murphy," I said.

"I love you more!" She responded. This saying became our thing. We would both often say, "I love you more." We had just made love to our spouse. We had just made a commitment to one person for the rest of our lives. Nothing in this world had ever felt better. I was hers. She was mine. We were married.

WAXY SITUATION

I stood up to walk away and go outside for a breather. The lightning bugs were putting on a show outside. As I walked past the big metal trash can, my boot clipped it. I almost tripped, making a very loud noise. I caught myself on the island, and I continued walking. The front barn lights were on. I could look down into our bedroom and see May still sound asleep. She always slept hard; nothing woke her up, even with the loud sound my boots made. She was still asleep. The light shimmered across her face; she was beautiful when she slept. I am a lucky man, I thought. I opened the back door.

My mind was unstable and racing. *Why did Raven just say that to me?* My thoughts continued. *Why could I not save that baby boy? Why did I take on so many projects at one time?*

I was stressed to the max. I went out to the barn and grabbed a vape pen. I didn't care much about getting drunk, and alcohol was not my thing. I liked a beer or two at night, but it was not taking the edge off. It was not doing the trick to ease my mind. Throughout my life, I would occasionally smoke pot. My friend bought me a wax vape pen. From what I understood, it was the strongest form of THC you could smoke. I grabbed it

137

and went back out onto our deck. I kicked back in a chair and watched the lightning bugs. I hit the vape pen, and simultaneously, Raven and her cousin Betty came walking outside. Raven said, "What is that smell?"

Betty looked at me and said, "See what I mean by naive?"

I honestly didn't give a shit at this point. I said, "It's marijuana, you know, weed? I had a little boy die in my arms a few weeks ago. I need something to ease my mind."

I was not in a good mood and really couldn't care less what either one of them thought. I was on my own property, at my own house, and in what was supposed to be the only place where my privacy was complete. They both had a look on their faces of disbelief as they were probably thinking, *Did he just say a little boy died in his arms a few weeks ago?*

After a long pause of silence, Raven spoke, "I have never smoked weed before." Seemed like a quick subject change.

Betty responded, "It is not that big of a deal, Raven. You would be surprised how many people do it."

I responded, "If you have never done it and you decide to try it, do it in a private setting. The first time May did it, she freaked out because she was not in a private setting. People get super paranoid their first few times. No, it is not a big deal, as

Betty just said. You will be fine as long as it is in a private setting." I no longer finished those words and thought, *Why am I still giving any type of fatherly advice to this girl? After what she just said and how uncomfortable she made me in my own house, she is never getting advice from me again.*

I stood up and dumped the rest of my beer over the edge of the deck. I was fed up and messed up in the head. I needed some rest. It was getting late. I was a newly promoted captain. I needed to get some sleep before heading to work the next day. I went in for a shower.

I typically would shave in the mornings before work. However, when I was going to bed late, I would shave the night before. I went into the bathroom and shaved. I then showered and went to bed. I remember lying down next to May, looking at her, and kissing her forehead. She made a rumbling sound, then looked up and smiled. I have always been the only person she was okay with interrupting her sleep. Any time I ever woke up May by kissing her face, she might rumble, but when she saw it was me, she would shower me with the biggest smile. At this point, May still loved me unconditionally, and I never imagined anything would change her love for me.

Knock! Knock!

As I sat on the bathroom tub ledge, that wasn't the only thing I was aware of. The sound of the knock on the door was bothering me. As a man, when you know you have to tell your wife something that you don't look forward to, it haunts you until you let it out. You know the saying, "The truth will set you free." If I hid anything from May throughout our marriage, my conscience ate at me, even for small little things. I would be open and honest about everything. What just occurred with this babysitter shaving the back of my head couldn't stay secret. How was I going to tell her? When was I going to find time to tell her without kids around? What was her reaction going to be? I had no negative intention when I let this female shave the back of my head. In that split moment, my only thought was, *I really don't want to miss a spot on the back of my head.*

It was a split-second decision. A poor decision. I knew what Raven had said to me less than a week prior. It hit me while I was sitting on that bathtub ledge that I had done the opposite of pushing her away from me. I had just allowed her to do something only May was allowed to do. Shave the back of my head. *Dumb D.J., Dumb!* I thought. *May is going to be pissed. This situation will drag on for months.* It was going to hurt May's feelings. She didn't deserve to feel insecure or sad about a situation with me and any female. Let alone this babysitter who was starting to feel evil to me. Little did I know what was coming moments later.

Our house had no privacy. We loved the property. We loved the barns. We especially loved the house after the remodel. However, it had two bedrooms and one bathroom, and seven and a half people living there. May and I, five kids, and a babysitter, who was now living with us half the time. If you walked in the front door, it was mostly wide open. A big living room opened up to the dining room and led to the kitchen. The renovations in the house caused some awkward room layouts.

If you walked through the kitchen, down one step into the landing area, and continued one more step, you entered our bedroom and laundry room, which had no door. Across from the washer and dryer, we kept shoeboxes filled with the kid's shoes. I would say this room was awkward, more than unique. There was a small private spot in the bedroom that people from the kitchen couldn't see. This was my spot to get dressed. I was that working man who was always in a rush. Grabbing my clothes and walking back through the house to find a room with a door did not cross my mind. My mindset was, get dressed fast and get to work. I could throw some clothes on in just a few seconds and be out in the garage and leave for work.

Every day when I would get out of the shower, I walked fast with my towel around my waist into our bedroom, and I would finish drying off in this little private area. I would then put my towel back around my waist and find my work clothes on top of the dryer in the bedroom. Then I would go back to the little private spot and get dressed quickly. Once I finished putting my clothes on, I would open the door going out to the garage and put on my socks and shoes while sitting on the

141

steps. From there, I could head out for the day to work. It was my routine. I never thought too much about it. It was my house, my bedroom, my private setting. I also never thought much about walking through the house in a towel. Again, this was my house, my private setting. May would sometimes say, "You should take your clothes into the bathroom and get dressed in there." It kinda made me mad. I would think, *This is our house May. This is our bedroom. I am the man of the house, and this is the only place that I should feel comfortable walking through my house with a towel around my waist.* I would also think, *We go swimming multiple times a week. When we go swimming, you women are in bikinis, and I'm in a little bathing suit. Is the setting any different than while swimming?*

Yes, it is. However, that setting is public. My house should be my only place for privacy. Raven was no longer what one would describe as a "typical babysitter." She was now living with us half the time. I paid her $200 a week. She ate our food. She slept in our living room. She had it made. She also felt wanted at our house. And she absolutely hated her mom and stepdad. She was comfortable in our home. She hated being at her house. That is why she asked to start staying with us. Giving her that comfort, I felt she understood whose house she was in. It was May's and my house. I paid the bills, I paid her every single week, and Raven needed to respect my privacy. Whether or not May liked it, that is how I felt.

DELIRIOUS

Knock! Knock!

The sound hit my brain again. I stood up from sitting on the tub edge. I only had a couple of hours of work that morning I had to complete. I had decided that when I was done with these couple hours of work, I was going to attempt to sleep in a bedroom with five kids running around and no door. This was my only option. I also had made up my mind that I was not taking the immediate release Adderall anymore. It was obvious after four days of no sleep that this shit was truly like "poor man's cocaine" for me. Sleep was way more important to me, and I had just slipped up from no sleep, making a poor decision to let this babysitter shave the back of my head.

I stood up, took the green towel off my head, and placed it around my waist. I brushed my teeth. All I had to do was grab some tools and materials for a job, take it to the guys, and I could hopefully find some rest because I was not taking this medication anymore. I stepped out of the bathroom. As I walked into the open area, I saw a couple of my kids. I remember smiling at them as they played, and simultaneously, I got so dizzy that I thought I was going to pass out. This had never happened to me before. It was that feeling of standing up too fast, and you're like, "Woah." Only this feeling was times ten. I still can't believe I didn't go down. I caught myself on this large dining room table. I composed myself, still a little dizzy, with the thought, *Get your work done,*

143

get some sleep! I walked through the kitchen and remembered thinking, *Where's Raven?* Another quick thought *Oh, she must be in the back bedrooms; I had not looked in there.*

I continued walking through the kitchen, I looked into our bedroom and thought, *The coast is clear. No one is in my room.* I went to step down into my bedroom, and my body was shifting and stepping towards my little private spot where I would dry off quickly each day. Simultaneously I grabbed my towel with my right hand and removed the knot in the towel with my left hand. I was now holding the towel with just my right hand. I had already looked up into the bedroom. No one was in there. I took one step at an angle down the last step so I could land in my little private spot and dry off. At this point, I was looking down at my towel. I also remember thinking, *Man, I need to lose some weight—a* thought I had almost every day.

PREGO MUNCHIES

When May was pregnant, it was like I was pregnant, craving food like her. She loved, loved food. She loved my cooking, and I loved to eat. We were "foodies." The money we wasted was often spent at new restaurants or going out to eat. We loved date nights and trying new foods. I would like to try new breweries and a new beer I had never tasted. May loved to try a new Malbec or some type of dry red wine. We would get appetizers every time. We almost always tried a different entree. Trying new foods was our thing. We enjoyed this part of our lives together. We had five children in ten years. I can't tell you how many times people said, "Y'all are crazy!"

We were crazy, crazy in love. We always had this vision of big Christmas gatherings and traveling to visit our kids when they got older and had their own children. We shared many of the same interests.

One of those interests was our late-night cereal splurges. May loved a bowl of cereal before bed during every pregnancy. I don't think she ever had to make her own bowl of cereal. I was her man, the provider of food. I didn't just grab her cereal. I grabbed our cereal. We would sit and eat cereal in bed. I always put a little extra milk in our bowls, brought the entire box, and sat it in between us. Two bowls each was common. Over ten years, with that late-night cereal habit, I was up to 230 pounds. I had a belly, and May didn't care. May knew I gained pregnancy weight with her. In a way, she probably felt more secure knowing that as she gained pregnancy weight, I was right there with her along for the ride.

I was a little under 200 pounds when we met. May fluctuated her weight throughout her pregnancies. She would get up to 180 pounds, but she was always diligent about losing her so-called "baby fat." Her baby fat never bothered me. I loved May at 180 pounds as much as I loved her at 120 pounds. However, May did care. She would get on strict diets and exercise routines after each childbirth. She knew I couldn't care less either way. She did this for her own self-confidence.

It always surprised May that I would say her weight didn't bother me. I think at the beginning of our relationship, she thought I was lying. As time went on, she realized I wasn't. May could be any weight; I loved her body, and I made her feel confident every step of the way. I have always liked a natural-looking woman. I was never a "boob guy," as most men would describe themselves. I was a "butt guy." May had a nice butt and sexy legs. That is what I liked. I have never liked a lot of make-up. I preferred no makeup. I liked everything natural. Natural fingernails, natural boobs, natural face, and natural personality. This was how God created me. Fake boobs were not attractive to me. Too much makeup, no thanks. Give me a pretty smile and nice butt, and I was good to go. May had the most beautiful smile and the nicest butt! I hoped these two characteristics would never fade.

Growing up without sisters, I never learned how obsessed women were with their self-image, starting at a very young age. May grew up between two brothers as the middle child. Her brothers, as you can imagine, treated her like any other brother treats their sister. May was called everything, including "chubby" or "fat." Her brothers were just brothers. They never intended to truly make her feel fat or destroy her confidence. However, it did. I think it amazed May that I never once, through all the pregnancies, said anything to harm her self-image or confidence. I never missed a day telling her how much I loved her and how beautiful she was, no matter the weight she carried. That included all the pregnancies. I thought she was beautiful just the way she was, and I told her every single day. "May, YOU'RE BEAUTIFUL!"

She would often say, "Quit lying."

That just made me repeat it," No, I'm serious. You are the most beautiful thing I have ever laid my eyes on."

She would reply, "Whatever, but thank you." Eventually, she believed me. May was the most stunning woman my eyes had ever seen.

As a kid, I had the biggest crush on Shania Twain. I would tell my mom, "I'm going to marry her someday." Shania had everything I wanted. Dark hair, dark eyes, big smile. I was probably only seven years old, and I thought I was in love with Shania. May's image is almost identical. I found my Shania Twain in real life. I married my version of Shania. May, however, couldn't sing. I thought her voice was cute. When May was in a great mood and started singing, we all knew she was in a great mood because she didn't like hearing her voice. Head to toe, inside and out, May was my girl. I would encourage her to sing. She rarely would, but when she did, it made everyone happy!

MONEY, MONEY, MONEY

The only thing that ever bothered me with May was when I had to tell her "no," to anything or when I disagreed with something she wanted to buy or do. May grew up with an uncle and a grandma who simply never told her no. She could ask for anything, and the answer was, "Yes, baby, anything for you."

May was now in a committed marriage. Everything we did was agreed upon, for the most part. At the time, I was the primary breadwinner. I had bills to pay, and I hated credit card debt or unnecessary purchases. Especially if it affected paying our bills. Having five kids at a young age came with a financial strain. That financial strain never went away. No matter how much I worked, no matter how much she worked, we never got ahead. Our bills were paid. We had food on the table. We had nice vehicles. But we never got ahead. We liked eating out too much. We liked nice things. May liked nice things. May's favorite reality show is "The Real Housewives." May would probably sign up as a real housewife and be on the show if given the opportunity. However, that was not our life. We were middle class, we both worked, we were spitting out kids left and right, and money was a struggle. The American dream isn't so dreamy if you experience financial strain.

They say, "Money is the root of all evil." I firmly believe it is. I couldn't say yes to everything May wanted. It was simply impossible. I wish I could have; it would have alleviated a lot of our arguments. May came to me once and said she wanted a Coach Diaper Bag. We just had our second child, Scarlette. We had sold our house and were living in my grandmother's house, trying to save up money to put down on what we thought at the time as our "dream home." I thought, *Coach Diaper Bag?*

She wanted a coach diaper bag to carry diapers and wipes. This seemed crazy to me. I told her no. And as with any time I told her no, it resulted in an argument. May was good with words. She could convince anyone why something was worth purchasing, a vacation we needed to take, or anything else she wanted from life. As you can imagine, it caused an argument. I gave in often; however, this time, I was not giving in. Time after time, I told her no to the Coach diaper bag. What did May do? She bought her coach diaper bag anyway. These situations occurred often.

It wasn't that I didn't want her to have the Coach diaper bag. To me, it was simply unnecessary when we were trying to buy a 5,000 SF home to raise our children in. We needed a down payment more than a fancy diaper bag. We wanted our kids to have everything, but May wanted everything as well. Every single time I told her no, if she felt she had to have it or had to do it, she got her way. There was not one single time when I would tell her no that she would respond, "Okay, I understand!"

It was a battle to get her way at all times. Many times, she would give up, knowing I was not going to give in. But if she gave up on me, it was time to call her grandma. "Hey Nana (she would call her grandma), how are you?"

Eventually, the conversation led to May saying, "Ya, D.J. and I want a new nursery furniture set, but we can't afford it. I found a slightly used set that is nice on Facebook, but we just don't have the money for it right now."

Guess what? Nana would say, "Well, sweetie, how much is it?" And sure enough, I would be instructed to go pick up Demi's new nursery furniture set.

I can still hear May say, "Hey baby, Nana volunteered to buy that $500 nursery furniture set I wanted that you said we didn't have the money for. Can you go pick up the money from Nana and then take the truck to go pick it up?"

I would say, "Ya, I guess." May never realized that I not only felt belittled, but I also felt like I was not making enough money and got this feeling of, *I can't provide for my family.*

Over time, situation after situation, it started to bother me a lot. I never had enough money. May always wanted more and more. I would try to talk to her about it, but it was in one ear out the other. I was feeling almost worthless, a man who couldn't provide enough for his family. If a man feels like he can't provide for his family, it starts to get to him. You become hard on yourself. You start to resent yourself. When this happens, good men do one thing. PUSH HARDER! WORK MORE! With the thought, "PROVIDE EVERYTHING!"

PRIDE

When such thoughts take hold, they never go away. Something edges into your life when you push for someone else's happiness through unobtainable material items. What crept into my life was PRIDE – one of the Seven Deadly Sins. Books have been written. Movies have been made. Churches talk about it. The Seven Deadly Sins: Pride, greed, wrath, envy, lust, gluttony, and sloth. We are all human. We all are imperfect. Of these deadly sins, pride is potentially the most dangerous. Why? Because those with pride often don't realize nor admit to being prideful. The others are easier to take action to overcome. If you eat too much, if you prioritize money, then you can admit your sin. Pride is deceiving. They all eventually lead to death. However, pride leads to destruction before death. I was pushing so hard to make May happy and satisfied. I wanted May to be proud of me. The worst aspect of this was I didn't recognize I needed to slow down and raise my family differently. Destruction was bound to happen. This destruction was going to get my attention and break me down. Humility was coming!

By no means am I blaming anyone else other than myself for my own growing pride. Every marriage has struggles. I could have just let everything roll off my shoulders when I started to think I was not adequately providing for my family. I was providing for my family. However, it didn't feel like enough, and so pride found its way into my life. I never was, as I would say, "proud of myself." I wanted everyone around me to be proud of my accomplishments, especially May. Pride was slowly overrunning my life. And it was starting to take away my joy. Often, by the time people realize they're "full of pride," destruction has already occurred.

I was an all-in-or-nothing type of person. I was either going to do something as best as I could or not at all. That applied to all aspects of my life. Sports, fatherhood, and especially as a husband. I wanted to be the best I possibly could. When I became full of pride, this "all or nothing" attitude was on full display, but I had no clue. God could see it. God knew it would take me losing everything to strip me of my pride. Multiple times God had laid me down and was probably saying, "D.J. take this time with your torn ACL to evaluate your life." I never heard the message. I was driven to make my ACL stronger than ever, not take a step back in life and say, *Am I working too much? Are my priorities straight? Is my life leading to destruction?* Yes, my life was leading to chaos, and it was going to be in a way I never foresaw.

My pride was coming to the surface of my personality. Others were starting to see a different D.J. It began with my crew. The guys who worked for me over the years were a loyal crew. I had always been a happy, enthusiastic guy. I remember showing up to a job they were working on. I had not checked up on them in almost a week. I was busy remodeling my house to give May everything she wanted so she would be comfortable. I was losing money by not being on the job, but May's happiness was more important to me. Day after day, I kept thinking I would get to a finish point. I was doing a lot of it on my own; the process was slow.

THE FELLAS

One day I pulled up to the big job. The guys were all standing outside smoking their cigarettes. Ezra was the first to spout off, "Well, hello stranger!"

Followed by Wyatt, "Hey buddy, nice to see you for once!"

The others didn't need to say anything. Enough had been spoken. I got the point as I replied, "Hey, fellas, good to see you! How's the progress coming along?"

Wyatt was the job site boss man, he said, "It is coming along slow, buddy. Good work takes time. Progress would speed up if you decided to come and join us sometime. You think you are going to come to work with us anytime soon?"

I replied, "I will try, buddy, deep down, knowing I had so much still left to finish my house remodel."

Ezra randomly spoke up, "Hey buddy, we are all kind of bothered by something, and we want to talk with you about it." I thought for sure something had gone wrong with the job.

Wyatt responded, "Ya, buddy, you got a second?" I responded, "Ya, no problem, what's up?"

Ezra spoke first, "Buddy, we are worried about that girl you have babysitting for you. She is acting and talking funny around you."

Wyatt continued, "Buddy, I know you don't want to hear any of this. We just want to make sure you are smart and stay safe."

I gave them a look like *Whatever, guys, continue.* They knew my looks, and I didn't have to say anything. They continued. Todd didn't say much usually, but he chimed in, "D.J., we are serious. We are not just noticing instances with you, she's doing and saying things around us when we are at your house, making us uncomfortable." Though Todd was a big dude, he was far from brave around me. His words shocked me. I knew it had to take a lot of courage to say that to me.

It was Tim's turn. Tim normally said nothing to me unless I asked a work question. Tim spoke, "D.J., we are looking out for your best interest." A man of few words just hit my soul. All four guys together agreed on one thing. Raven was a problem for me.

Ezra, who was never short on words, continued, "Deej, (his nickname for me), we are being serious, man. She wears almost see-through spandex.

154

She walks like she wants all the attention on her; she bends over in an unnatural way, and she's way too nice to you, D.J. By nice, I mean she has a thing for you, bro! You need to open your eyes up!"

Before I could say anything, Wyatt spoke again, "Buddy, listen, that girl is no good, man. I don't know how else to say it. She's evil, and she's up to no good with you. The other day she started asking us questions when we picked up some equipment from your house. They were questions like a wife would ask. 'Where's D.J.? What time will he be home? Is he not working with you guys today? I know he's not at the fire station today.'"

I interrupted, "Wait, what? She said that shit?"

Todd spoke dramatically, "YA MAN! That girl is no bueno, bro!"

I looked over at Tim as he gave me a look like, "We've been trying to tell you!" He was rolling his eyes and shaking his head in disbelief that I had not caught on to any of this yet.

I continued, "Guys are you sure? I have always just treated her like a daughter!"

Wyatt, who was my best friend at the time and one of the few people who felt comfortable telling me like it was, said, "D.J.! (He never called me by name, it was always 'buddy'), LISTEN TO ME! That girl wants more from you, we all see. We have all been giving you hints here and there.

This is us telling you directly to get your head out of your ass and get that girl out of your house!" *Holy shit!* I thought quietly.

Ezra continued, "D.J., we are having this conversation because we care about you, we love you, and we don't want to see anything bad happen."

I defensively spouted off, "Anything bad happen? I would never do anything to hurt May. You guys know how much I love her! Nothing bad is going to happen! "

I was thrown off, and I felt cornered. They knew it.

Tim said in the gentlest voice, "Buddy, we know the person you are. It is not you, it's her." They all replied together with head shakes of "Yes."

Wyatt said, "We will stop talking about it. Just be careful, buddy. We love you."

I replied, "I love you guys too. Come show me your progress. I will be fine. I have no feelings for that girl. She's only 15 years old, guys."

Todd spoke up again, "Buddy, she doesn't look like a 15-year-old, she doesn't dress like a 15-year-old, and she doesn't act like a 15-year-old." We all paused for a second as we gathered our thoughts. I wanted this conversation over so badly. But it was not over.

Ezra spoke again, "Remember a week or so ago when you told us you were doing estimates at your table, and she got off the bus crying? You glanced outside, and she kicked your dog off the porch because your dog was in the way of the door?"

I replied, "Yes."

Ezra continued, "Do you remember that conversation you had with her?" I again replied, "Yes."

Ezra continued, "What was that conversation you shared with us you had with her?"

I repeated the story, "I glanced outside as I was typing estimates at the table. I saw her kick my dog aggressively off the front porch. When she came inside, I asked her what was wrong. She said people at school were making fun of her. I told her she needed to be self-confident and have things to tell herself at moments like that in school. I told her that May struggled at that same age when she was bullied, and May didn't have a father figure to pick her up when she was down."

Wyatt responded, "Uh, huh, and?"

I continued, "I told her to tell herself things to pick herself up. I told herself things such as, "I'm a strong person. Only God is my judge."

Wyatt responded again, "Uh huh and?"

"And I told her she needed to be secure in herself and say things to herself such as 'I have pretty

eyes, and I am pretty in the eyes of God." Ezra spoke, "Bingo!"

"Bingo, what?" I said.

Wyatt continued his lecture, "Buddy, though you may think you're a father figure and that you're only being helpful and giving advice. D.J., you're the nicest guy. We all believe that you only have the best interest at heart for everyone around you. You have always treated all of us well. That girl didn't take that comment as 'He's giving fatherly advice'. Raven took that comment as 'D.J. thinks I have pretty eyes. D.J. thinks I'm attractive. D.J. cares about my feelings."

Wyatt continued, "You have to realize that not everyone in this world is a nice person like you. We all know you have no feelings for that girl. So, be careful. All four of us believe she has more than just a thing for you."

I looked around at the guys as they all shook their heads up and down. My guys had cornered me. They were concerned enough that they knew they needed to bring this to my attention. I was the type of person who fits the definition of "naïve." I treated everyone like a brother or sister in Christ. I loved people. I gave people the benefit of the doubt in all circumstances. I was always forgiving and usually the first to apologize. I hated it when anyone was upset with me, and I would go above and beyond to keep everyone happy around me.

THE REALIZATION

That same day, after the conversation, I went to drop off dog food at the house. I drove around the back of the house where his food was. His dog bowl was dirty, so I went inside to clean it. May was at work, Raven was watching the kids. Raven saw me cleaning the dog bowl and pranced into the kitchen. She explained she was writing an essay for school and said, "You know, I have always wanted to have five kids and to live in the country!" I turned around and looked at her knowing I had five kids and lived in the country. My mouth dropped, and I felt confused. I thought to myself, *What 15-year-old would say that?*

When I made eye contact with her, she saw my intense, baffled look. I replied, "Well, someday you and your future husband can do just that. Focus on your education, and you will get there someday." I didn't make this comment in my normal sweet tone. I finished the comment and left the house again. I had multiple customers needing estimates before I could finish my day and make it home to my family.

As I drove away from the house, I started recalling every single comment and analyzed everything. The fellas had cornered me, and just moments later, this babysitter made the most random/strangest comment. Then I remembered that when my mom was at the house a few days prior, Raven said to her, "You know I am very concerned about D.J. and May's marriage. D.J. is working all the time, and May seems to be unhappy with him."

My mom felt obligated to relay this comment to me and added that it threw her off guard. Other memories started to jolt into my mind, causing my neck to tighten up.

My brother, Matt, had also recently commented, "No girl has ever made me uncomfortable before besides Raven."

My other free-spirited buddy, who could care less about anything in the world, was working in my house. He walked up to me and said, "WHAT IS UP with that babysitter? She's a little over the top, don't you think?" Everything he said was always so free-spirited and innocent, though he never held back any thoughts that rose in his mind.

A subcontractor I hired to help me finish the remodeling. He was a devout Christian man who had called me and said, "Hey man, I'm not going to work at your house anymore unless that girl is not there."

My response was, "WHAT? Are you serious?"

He was dead serious and gave me multiple examples of instances that had occurred. Person after person. Story after story. And it hit me! The brick fell from the sky and smacked me in the forehead. The fellas were right. I needed to get this female out of my house, but how?

If it was any other babysitter, any other female, I wouldn't have hesitated to act quickly. I would have called May right then and there at this world-shattering/mind-boggling moment. However, this conversation with May was not going to be easy. This conversation was going to cause an argument.

This conversation was going to be hard, and I knew it would linger for months. Raven and May were close. Raven's mom babysat May as a kid. There was a family history. Raven and May were together all the time. May thought the world of Raven. May also felt like she "needed" Raven to help with the kids. I rarely saw May with the kids without Raven. Raven was like May's personal kid assistant. Raven had just returned from a vacation with my side of the family. May insisted on Raven going with my family on that vacation. At the time, I had too many projects going on to be asked to stay home, May was pissed. During the vacation, May relaxed and was carefree while Raven took care of the kids. It seemed that May really needed Raven – so much so that I questioned how May would respond to me saying, "Get this girl out of our house!"

Not to mention, Raven's mom was "Crazy Karen!" How was Karen going to respond? What problems was Karen going to create in, her daughter?" I had so many worries about breaking this news to May. I even questioned if May would somehow blame me. Followed by Raven blaming me, then here would come "Crazy Karen!" I had a problem on my hands, and I simply didn't know how to go about resolving it. I had so much going on at that time that I decided to wait it out. This was the worst decision of my life. To this day, I still say. The worst decision of my entire life. I deeply regretted not getting rid of this girl and getting her away from our house.

THE DRESS

The day wasn't over, and the comments from Raven echoed in my head. This girl didn't just want me; she wanted May's life. My phone rang. It was my cousin Annie. She said, "Hey, D.J., my girls want to walk down to your house and hang out for a couple of hours before their dad comes to get them. Do you mind if they come hang out?"

I responded, " No, I don't mind at all. The babysitter is there with the kids, and I'll be home shortly. I'll let the babysitter know."

Annie continued, "Sounds good. Hey, cuz?" Anytime Annie said "Hey cuz", I knew she had something serious to say that she didn't want to say.

I replied, " Ya Annie?" I knew something was about to come out of her mouth that I did not want to hear. Annie was like a sister to me all through our childhood and into adulthood. Annie spoke, " DJ, I don't like that girl babysitter you got. She struts around your house like she's your wife. And the way she looks at you is not okay. I know you probably don't want to hear this, but, you feel me?"

Head down on the phone, already lectured once today on the exact same topic I responded, "Yes Annie, I hear you. I love you, Annie. Annie got her message to me and probably knew by my reaction I didn't want to get into this conversation.

She said, "I love you too, DJ, and I am only looking out for my cuzzo."

I replied, "You always have looked out for me. Thank you. Call me later?" We hung up. My head immediately fell again as I could only gather one word that I said out loud to myself, "FUUUCCK-KKKK!"

I picked up the phone and called Raven. She answered on the first ring. "Heyyy DJ!" The enthusiastic tone of someone excited to speak to me had never felt so evil rushing through my body.

"Hey Raven, my little cousins are walking down to the house to hang out with the kids. Their dad, Cody, is picking them up in an hour or so and I'll also be home around the same time."

Raven responded, "Sounds good, DJ. Whatever you need. Bye, see you soon!"

I was so irritated with her and just said,"Thanks, bye."

A couple of hours went by, and I was on my way home. I pulled in the driveway, and Cody happened to be there at the exact same time, picking up his girls. I parked in the front of the house and walked up towards the front door so I could say hi to Cody. I could see Cody was standing right inside the front door. I opened the door, and Cody turned and looked at me with a surprised, eye wide-open, look on his face. Before I could even say what's up to him, I could clearly tell by his expression that something else was going on. Cody looked uncomfortable, and I had no idea why. I turned my eyes away from Cody and looked into the living room. As I thought, *What was Cody seeing that had him giving me such a strange look?*

As my eyes turned towards the center of the room, I made eye contact with Raven, who was standing in the center of the room. Raven noticed that I had made eye contact with her. She began to swing her arms up and out like you would see a princess in movie do. As she swung her arms up, I look down at her attire. My face was now more surprised and shocked than Cody's. Raven had my wife's royal blue dress on. This dress was not a typical dress. This dress was my all-time favorite dress I had ever seen on a woman. Only it was my favorite dress on my May, not this 15-year-old babysitter named Raven. May wore this dress for her 21st birthday. It was revealing, sexy, and exotic. The moment I saw May with this dress on many years prior, it was like I was seeing a goddess. May had never looked sexier than when she wore that dress. Now, I was standing looking at Raven in my wife's dress. Raven opened her arms, palms up, real wide, and said, "Look, DJ, we're playing dress up!" As she simultaneously spun around in a circle.

Cody and I immediately looked at each other, and I will never forget the shocked look we both gave to each other. He and I were both thinking the same thing. *What the fuck is going on?* Here Raven was, breasts halfway out, in May's dress and dancing. I became so uncomfortable I didn't say hi or chat at all with Cody. I didn't say hi to my little cousins. I didn't even say hi to my own children. I quickly said, "I'm not done at the job site yet. I just came home to grab a tool, and I'll be back after bit." I was shaken. Troubled. And didn't know what else to do other than get out of the house.

The biggest mistake of my life is what I didn't do next. I should have driven straight to the hospital where May was working. Tell her to come outside. Explain everything. And get this female out of our house. Instead, I drove to the closest Home Improvement store and placed orders that I needed for the next day. By far the biggest mistake I had ever made in my life was the decision I made after scurrying out of that house as fast as I could get out. Not going to my wife and laying it all out. At this point, I shouldn't have cared if it was going to cause a fight or not.

The dominos were falling and falling quickly. I didn't get this girl out of my house. I had not told May my concerns. I had listened to Raven speak of family and fantasies. Annie had just told me, "This babysitter is walking around your house as if she is the wife." Hours later, Raven was in May's

165

dress. And now I had let her shave the back of my head. Was I somehow involved in some type of witchcraft bullshit? Seemed like a crazy thought but felt real in an odd way. After four days of only a few hours of sleep, I wasn't thinking clearly.

THREE SECONDS

Knock! Knock!

The sound of a knock jarred me while I started walking in my towel toward our bedroom. I liked having our laundry room in the bedroom. May hated it, I understood why. May wanted a master bedroom the size of some people's homes with fancy everything, a jacuzzi tub, and everything else you can imagine. However, that was not our current situation. We decided to buy a small house for the land. The laundry room was our bedroom, and that was our only option with five kids. Next to the washer and dryer was a closet pantry for food. Across from the pantry was this safe spot where I could have the little bit of privacy I needed to get dressed. That wall extended out just enough to where no one could see me. Right next to my safe spot of privacy on the ground were shoe boxes for all the kids. The wall that stuck out stuck out enough that you couldn't see the shoe boxes until you stepped into the bedroom. I looked down at the whole bedroom. No one was in my bedroom. No one was behind me, I had just walked through the entire house and surveyed everything except for the two back bedrooms.

Raven must have been in one of the bedrooms on the other side of the house, I thought. I looked down and grabbed my green towel with my right hand to bring it up to my body to finish drying off. Simultaneously, I reached down with my left hand and untied the twisted knot. I turned my body towards the safe spot behind the wall to dry off fully. It was habit. I liked steaming hot showers. I may have been dry before leaving the bathroom but sweat would continue to pour out of my body. I would always need to dry off twice. I stepped down one step, then two steps with my head down. If you have ever been caught off guard and almost ran into someone, this was that moment. On a level floor, when this happens, you jump back. But I was going down steps with momentum carrying me forward. I undid the knot while looking down. I took the final step into my bedroom. I was heading down the steps and now Raven was an inch away from my face staring at me. *What the fuck*? I thought! I remember the surreal comment. I was beyond tired, in a fog, and now pissed. I knew what she was up to, this was no accident! I spouted off, "Fantasize if you want, but I will never cheat on my wife!"

I was caught off guard. I was in my private space. She was in it. I was in my bedroom to get dressed. She knew I would be heading that way. I was still holding my towel with my right hand. I had undone the knot with my left. I was fully naked with this 15-year-old female babysitter standing in front of me, all the while recalling everything everyone had been telling me for a month leading up to this moment. Her eyes went from an "oops!" look of this was somehow just an innocent mistake to a completely shocked look after my response. I was still holding my towel in my right hand. I reached my left hand back around my body, put my towel back on across my front section, and walked past her. She could tell I was pissed. She walked away quickly. This entire event in my life was less than three seconds. I'll repeat: the entire incident, from the step down onto the ground behind the wall to Raven popping up, and my irritated brusque response was about three seconds. I had never dried off, dressed, and left the house that fast in my life. I jumped in my truck and left. Now I had a big problem on my hands. It felt like there was no way to fix it. Did those three seconds just ruin my entire life? How was I going to tell May that the babysitter shaved the back of my head and now saw me completely naked?

I drove off. I didn't even grab the stuff I needed for the guys at the job site that morning. It was a couple of cheap things so I said to myself, *I will just go buy new items and take it to them.* As I was driving, I realized how fucked up everything was that had just happened. I needed to tell May, right now! I called her, no answer. I texted, "Call me."

No reply. May was at work, and she was busy. I tried calling again, but no answer. She finally calls back, "Hey babe, I'm busy. Can we talk later? I don't have time right now."

I replied, "Sure." No way was I going to bombard her with this story when she was trying to keep patients alive in an ICU.

I dropped off the items to my crew without any conversation; they could tell something was wrong. I left quickly. What was I going to do? How and when was I going to tell May? I went back to the house to handle this entire situation with Raven myself. I was past my breaking point with her. I had been so good to her, like a dad, for almost two years. Now this! I was intending to just tell her straight up everything that was transpiring was unacceptable. I also wanted to tell her that my reaction to my words, "Fantasize if you want, but I'll never cheat on my wife," was unacceptable and I didn't mean it literally. I was just going to explain that I reacted inappropriately from lack of sleep. I walked in the back door. Raven was doing the dishes. I never saw her do dishes. I could tell she was bothered. I could hear a cartoon on the TV and knew the kids were watching the television.

THE EVIL GRANDFATHER

I said, "Raven, can you step outside for a moment so I can talk to you?"

"Sure." She replied. We stepped outside. I wanted to apologize for my reaction before getting into the rest of my situation with her.

"I'm sorry for what just happened, I didn't mean to say those words." Before I could finish that statement, Raven started shaking. Almost like a seizure. I thought, *What the fuck?*

She started speaking, "When I was a kid, I was molested by my grandfather. I have never told anyone in my entire life, not even my mom."

She shook for a few seconds more and continued. "What just happened brought all those memories back to me. I... I.. I…"

I stopped her, I replied, "Raven, I didn't touch you, you caught me off guard in my bedroom." Raven continued, "I know, I know, but the memory of being molested came back."

Raven was still shaking uncontrollably. Somehow, I was now "apparently," the cause for surfacing a traumatic memory she had as a child that was hidden deep in her soul. Immediately I knew I was not going to be able to bring up all the inappropriate situations she was the root cause of. This entire situation went from horribly awkward to terrifying. I also knew I was now going to get blamed by May for a circumstance that happened. I could just hear May say, "I TOLD YOU TO TAKE YOUR CLOTHES INTO THE BATHROOM TO GET DRESSED!"

I continued, "I'm sorry for whatever happened with you and your grandfather, Raven. That is terrible."

Raven, while still shaking, quickly responded, "Please don't tell anyone about what I just told you.

My mom doesn't even know. NO ONE KNOWS!"

170

She was shaking so bad it looked like she was in a seizure. However, part of me felt as if it was a grab for attention because it looked fake. I replied, "I won't, I won't say a word, I swear, I will pinky promise to never tell anyone."

She stuck out her pinky. I was just saying that as a figure of speech, not wanting to lock pinkies. She wanted the pinky promise. The situation felt unreal. As if I was in a lifetime movie. The drama was real. I knew I couldn't recount all the situations where this girl had made so many people uncomfortable. But I felt obliged to address one of the many. I touched her shoulder and said, "I am so sorry this situation brought this horrible memory back to your mind."

I continued, "But Raven you know what you have been doing and you know what you said two nights ago in my living room."

I saw fury enter Raven's eyes. All of a sudden, she stopped shaking and with anger responded. "I didn't do or say ANYTHING!"

I replied, "Raven, yes you did, and you know you did, and you know it was inappropriate." She responded, "NO, I DID NOT!"

I looked at her and realized at that moment she was going to defend herself to everyone, especially May, her mom, and anyone else she told this story to. To put it simply, I realized I was in for a nightmare. That nightmare, I thought, was only going to be with my wife. I never imagined it would be the worst nightmare of any man's life.

I BLINKED

I shook my head, walked past her, and left the house again. All I could think about was quickly finishing the last few things I needed to get done for work and SLEEP. Sleep wouldn't come easily, and I also knew there was no way was I going to be around that female ever again. I was not even considering taking her home in the same vehicle with me. I was stuck in a very messed up situation. I was gone for maybe twenty minutes, and May called, "Hey, I don't have time to talk, but I need you to go home to be with the kids. Raven called and said she was not feeling good, and her parents were picking her up. Can you head home from work now?"

I replied, "Yes, I can."

She quickly responded, "Okay, thanks, love you, bye!" I tried to get a word in, "Hey, May!"

She hung up. That night, I got the kids to bed early. I had full intentions of telling May everything when she got home. May got off work at 7. Done with her report by 7:30. Home by 8 at the latest. I had kids all in bed by 7:30. I lay down on the bed, the first day off the medicine, and blinked. It was 7:30 a.m. the next morning. I woke up to May shaking me, "Hey babe, you need to get up for work." I had to be at work by 8. I was supposed to be there by 7:30 as an officer.

"Oh shit," I said aloud. I jumped up, got dressed, and sprinted off to work. I arrived at work shortly before 8 a.m. I was now at work as a newly appointed officer with my life in turmoil, and we had a full day of training.

A DAY FROM HELL

My battalion Chief couldn't stand me. He called, "Hey!" No way was he going to call me captain or even my name. The disrespect was real. When I was promoted, he had his pick of who should be promoted, and it was not me. I replied, "Yes, Chief?"

He continued, "I need your crew at training by 8:30 a.m. Feed them boys and head over as soon as possible."

"Yes, sir," I replied. We headed off for training. We had a new ladder truck that the training was for. The Chief wanted everyone to know how to operate it. The entire time I tried to appear as if everything was fine, and I was normal. A few of the guys made comments, "D.J., you good bro?"

They could tell something was bothering me. I was not my normal self. We finished up training around noon. Once we were done, we headed to the grocery store. Meijer was the closest store to our firehouse. After getting done at Meijer, it was around 1:00 by the time we got back to the station. We had back-to-back medical calls. Nothing serious, just everyday stuff. A seizure and an overdose. We could count on those types of calls

173

about every single day shortly after lunch in our district. We finished the medical calls and I saw a missed call from May. After the missed call, she sent a text saying, "Call me!"

May never just said, "Call me!" Her texts were more like, "Hey baby, call me when you get a chance." I knew something was wrong. We got back to the station, and before I was going to call May back, I knew I needed to get the reports done from the two calls. I finished up the reports and stepped outside to call May back.

I had absolutely zero intention of telling May anything over the phone. I needed to do it in person. She needed to hear the entire story. I knew if I told May on the phone, it could be catastrophic if I was not able to tell her the entire story. The phone rang. On the first ring, she picks up, "Hello." She said in a half-pissed tone.

I responded, "Hey, babe."

She started in right away, "Hey! Sooo, Raven!" My heart sank. I replied, "Ya, what about her?"

May continued, "Raven is all of a sudden acting really strange. I asked her if she wanted to ride along with me today while I ran some errands. She didn't respond to texts nor answer my calls. So, I tried calling a few more times. She didn't answer. So, then I called her mom."

When I heard what May said Crazy Karen had told her, my heart had never fallen so fast in my life. This woman was the definition of psychotic. If Raven spun this story in any other way other than the truth, I was in for a nightmare beyond my imagination. May continued, "So then I called her mom, and Karen said, 'May, something happened, and Raven won't be watching your kids anymore. She feels uncomfortable, and you need to talk to your husband.'" I had never felt this horrible in my life. The way Raven reacted came back to me. I knew this story was going to be much different than the truth. I would now have to tell May something over the phone before I could see her in person.

I spoke, "May I need to tell you something, and I need you to hear the entire story." May snapped back, "What the fuck is going on, D.J.?"

I continued, "May, I got out of the shower yesterday, and I was caught off guard in our bedroom. I was exposed in front of Raven.".

I tried to continue talking, but May cut me off, "What the fuck do you mean exposed? Exposed how?

Like naked?"

I replied, "Yes, May, I was naked. I didn't touch her; I was caught off guard; please listen to the entire story."

I didn't even finish the whole sentence before May hung up. I called May many times that night, but she refused to answer. I refused to text anything.

I wanted her to hear me out. If I had to guess, without ever hearing her husband's side of the story. Knowing May like I do, she probably drove straight over to their house and got down to the bottom of the story from Raven's side. God forbid that May listen to her husband and hear his side first. Nope, May went into a frenzy immediately. That night, May never answered any of my phone calls. As any man in this situation would say, *I was pretty much fucked!*

I started to realize it was going to be a month or more before May and I were normal again. Never did I think "normal," would potentially never exist for us again. And not once did I think it could lead to problems beyond my imagination.

SIDES CHOSEN

The next morning, May had to work. She sent me a text saying, "Raven is watching our kids, don't fucking talk to her. Don't even fucking go inside. I put your work clothes outside in the first barn. Again, don't fucking bother her. One more thing, don't come home tonight!"

I was getting off a 24-hour shift, and my life was ending. My May had made her mind up that I was the guilty one, and Raven was still allowed at our house. So, obviously, she had picked a side. I did exactly as she wished. I went home, grabbed my work clothes, and headed towards the job where my crew was. I was shocked and distraught. An intense sadness came over me like never before. I drove out of the driveway towards the job and parked at the church down the street from my house. I parked and started bawling my eyes out. I was crying uncontrollably. I called my dad, but he didn't answer. I called my mom; she picked up. I have no clue exactly what I said. All I remember is my mom was out of state, and she said, "I will be back in two days, and I will head straight to your house."

I couldn't stop crying, and May refused to talk to me. I never went to work that day. I was in such shock, I honestly can't remember much. At one point during that day, May called. I was balling my eyes out. "Hello?"

May only said a few words, "Hey, dumb ass, since you showed your dick to our babysitter, don't come home until after your fire department shift tomorrow."

I tried to squeeze a few words in, "May wait..." She hung up. May had made up her mind. I was the enemy. Raven was somehow a victim. And I had no clue what story Raven, a 15-year-old, was telling everyone.

LIVING IN SHOCK

The anger in May's voice haunted me. I had never felt so alone. So terrified. So afraid. So disappointed in myself for not listening to the people in my life. I should have listened to my workers. I should have gotten this girl out of my house. How was all this real? It was real, and it was now my life. I couldn't stop crying. The church where I was sitting was across the street from my cousin's house. I knew I couldn't stay parked at this spot. I knew of an abandoned church out in the country in the middle of nowhere. I drove to the church, parked, laid my seat back, and cried. As I was crying, I had every thought possible for a person in complete shock, including thinking that I was going to wake up and it would all just be a bad nightmare. I cried myself to sleep and remembered the last thought: *No way is this real!*

I woke up to an ambulance flying down an adjacent country road. I was hoping to wake up in bed next to May and just hold her to tell her about a horrible nightmare I had. My first thought was, *D.J., you're in survival mode. What is your next step?* It was late afternoon. I called a friend that no one would think I would go to. I said, "Hey man, I need a place to sleep for just one night."

He replied without hesitation, "No problem, man, come by."

I drove straight there. I walked in, and he could tell something was terribly wrong. He said, "Hey man, everything okay?"

I didn't know what to say. I was not in the right mind to get into the whole story. I just responded and said, "No, I am going through some crazy shit and can't talk about it right now."

He responded, "No worries, man, I'll show you my spare bedroom."

Worries were all I had. I truly didn't expect what was to come in the days ahead. I walked into the spare bedroom and said, "Thank you for letting me crash here tonight. I really appreciate it, man."

My voice was sad. He knew it was serious. He responded, "No problem, try to get some rest."

I lay down in bed and felt like my life was ending. Little did I know the worries were only beginning. I took the pillow and placed it over my head and sobbed for hours before I fell asleep.

"GOODBYE, D.J."

I woke up and went to the fire station the next day. I had no choice. I had to go to work. I must have had the most blank stare of shock on my face the entire day. Multiple times, the guys said, "D.J., you good?" I'm okay guys. I tried to hide from them the entire day. Multiple times I got in my truck and just cried. I parked my truck in a spot where they couldn't see me. They probably thought I was on the phone all day. I was out there crying. I was losing my May. I was losing my life as I knew it. I kept thinking, *Surely May will listen to my side eventually.*

Around 10 p.m., my phone rings. It was May, "D.J. I know what happened. I want you to know that I am doing what I think is the best decision for our children."

I didn't even try to understand what she was talking about. I wanted so badly to give her just a glimpse of the truth. I responded, "May, please listen to me, please, I'm begging you. This is not what you think it is."

Without knowing it, May was about to speak the last words for weeks to come and it pierced my soul. She was not going to listen to anything I had to say. She spoke the most heartbreaking words a husband who adores his wife could ever hear, "Goodbye, D.J.," and hung up. My heart sank again, each time it sank lower than the last. There was a streetlight outside that glared into the fire station bedroom where you could barely see the light blue walls. I stared at the wall in front of me all night. The men I worked with were just a locker over also sleeping. I tried hard to not cry that night. It was the longest night of my life. "Goodbye, D.J.," echoed on repeat in my mind. My emotions were as bipolar as you can imagine. How could all this be happening?

EMPTY HOUSE

The next morning, I rushed home, thinking I would force my way in to talk to May. It was too late, she had left the house with the kids, and she was gone. The kids' clothes were gone. Her clothes were gone. Everything they needed for everyday life was gone. My precious May had listened to a 15-year old's story before ever listening to her husband's account of what happened. She took Raven's story as truthful, and I didn't even know what this girl's side of the story was. She left. Our home was empty. My children were all gone. My life felt like it had ended. My house and my heart were empty. I sat outside and cried for hours. In my entire life, I had only cried a few times. My parents' divorce and my grandparents' funerals were the only moments I could remember crying as an adult. And now this. I couldn't fathom my life without May. I couldn't live my life without my children. My sadness turned to anger and back to sadness. This cycle continued for weeks. I had four days off from the fire station. How was I going to survive the next four days without my family? How was I going to survive one day without my family? I was a family man. My children and my wife were the only things I truly cared about. Was I the best husband in the world? No. Was I the best dad in the world? No. But my family was all I genuinely cared about. Nothing else in the world mattered to me. At this moment I realized like never before, just how important they were to me. They were my entire life, and they were gone.

Later that day my mom showed up at the house. She brought my favorite gyro salad hoping it would cheer me up. I remember eating the salad thinking it had no flavor. Even my taste buds were numb. We had not talked on the phone much at all, so I was filling her in for the first time on everything that transpired. I sat down at the end of my big farmhouse table and started telling my mom the entire story. Then my brother showed up. I told them both the entire story. The looks and expressions on their faces were mouth-dropping. When I finished my brother said, "You know I could see that girl going to the authorities."

I looked up at him and responded, "Authorities? For what?" Matt continued, "D.J., how old is she?"

I replied, "She turned 15 a few months ago, but I don't remember her birthday."

Matt spoke again, "Ya, man, she's underage. If she goes to a detective and makes up her side of the story, you could be in some shit."

I thought to myself, "Surely, after almost two years of the girl knowing who I am as a person, surely, surely, she won't do that."

My mom chimed in, "D.J., don't put it past her. You know none of us ever had a good feeling about her."

My world ended right then and there. I knew everything that had already transpired with that girl up to this point. I knew May's reaction was insane. I then said out loud to my mom and brother, "She's going to the authorities."

I pushed the salad off to the side. My face dropped into my arms and crossed on the table as I thought to myself, "My life is over."

LAST DAYS AT THE FIREHOUSE

Four days later was my first day back at work and the driver of the truck was out on vacation. They had to call in overtime to fill his spot. A friend of mine, Lenny, who was much older than me was the one who got called in for overtime to fill in for the absent driver. He had been married and divorced multiple times with crazy women, as he would often say. Lenny was a good guy, around 50 years old, with terrible judgment of women. I heard all his stories in the past of all the women he had been with. He never could pick the right one. Lenny asked me multiple times throughout the day, "D.J., what is going on with you? I can tell something isn't right."

Eventually, I couldn't take it. I told him the short version of the story. When I finished, he looked at me straight-faced and said, "Uhhh you're fucked man."

After telling him the condensed version of the story, it hit me, Lenny was really good friends with the Fire Chief. Not any chief. THE FIRE CHIEF! The man in charge of all of us was thick as thieves with this man. Lenny also had a hard time controlling his tongue with the Fire Chief. I thought to myself, *Oh shit, I told the wrong person.* But it doesn't matter. Everyone was going to find out whatever this girl's story was in a matter of time. I was fucked either way.

Later that day at 3:45 we had a medical call. It was a quick call, and we were back at the firehouse within 10 minutes. When we got back, I grabbed my phone and had a missed call from a local number. There was a voicemail. I listened to a young man's voice that sounded as arrogant as you can imagine saying, "Hello Mr. Durand Murphy, this is Detective Semon representing the Sheriff's department. Can you give me a call back at your convenience? I have a few questions for you."

Right then I knew Raven had gone to the authorities, and the shock hit my soul all over again. I looked at the clock. It was 4:01. I called back and got an automated message that you must call between the hours of 8 a.m. and 4 p.m. I called Cole, my other fire buddy. Cole was the Chief. Cole knew everyone. I knew Cole could get Detective Semon's cell number. Cole answered, "Yo! D.J., what's up?"

I spoke, "Hey man, I need a favor without questions." Cole responded, "Shoot (as in go ahead whatcha got?)"

I continued, "I need Detective Semon's cell number, who works at the Sheriff's Department." Cole didn't hesitate, "I got you. Give me a minute. I don't have his number, but I will get it." A few minutes later Cole called back and said, "Hey bro, what is going on?"

I responded, "Why do you say it like that?"

He continued, "I got a text back from another Detective on behalf of Detective Semon and it reads, 'Tell Durand Murphy that Detective Semon said that he needs to follow the instructions given to him in his voicemail. Durand Murphy needs to call on a business day between the hours of eight to four and he won't be giving out his cell phone number.' "

Cole continued, "So I'm going to ask again, what the fuck is going on D.J.?"

That was the moment I knew this Detective Semon, like May, had already made up his mind. I was guilty of whatever Raven said. Whatever Raven's story was, I had no clue what she had told the authorities. My mind wandered, *What could she have possibly said?*

I was unsure, but whatever it was, it was not good. I responded to Cole, "Buddy, all I can say is I am about to be in some shit, and it is not good."

Cole responded, "I'm coming to see you right now."

I waited outside. When he arrived, I told him the same shortened story I had told Lenny. Cole was in disbelief. His last words to me were, "Lawyer up!" Up until this point, I had not thought about hiring an attorney. Cole was right, I needed a lawyer, and I needed one fast.

QUICK DECISION

Weeks before all this happened, we had just finished a job for a family. The men and I became friends with them. The husband's name was Oliver. Oliver was an attorney. The wife, Alora, was a realtor. Often, I would work in homes by myself around pretty women. Alora was no exception. She was not just pretty. She had an awesome personality, and she was an athlete. She was just a cool chick. Oliver, her husband, was full of himself. I found out later he was not a respected attorney. He walked around like he was this big-shot attorney, but he was not anywhere close to being a respectable attorney. At the time, though, he was the only friend I had who was an attorney. I had worked multiple days around his wife, often alone in the same house as Alora. I knew I had gained Oliver's trust. Throughout my career, I never once in my entire time at the fire station in my uniform, nor ever working in a house with women, made any inappropriate/sexual comments. I never made any passes at any woman. I was a stand-up and respectable man with dignity. I never came onto or made a pass to a woman in my entire marriage. Not once, ever. Even before I was married, I had respect for clients. Was I nice? Absolutely! I had a business, and people needed to see that I was nice.

From the moment May asked me, "D.J., Are we exclusive?" On a Skype call before she ever came home from Germany, I was faithful. Not just in public. I was faithful in secret. As I said before, I saved all my sexual desires and intentions for one woman. I was going to my grave a loyal man. May was my entire life. She was all I ever wanted. I wanted her to always think of me as a stand-up, honorable man. Before Raven, she never doubted me. As soon as Cole left the fire station, I thought, "I'm calling Oliver."

Oliver had to know that I just finished a professional job for him and never made his wife feel the slightest bit uncomfortable. I texted Oliver, "Call me ASAP!"

Oliver called, "What's up, man? Why ASAP?"

"Listen, man, I'm about to tell you a crazy ass story, it has blown way out of proportion, and I have no clue what is about to happen. I need an attorney, and I need one now." I told Oliver the entire story. Oliver was speechless throughout and then had some questions at the end,

"Have you talked to the Sheriff?"

I responded, "No, I tried and was willing to, and here is how that went down."

When I finished, Oliver and I agreed that Detective Semon already had made up his mind and that I would retain him for $500. Oliver advised me not to answer questions from the Sheriff. The idea was that if I went in to answer questions, anything I said could be used against me in a court of law. If I could go back to this moment in life, I would have ignored the attorney and walked into Detective Semon's office and answered all his questions. I was not guilty of any crime. I should have gone in and told my side of the story. Unfortunately, in the heat of everything, especially with May leaving and my state of mind, I made decisions that didn't help. May leaving with the kids messed me up. Nothing felt real. I had never experienced anything close to this situation in my life.

UNPAID LEAVE OF ABSENCE

We lived in a small city. Everyone knew everyone. My case was no exception. Oliver called the Detective to get some information. Oliver then called the prosecutor who was going to be assigned to the case. After Oliver spoke with them, he called me and said, "Bad news, buddy, you're getting charged with some type of felony."

I got pissed, "Felony? What felony did I commit? I didn't touch that girl. It was in my bedroom! She caught me off guard! Are the words I spoke a felony!?"

I had never been so mad in my life. I had lost my wife and my kids, and now I was being told I was getting charged with a felony! None of it seemed real. I had more questions for Oliver... If they don't know the charge, how do they know it's a felony?"

Oliver continued, "That was the same question I asked. I was told that the girl's mother wants you charged with a felony, so they're going to find a felony charge that fits the description."

"Description of what?" I replied with frustration.

Oliver spoke the most haunting words I could've heard, "D.J., I know you're a good dude, and I believe your side of the story, but according to the prosecutor, Raven is saying you approached her, dropped your towel on the floor, and said, 'This is for your fantasies.'"

"Wait, WHAT? Repeat what you just said!" I replied.

Oliver didn't repeat but said, "D.J., you heard me correctly." I went silent.

After a few short moments, Oliver continued, saying, "D.J., there's something else the detective said that startled me a little."

I said, "Go on..."

Oliver's words continued getting worse, "The detective said the word, 'grooming,' as in he was accusing you of grooming this girl."

I replied, "Grooming? What does that even mean?"

Oliver again spoke, and it felt like an increasingly horrible nightmare, "Grooming... As in, you were grooming her for years to someday seduce her."

I replied, "Oliver, I'm going to hang up and let all this sink in and probably vomit somewhere. I have zero feelings toward that girl. I'll talk to you soon." We hung up, and when I thought things couldn't get any worse, they did, in a major way. I was just told I was being charged with a felony.

My wife had already left with the kids. I felt as if I was better off dead than alive.

I was due to return to work at the fire station the next day. The last thing I was going to allow to happen was for a Sheriff to pull into the firehouse and arrest me on unknown felony charges. I called the Chief of the department, Chief Clark. "Hey, Chief, It's D.J." He played dumb. I knew that Lenny had already talked to him.

He responded, "What's up, D.J. Everything good, man?"

I continued, "I would like to request an unpaid leave of absence from the city. I am going through some shit right now that I can't talk about at this time."

He was prepared and responded, "No problem, come on in, man, I'll have the paperwork ready."

I drove up to the fire station where his office was. I walked in and signed up for an indefinite, unpaid leave of absence. If you ask for unpaid, they will let you go on a leave of absence as long as you would like. It was quick, and no one asked any questions. I was now on an unpaid leave of absence. I was soon to face an unknown felony criminal charge. I lost my wife and kids. I had no clue where to turn next.

FAITH TESTED

The next few days following my approval for an unpaid leave of absence were awful. It finally hit me. The only way I would survive this time in my life was with Jesus. I threw away the damn Adderall. Never again was I going to take "medicine," which kept me up for four straight days. I threw away the marijuana vape pen. I threw away any alcohol in my house. I was about to commit my life to God, cry out to Jesus, and ask the Holy Spirit for power to get through this. The devil began the battle with a full-blown attack on my life. It felt like a battle between good and evil. I had to be sober and diligent with every step I took. The effortless way out was putting a bullet through my head. No way was I going to even consider suicide. I would say the words, "I'm better off dead!" However, it was a figure of speech. I knew I was not going to resort to taking my own life all because of a girl's one-sided story. I needed my faith to carry me through this trial of life.

Oliver called a few days later and said, "Hey man, I tried to convince the prosecutor to charge you with a misdemeanor. Nothing seems to be working. They are going after a felony charge."

"What is the felony charge?" I responded. Oliver was as distraught as I was. Though he was not the sharpest attorney, he couldn't believe what was happening to my life.

He responded, "D.J., I really don't know. I could take a guess, but that does you no good. All I can

191

say is you're getting charged. It is likely to be a felony, and I'm sorry, man. I tried so hard to persuade the prosecutor to at least give you a misdemeanor. He's not budging. They want a felony."

My final question to Oliver was, "Who are they?"

Oliver replied, "The prosecutor, Detective Semon, and Karen, Raven's mother." I replied, "Oh great! Crazy Karen is involved in the decision. Ruthless."

Later that day, May called and went on a rant. I had not heard from her in days. I missed her terribly. Even though she had never listened to my side of the story, left and took the kids, and refused to let me speak, I still loved this woman. May was everything to me and the mother of our children. May's first words of her rant after not speaking for multiple days, "Is this the guy that showed his dick to our 15-year-old babysitter?"

I said nothing; it was pointless. She waited a split second and continued, "Just wanted to let you know that the Detective just called me and said you were getting charged with a felony. I hope you realize everything that I have to do is for our children's protection. I have made decisions, and you need to remember what I just said!"

She hung up. I never got a word in, and I had no idea what she was going to do. The entire situation was unraveling. The community was starting to hear whispers of what D.J. did. May had made up her mind. I had no idea what she meant by

"I have to make decisions that are best for our children."

All I knew was I needed to take a drive. I was not sure where I was going to go. I needed to drive and get out of the city before being arrested and charged. Everything in my life was ending as I knew it. Very few people knew the truth. I was the entire city's #1 enemy, and I had not even been charged yet. May hated me. I was struggling from just a few days without her, let alone not seeing my kids, which added to the sorrow. It didn't seem real, but it was. I would often wake up in the morning and think, *Is this all a nightmare?* All it took was a quick listen every morning. No kids running around and yelling. I thought every morning, *Nope, not a nightmare. This is really happening.* Waking up every day to the sound of silence was making me feel dead, and I couldn't fathom how May Murphy was not even allowing me to tell any part of my side of this insanity.

THE CHAPEL

After the phone call with May and hearing her terrible words, something was telling me to drive. I had accepted the fact that I was about to be arrested on unknown felony charges. On this afternoon day, something just told me to start driving. I started driving East, and I stayed in the countryside off the main roads. I just drove. I drove for an hour without a clue where exactly I was heading. It was like the Holy Spirit was telling me to drive so I was just following that guidance. Then God spoke to me, "Find a 24-hour Chapel."

These words came like a rushing wind into my soul. So now I was on a journey in the middle of nowhere, and where would I find a 24-hour Chapel?

Occasionally, in the Catholic Church, there are chapels that allow access to prayer at any time without needing to keep the church doors unlocked. In the Catholic Faith, we believe that the Holy Eucharist (the body and blood of Jesus Christ) is real, not a symbol. The Holy Eucharist is present at all times in these Chapels. You can feel the presence of Jesus Christ in the Chapel when you walk through the doors. For a non-Catholic, it is hard to explain the feeling, but there's so much power in one's prayers in the Chapel.

A non-Catholic once told me, "There's nothing more powerful than the blood of Jesus Christ!" Jesus is present everywhere and comes to anyone who calls out His name. I have nothing against any other religion or nondenominational beliefs. At this time in my life, at this moment, I needed Jesus more than ever before. So, I was going to follow the words, "Find a 24-hour Chapel."

"Find a Chapel," God said. Okay, I will.

I started calling Catholic churches east of the direction I was headed and asked one question, "Hi, I was wondering if you had a 24-hour chapel available?"

The responses were very interesting. I had to call multiple churches to find a 24-hour chapel. I heard everything in the responses from, "Sir, are you okay?" "May I ask why you're looking for a 24-hour chapel?" "Why do you need a 24-hour chapel?" The list goes on.

One lady even said, "Sir, do you have any intention of harming yourself?"

My response was the same to every question: "I need somewhere to pray for as long as I need to pray."

Of all the churches I called, one lady said, "Sir, something is telling me you need this Chapel. I'm going to give you more information."

I responded, "Ma'am, thank you so much!"

This amazing lady called back, "Sir, I found you one!" She gave me an address and said, "Sir, Jesus loves you!"

I responded, "Yes, I know. Thank you so much for finding a Chapel for me to go pray." I looked up the address on my phone's GPS. I still had a two-hour drive to get to this location. I drove another hour, still in the countryside, and realized not only was I in the middle of nowhere, but the Chapel was also in the middle of nowhere. There were corn fields for miles and nothing else in view. An hour into the two-hour drive, I saw a gas station in the 'boondocks.' I stopped, tired, beaten down, and exhausted. The question crossed my mind:

Am I making the right decision? Or should I turn around? Am I running away from a horrible situation?

I parked at the gas pump. I thought, *Might as well get gas while I am here and grab a drink.* When I finished pumping gas, I walked into the gas station. I said to God, "God, if you want me to continue to this Chapel, you need to give me a sign."

When I walked into the gas station, I had to use the restroom. In the bathroom, I heard music on the speaker inside the bathroom. I thought, *What is this song?* At a gas station in the middle of nowhere? The song was "Cry Out To Jesus" by the artist Third Day. Standing in a bathroom in the middle of nowhere, I started tearing up. God just answered me.

The entire point of heading to this Chapel was to do one thing, "CRY OUT TO JESUS!" I wiped my tears, washed my hands, got my drink, and drove another hour to the Chapel, confirmed with this one song on repeat. "Cry out to Jesus".

"There is hope for the helpless, rest for the weary, and love for the broken-hearted. And there is grace and forgiveness, mercy, and healing. He'll meet you wherever you are. Cry out to Jesus!"

I felt helpless, weary, and broken-hearted. I knew this Chapel was going to give me some clarity and strength. I cried the entire final hour of the drive. I was getting close. I had in mind that I was looking for a little building next to a church identified as a Chapel. I looked in the distance and saw this long road leading back to a church. I thought, *Okay, I am here.*

I looked around. I had never been so amazed at what I saw. Beautiful trees, ponds, and a walking trail. This church property was immaculate. I saw in the distance this huge, beautiful church. I pulled up around the back and parked. I got out of my truck, not knowing who might help me. A maintenance man met me in the parking lot and said, "Are you the guy who called asking for a 24-hour chapel?"

I replied, "Yes, sir."

He continued with the same questions everyone asked. I responded to his questions and said, "No, I have no intention of causing any harm to the chapel, to myself, or anyone. I need somewhere to pray without interruption. Please let me go pray as long as I need to pray."

He looked at me and said, "You realize no one has ever asked to do something like this before, and why we are a little nervous?"

I continued, "I understand, sir. I just want a safe place to pray."

I was wearing shorts. I pulled out my pockets, took off my hat, and said, "I have nothing dangerous on me. I just want to pray in a Chapel."

He replied, "Okay, follow me."

He led me into what I thought was the Church and was then going to lead me to a separate place where the Chapel was. He said, "Here's the Chapel."

I was in disbelief. I replied, "Your Chapel isn't a separate place?"

He said, "No sir, our Chapel is our church, take as long as you would like, just be safe."

I looked at the back wall behind the Altar and saw the most beautiful crucifixion of Jesus Christ I had ever seen. It was enormous. By enormous if I had to guess it was probably 20 feet wide by 40 feet tall. I had never seen anything close to it. I blurted out, "WOW!"

He replied, "Ya, I know. That crucifixion of Jesus Christ was made with more than 1 million pieces of glass."

I replied, "It's the most beautiful thing I have ever seen!"

"Yes, it is," he said. At that, he walked out, leaving me alone. God didn't lead me to the normal small, roomed Chapel separate from the church. He led me to something so magnificent you would have to see it with your own eyes to believe. I had my Bible, my rosary, and myself. I was ready to Cry out to Jesus. I found my spot. I got on my knees. I started to pray. I started to cry. I started to ask so many questions. *God, why is this happening to me? What is the point of all this? How could this be?*

I heard a noise from above. On the second level, a woman had sat down back behind me up above. This woman must have been informed that a man called and said, "I need a 24-hour chapel." Maybe it was the woman who found this chapel for me. I never spoke to her. She stayed there for hours. I was not sure if she was there to watch over me or not. She was probably praying for me the entire time.

Eventually, she left. I stayed in this Chapel all night. It was the first time in a week that I felt safe. The sun had come up. I decided to take a walk on the trail I had seen outside. As I was walking out of the Chapel, a retired Priest stopped me. "Sir, would you like us to pray for you?"

I replied, "Yes, please pray for me, my wife, and my kids." He continued, "What is your name?"

I said, "D.J."

Without hesitation, this retired priest I had never met before in a state I had never even been to said, "Durand Joseph?"

I looked at him in unbelief and said, "Yes, how did you know that?"

He responded, "It just came to me. We will pray for you. Are you coming back?" "Yes, I'm coming back again to pray. I just need some fresh air."

He replied, "Take as much time as you need." SOLITUDE

I started to walk this beautiful path on this enormous, beautiful property in the middle of nowhere. I remembered a conversation I had with my local priest, who I went to right after signing the unpaid leave of absence paperwork. His name is Father Alphonse. I trusted him. I reached out to him and said, "I need to come talk to you ASAP."

Without hesitation, he said, "Come see me now if you like."

I left the fire station after signing away my career and went to see him. When I sat down with him, he said, "Let us pray first."

He prayed, and I told him the entire story. Afterward, I started venting my feelings as I continued speaking and said, "I don't understand why I am going through this! I am going to be charged with a crime that is going to make me look like a pedophile. I don't understand why I am going through all this. I feel like I am being punished, and I don't masturbate, I don't look at pornographic material, and I don't allow myself to have sexual thoughts of other women. I save all my sexual energy for my wife, and I say this with all honesty!"

My venting rant continued, "And, I am going to be in the newspaper because I am a local officer, I am going to be labeled, People are going to hate me. I am losing my wife and kids. I am going to have to sell everything to pay attorney fees and afford to survive. Father Alphonse, I DO NOT UNDERSTAND!"

He looked at me and said, "WOW!"

I had just told him the entire story of everything that happened and why I couldn't understand how of all the possible trials I could have experienced, why this, and why me? After saying, "WOW!" he paused and continued,

"I believe everything you just told me, D.J. I know the person, husband, and father you are. If you have no struggle with lust, then God is working on something else."

I replied, "What do you mean?"

He said, "God is working on some other evil in your life right now that you are unaware of." "Okay?" I said.

He continued, "I'm going to ask you some questions. Is that okay?" "Yes," I said.

Father Alphonse began to ask me all sorts of questions. I answered them all honestly. When he was done asking all the questions, he began telling me how early in his Priesthood he began to study demons. He wanted to learn a demon's characteristics so he could understand more about how to help people struggling with different evil sins of this world. He said he studied for some time and had to stop

because he said, "In all honesty, I was getting scared."

I asked, "Why were you getting scared? You're a Priest."

He continued, "I learned that the spiritual world around us is real. It is physical, not just a figment of our imagination. The demonic world is as real as the spiritual world of God and is constantly trying to attack us, much like God's spiritual presence is trying to protect us."

I looked at him and shook my head as if to say, "Go on…"

He continued, "I was spending more time learning about demons than I was about God, Jesus, Angels, Saints, etc. I stopped myself, and I will never again study the demonic world ever again." When he finished these words, I realized that even the best men and women need to focus their eyes on Jesus and stay away from the evil world we live in, or any of us could end up in trouble.

Our conversation continued, and he said, "Okay, now that you have answered all these questions, I think I know what God is working on with you."

"Tell me," I said. He replied, "Pride."

At that moment, in all honesty, I had no idea I had any issues with pride. I always perceived pride as a characteristic of someone feeling arrogant about their actual or perceived superiority over others. He asked more questions and said, "You do not have to be proud of yourself for your accomplishments." He continued, "Do you want your wife to be proud of you? Do you want your kids to be proud of you? How about family members? Do you want your parents or grandparents to be proud of you?" The list was piling up. At that moment, I realized as I said out loud, "Oh my, you're right. I am full of pride, and I didn't even know it."

I wanted all those family members in my life to be proud of me, especially May. My final question to him was, "How do I get rid of pride?"

He said, "The Demon of Pride is one of the strongest Demons, if not the strongest. The way you get rid of pride takes time, but you can do it."

He said, "You have to commit yourself to the prayer of the removal of pride; you have to find a way to live a simpler life; you have to find solitude as often as possible; you have to trust and believe in everything you are doing."

I replied, "Solitude? Describe solitude to me because I don't usually sit still for very long."

He spoke his last bit of advice as he said, "Study solitude, find solitude; solitude can be a physical emotion that overcomes your body and soul, and you need it. Solitude will bring you peace. Solitude will help bring simplicity to your life. And that is what you need to remove pride."

We concluded our meeting in prayer, and I left thinking, "How am I going to find solitude?"

As I started walking on this beautiful trail, the scenery was amazing. I just spent an entire night in a beautiful Chapel in the presence of Jesus in tearful prayer. I had my rosary in my pocket. I pulled it out and started praying the rosary while walking ever so slowly. I said, "God, give me solitude on this walk," I was by myself with the sun shining, and everything around me was quiet. Twenty minutes later, I finished the rosary. I said aloud in a whisper, "God, I don't understand the situation I'm going through; I give it all to you. Take my worries away. Your child needs you. Help me and take away the pain and sadness."

Immediately after saying those words, a sensation came over my body--most amazingly, almost indescribably, a feeling of calm came over me. For a moment, all my worries, all my sadness, all my fears, all of it was gone. I stopped, looked up to the heavens, and said, "Solitude!"

Little did I know how important solitude was going to be in my life for the months to come.

MANIC OR SHOCK?

I went back to the Chapel for most of the day, and later that night, I found a hotel where I stayed for one night. I knew I had to get back home soon because there was going to be a warrant out for my arrest. That night in the hotel was tough. Solitude can disappear quickly if you become consumed with worries. However, solitude through Jesus can come back just as fast if you fall to your knees and your worries are, in a sense, "prayed away." My phone rang, it was May. She was staying at her mom's house, and the kids were put to bed. I could tell she had been drinking some wine.

Drunk or not, it was the first time May let me speak. May seemed like she was in shock. I was in shock as well, so I understood. Then, I thought of something that had never occurred to me. Was it shock? Or did May have an issue with manic depression?

May would go through phases of the highest of high happiness, then the lowest of lows with anger and sadness. May could function with little sleep and still have high levels of energy. May would go from completely normal to an all-out brawl argument over the smallest things. At the time, I didn't understand any of these characteristic traits. Most of the time, I blamed myself for not being able to stay calm and keep her calm. I would voice my opinion as any person would during a disagreement. However, our disagreements always started with the smallest things. Such as why I thought I should put garlic in the gravy or why we didn't need expensive high-thread-count bed sheets. Our fights never started with serious subjects. Our fights always started over what men often describe as "The dumbest shit." A disagreement on thread count on bed sheets would escalate quickly if I didn't just agree with whatever May wanted. Her anger would erupt quickly. I would just give up and try to walk away, and May would follow. May tended to back me into corners during arguments. At times, she would lay her hands on me. Sometimes, it would be pushing my chest back. Other times, it would be grabbing my face to look at her while she was scolding me. The worst was when she would grasp my mouth and tell me to shut the fuck up and listen. I always maintained self-control and didn't react. This was challenging at times.

When you're backed into a corner of a bedroom, and someone is pointing and screaming at you, a lot of thoughts come across your mind. In those moments, May was oblivious to her actions. She justified them. Was I the best husband during those moments? Absolutely not. I would argue my point. "We don't need $200 sheets for our bed, May!" The fight was then on. I knew how May fought before this insane and unbelievable situation of her husband, soon to be arrested, was about to take place. I knew May was going to react in the craziest way possible. However, May took it to another level. She refused to even listen to my side. She moved out. She withheld the children from me. But the worst was yet to come.

DRUNK CALL

The phone rang. I had shut my phone off the entire time at the Chapel. I told my mom before pulling into the Chapel, "People are going to call you and ask, where is D.J.?"

I told her to make sure everyone knew that I was not doing anything stupid. I was simply finding somewhere to go pray where no one could find me. Shortly after checking into the hotel, I turned my phone back on. My phone rang almost immediately. It was around 10 p.m.. May had a few glasses of wine and was going to give me the business. I was just hoping she would listen even if for just a moment. May told me how I was ruining her life, how I made the biggest mistake of my life. So on and so forth. I was the worst person in the world. I did catch a few moments to open her mind up saying, "May, this girl is not innocent! May, if you're not going to listen to me, please call Wyatt, my brother, or anyone who was around Raven at the house."

May didn't like to hear any of that. May said, "You need to sincerely apologize to her, or I will never take you back."

The conversation was nothing but a mess. We went back and forth. I was trying to open up her mind. She said I was being defensive and repeated that I needed to apologize. I can't tell you how many moments in our marriage she has manipulated me into apologizing or doing something that I later regretted. I love May so much that I would do almost anything to keep her next to me. I would jump off a mountain and try to fly just to keep my May. She and I had five children, and I was going to do everything I could to keep our family together. The conversation was not going anywhere.

Around midnight, I finally said, "May, can I pray with you?" She replied, "SURE!"

I started to pray. May might not realize it, but throughout our entire marriage, when I prayed with her at night, she would always feel a sense of calm come over her soul, and every single time she would fall asleep. This night, on the phone, was no different. May fell asleep. I prayed over May on the phone for thirty minutes. She didn't speak a word. When I finished, I said, "May?"

She was out. I put the phone on speaker that night and listened to her breathing as she slept for three hours. I missed listening to her breathe while she was sleeping. Her breaths were followed by gasps as she slept. This situation was haunting her. I felt so horrible for her. Her husband was getting arrested, her life was in turmoil. I could tell by the way she took gasps of breath in her sleep. Listening to her sleep, I cried the entire time. All I wanted to do was hold her tight and comfort her. After hours of listening to her sleep, I heard her move. She woke up and hung up the phone. There goes my May. The closest thing I got to connecting with my wife at the time was listening to her sleep. When she woke up and hung up the phone, it was like another dagger to my soul.

NOOSE LETTER

"You need to apologize to her, or I will never take you back!" I realized an apology was going to go one of two ways. The first way it was going to confirm me as guilty to the prosecutor if Raven turned it in to the authorities.

The second outcome was Raven could look at it and say to her mother, "Mom, he did apologize sincerely; we should drop the charges."

Was I guilty of a crime? Absolutely not! Was I sorry? Yes, there was a part of me that felt bad for

Raven because of the trauma it brought to the surface for her. Being molested by a grandfather is awful. However, Raven was far from innocent, and she knew it. I was hesitant in writing the apology. May still had never listened to my side. She had her mind made up that Raven was innocent, and I was this horrible man.

"You need to apologize, or I will never take you back!" May's words echoed in my head. My pondering continued as I thought to myself *May was drinking, though. Does she even remember saying that? Does May want to see me in jail? Will she truly consider taking me back after an apology?*

This apology letter was a huge risk. I wanted my wife back, I wanted my kids back, I wanted my May back. In a way, I was blaming myself anyway. If I had just listened to everyone and got this female out of my house, this would have never happened.

My decision was made if May wanted me to apologize. I was going to apologize. The risk would be worth it for me if I got my family back. I wrote a simple apology for the incident and what it caused to surface for her. I wished her a happy life and hoped she accepted my apology. I had it delivered to Raven. This apology letter ended up being the death of me. Raven decided to hand it over to the authorities and show that I was admitting guilt, though I never gave any details of the incident or anything leading up to it. It ended up being used against me in the case. It was the worst decision I made the entire time. May later said, "I NEVER TOLD YOU TO WRITE THAT LETTER!"

But that is not how I remembered it. The apology did nothing other than help the criminal case against me. Raven and her crazy mom did not accept the apology. They were going for blood. I even offered to resign from my job completely in the apology letter. Nothing I said in the letter mattered. They wanted to see me behind bars. Raven had the mind of a 15-year-old. She was determined to show her mother, May, and the entire community that she was not only innocent but the victim! Raven knew how well-known I was in the community. This situation was either going to destroy her local community's reputation, or she had to go after mine.

After writing the noose letter, I called Oliver, my family's friend, a short-term defense attorney. Any good defense attorney on the planet would argue until they were blue in the face to stop a client facing criminal charges from submitting an apology letter. I explained to Oliver that my wife wanted me to apologize to Raven and that she may never take me back if I didn't. I went on to explain that I prayed about it and knew getting my family back was more important than anything to me. Oliver agreed that the letter could go either way, meaning Raven and her mother

210

drop the charges or hand the letter over to the prosecutor. Oliver should have done everything in his power to stop me. Defense attorneys usually understand that their client is in the most chaotic state of mind of their life. This means a good defense attorney is not just representing you in court. They are instructing you on good and bad decisions along the way. Oliver not only allowed me to convince him to submit the apology letter. Oliver even called the prosecutor to tell him that I was submitting a letter of apology with the hope that the charges would be dropped. Oliver allowed his client to submit an apology letter and called the prosecutor to tell him about it!

Knock! Knock!

"One second!" I opened the door to the hotel room. The housekeeping lady said,

"Sir, it's time for your check out." I responded, "Give me a few minutes, ma'am." Before I could even finish packing up my stuff, Oliver called back.

"D.J., bad news, Detective Semon just called and said you're being charged today, and there is about to be a warrant out for your arrest."

I responded, "Oliver, does this have anything to do with the apology letter I just submitted?" He defensively replied, "No way, man! You were getting arrested no matter what!"

"Okay, man," I replied. We hung up. The noose letter was exactly what the prosecutor and the detective were waiting for. They had zero evidence up until this point aside from a 15-year-old's story. I had just hung myself as a felon. As I sat in my truck, I thought, *Is this what May wanted? Is Oliver even on my side? What is happening!?*

FAITH AND MOMMA EVE

I was due to be arrested and charged with an unknown felony. The apology letter was evidence of my guilt to the prosecutor. As I drove back home, I called everyone who had been worried about me. To each person, I just said, "I am alive, I am going to be okay."

I had a childhood female friend, Faith, who I grew up with. She and I were close our whole lives. There is a picture of us as infants taking a bath together because our mommas were best friends. Faith and I had always been good friends, but we never dated once. Our friendship was more important. She was the only female friend I ever had like this. I trusted Faith. Faith trusted me. Faith was beautiful physically, emotionally, and spiritually. At the time, she lived with her boyfriend out in the country.

I called her, "Faith, I need to come to your house for a few hours."

She said, "Okay, let me call my boyfriend and make sure he's okay with it."

I responded, "Faith, I don't care if he's okay with it or not, I'm coming to your house for a few hours.

I'll explain later."

Faith responded, "Okay, D.J., I'll call him and let him know you're coming over." I had already been driving a few hours back from the Chapel. Shortly after our phone call, I arrived.

Faith's mom, Eve, is my second mom. Not blood-related, but she's my second momma. Eve is truly a gift from God to the world. She has a spiritual presence that always calms me down. Every time I have been in turmoil, I called her. Eve is wise. Before ever giving advice, she would go pray, find solitude, and then call you back. I could be shot ten times with bullet holes all over me, and she could somehow calm me down. She's simply an amazing second mom. I had called Eve multiple times throughout the entire crisis, and she was always there for me. Eve and her daughter Faith were close; they talked every day. I knew Eve had discussed my predicament with Faith, knowing I trusted them both. Faith had to be a little nervous, knowing that I was heading to her house. Faith didn't care, though, I was her non-blood brother, and she would do anything for me.

After arriving at Faith's house, I sat down on the couch. I explained to her that I just needed somewhere to hang out for a few hours because I was getting arrested that day. I informed her that as soon as the Sheriff called me, I would be heading to turn myself in. I said, "Faith, I don't want to give them (the Sheriffs) the satisfaction of arresting me at my house. I wanted them to go to my house, not find me, and be forced to call me to inform me that there was an arrest warrant for me. And then, I would go turn myself in."

Faith looked at me and said in the most ditzy way, "Well, okay then!"

I'm sure none of it seemed real to her, and it didn't seem real to me. Her boyfriend was gone, so I had a chance to tell her everything that transpired, from start to finish. I can't tell you how many times she repeated the word "WOW!"

ISSUED

I had not yet hired another attorney. Oliver was still my contact, but I knew that I would soon be interviewing other defense attorneys. Oliver called while I was still sitting on Faith's couch, "Hey man, your arrest warrant has been issued. The Sheriff's department is more than likely headed over to your house."

I responded, "Get in contact with someone there and inform them that I am not at home, and I will come to turn myself in."

Oliver responded, "Will do. When?" I replied, "I'll head that way now."

Oliver continued, "Okay, I'll let them know, D.J." I replied, "Thanks."

Oliver spoke again, "Hey, D.J.?" "Ya, man?" I said.

214

Oliver's last words to me were, "I'm sorry, man."

His apology didn't feel completely sincere. I was getting arrested. I'm sure he felt bad for me. However, his apology felt like he was saying sorry for thinking he could trust the prosecutor who I found out later was his buddy. I found out the hard way later that everyone in the crime community was tied together.

"It's okay, Oliver, I will get through this," were my last words to him. Oliver was friends with the prosecutor. I think he thought their friendship would help him stop a felony charge. It didn't. The felony charge had come, and I was on my way to turn myself in.

As I left Faith's house, I had the saddest expression Faith had ever seen on me. "Goodbye, Faith." Faith said, "D.J., wait!"

Faith came and hugged me and said, "I love you, buddy. You are one of the strongest, if not the strongest, men I have ever met. You will get through this."

I responded, "I love you, too, Faith, we'll talk soon."

Though I had just told Oliver that I would get through this, I didn't say that to Faith. With Oliver, I didn't want him to feel bad about not being able to get the charge knocked down to a misdemeanor. With Faith, I didn't want to lie. I had never, ever lied to her and we had been close with one another since birth. I remember walking out of Faith's house thinking *I really don't know if I am going to get through this.*

I was officially charged with a felony, I had lost my May, my children were gone, and my life was crumbling, to say the least. I had no idea what was to come. It seemed like I was constantly being surprised with more sad news and was living over and over in shock. I was living in fear. Living in fear is the most awful feeling in the world. Living with the unknown. Living not knowing what boulder was going to roll into my life next. The boulders kept tumbling into my life, and it felt like May had dug a grave that she wanted me to jump in.

There was a witch hunt taking place behind my back that I had no awareness of. I found out later that Detective Semon was a newly appointed young detective. He had a case on his hands that he was going to leverage to make a name for himself. He was going to be the Sheriff's detective who charged and arrested the captain of the fire department. This was his case and the way to become "locally famous and recognized." I later became convinced that this guy hated me for some reason. I was not convinced of this just because he believed some story a female named Raven came up with, making her look like a victim and making this guy named D.J. out to be a criminal.

Detective Semon was around my age; it was highly possible that we had crossed paths in some way in the past. I felt as if he had a personal vendetta against me. And the longer everything transpired, the more this felt true.

REMEMBER ME?

I was on my way to the Sheriff's department, but I needed to make one stop. I had a business bank account that only I could access. I needed bond money. No way was I going to let this Sheriff win the fight with the pleasure of me spending the night in a jail cell. Oliver had told me what the bond was. I stopped and got the cash. I was now heading to meet Sheriff Semon, a man I had never laid eyes on. I pulled into the parking lot. I pulled right up next to a Sheriff's' vehicle I saw in the parking lot. I just knew they were waiting for me. I had a plan! I would hand my captain's badge to this prick and let him know I wanted him to keep it as a memory of the guy he falsely charged and what this girl had been up to. I was going to let him know that Raven was not this innocent little girl he thought she was. I pulled up next to them. I had my captain's badge in hand. I had not met Detective Semon, but when I got out, I just knew by looking at the three Sheriffs which one was him. I said, "Detective Semon?"

He responded in the most arrogant and egotistical way you can imagine."YUP, THAT'S ME!"

I replied, "I have something I would like to give you as a memory of the man you are falsely charging."

By their reaction, you would have thought I brandished a gun out and pointed it at him. The three Sheriffs jumped me and slammed me up against my truck. No way was I going to fight back or resist. Though in the back of my mind, I knew he had caused my May to leave me. I thought to myself, *I would love to be in an alley with all three of these pricks by myself without guns.*

Though I was not resisting, they slammed me a couple of times against my truck as I said, "Woah, fellas, what are you doing? I'm turning myself in!"

Detective Semon couldn't wait to read my rights, and this was the first time I had heard exactly what I was being charged with. "Durand Murphy, you are being charged with Sexual Misconduct--Exposure with Objective to harm a minor! You have the right to remain silent. Anything you say can and will be held against you in the court of law!" It made him so happy to say that as he overly tightened the handcuffs.

"Remain silent!" I thought, *FUCK NO!* The entire walk into registration I let him know everything this female had done and how devious she was. He probably didn't listen to a word I said, but I do remember looking at the facial expression of another Sheriff who had a look on his face like, *What the fuck? Is he serious?*

I finished by saying, "There are two sides to every story!"

When they walked me into registration, it got more interesting. The lady at registration called me up. She read the charge. She needed to find the charge in the computer system, but she couldn't find it. She kept looking and still couldn't find it. She commented to me, "Apparently, there's a first time for everything!" She continued, "You're the first person in the history of this database to ever get charged with this crime."

I replied, "Sounds about right, and I'm not surprised."

She gave up looking and said, "You can go back and have a seat. I have to figure out how to put this charge in the computer system." I thought, *You have got to be kidding me!*

I was being charged with something unknown. The computer didn't have this charge in the system. This was unbelievable, and I continued to conclude that the prosecutor and Sheriff wanted to find anything to charge me with. Twenty minutes later, the woman at registration called me back up. "Durand Murphy, you can come back up here."

She continued, "I had to manually enter your charge into the notes and put the closest charge I could find into the box for the system to allow me to process you."

I replied, "Okay, ma'am."

I had nothing else to say. I thought to myself, "Not even the system wanted you to process me!"

I didn't dare speak; I had already said enough. I knew then I was not going down without a fight. This was not going to be a quick and easy plea agreement. I wanted a jury trial and was going to do whatever it took to get my day in court.

MUGGED

After processing, I was sent over for my mug shot. I didn't plan for this picture. Everyone has seen the attire jail workers wear when they are mowing the yards or picking up trash around the jail. I had on a blue and white striped shirt. I thought, *Oh! How perfect! My mugshot for the newspapers will make it look like I already have the jail uniform shirt on!*

The jailer took the first picture. He said he needed to take a few more as he said, "Sorry man, that is not what I am looking for." I thought, *What are you looking for? Is this a reality show?*

He started clicking a few more shots. He soon got what he wanted. He got a mugshot with big blue and white pinstripes and a look on my face like I was a freaking meth head. The mug shot of a lifetime for these people. The newspapers were going to love it! I got done with the mug shot and I overheard in the next office room the Sheriff talking about towing my truck away. I was not going to stay silent on this as I said in a smart-ass voice, "Hey guys! You are not towing my truck away; I have cash for my bond, and I am driving myself home!"

I should have ended that statement with, "You mother fuckers!" They all looked at me with disbelief as they thought, *Oh shit, he heard us talking, what do we do now?* They had no right to tow my truck away, and they knew it. However, they were not going to just let me go home that fast.

One of them responded, "D.J., you can go have a seat over there." As they pointed in a certain direction. I went and sat down, realizing they wanted to personalize the situation by calling me what everyone my whole life had called me, D.J., not Durand.

I started looking around at everyone. I recognized three people in jail whose lives I had helped from overdoses while working as an EMT with the fire department. I saw multiple other people I had run across from time to time. Seizures, domestic calls, etc. I shook my head in disbelief, thinking *How am I here?* I went from helping the people in jail to becoming one of them.

There was a guy sitting close to me who was "cracked out" (on meth) or some type of drug. He was itching his skin, shaking his leg uncontrollably, and looked like a mess. I don't think he even noticed me. He was just thinking about how fast he could get out of there and get some more drugs. Eventually, he looked over at me and said, "What is a guy like you in here for?"

This was the first time I had laughed in weeks. This cracked-out guy had just brought a smile to my face in the worst situation possible. I laughed quietly and said, "Buddy, I really don't know how I ended up here."

But what I did know, I thought quietly to myself, was that Raven was doing everything she could to make herself look innocent, and she wanted the attention. And her mother, "Crazy Karen," was going to have the last word in all of this travesty. And Prosecutor Shitbrick, real name Prosecutor Richard, was intimidated by Crazy Karen. I was convinced that Raven went to this extreme for one big reason. No way was she going to let May think that she was guilty of having feelings for her husband, and she loved the attention she was getting from her mom for the first time ever. Eventually, they let me bond out, and I was able to drive home.

This was a relief. I got this portion over with. It was going to get harder each day, but I was glad to be out of jail. Before I left, Detective Semon wanted to get the last words in. He said, "Hey, D.J., I look forward to when you're sitting in a jail cell!"

I thought, "Wow, this guy!"

I walked out, went to my truck, and drove home. I was out of tears for the night. I got home, and my brother and mom were waiting for me. I was full of anger. I vented for twenty minutes, and they so calmly just let me get it all out. My mom

and brother were there for one purpose – KEEP
D.J. ALIVE! Everyone knew what I was going
through was as traumatic of a life circumstance as
one could imagine.

SUPPORT

My brother had my back. He gave me all the
brotherly love with no judgment and words of en-
couragement to help me stay positive. He would
say, "D.J., this too will pass!"

Matt was also worried about money. Matt is a
financial advisor so he couldn't help but be concerned about money. He would produce all these
game plans for how to survive financially. He
would say, "Okay, you need to sell this and sell
that. Cancel this subscription. Do this, do that."

What Matt didn't realize at the time was that
money meant nothing to me. I couldn't even think
about money. Paying bills seemed irrelevant. I was
fighting for my life, fighting for my family, fighting for my freedom. I didn't have the fight in me
to find a way to pay bills. Throughout this entire
process, my mom, Lucy, was a saint. She knew everyone was blind to the situation and who her son
truly was. She stayed right by my side and never
left my house for a month.

Even later, she would come to check up on me
every day. She stopped her life completely and
understood that her task as a mother was to "help

my son survive the storm." I don't know what I would have done without her. Though I often just wanted to be alone, she guarded me in ways only a mother could do. When I needed to vent, I had someone to vent to without any judgment. When I needed to eat because I was not eating anything, she would cook something. When I needed groceries, she would go for me.

And she was being judged in the city as well. People knew me, people knew she was my mom, and everyone judged her as well. "How dare you come in public knowing you raised that piece of shit son of yours!" People had ruthless words and thoughts. My mom and I could feel them as we went out in public. When you are going through a situation like this, you try so hard to block everyone and everything out. However, that was almost impossible. I was living through the darkest of the darkest days of my life. May leaving with the kids eviscerated my soul, and that was only one of the many problems I had to deal with. Following the day after the arrest, it just got worse. Much worse!

FAKE NEWS!

The next morning, all hell broke loose in my life. I was on the front page of every newspaper. I was on every news channel. I didn't just hit the local newspaper. It hit national newspapers. It hit news channels on TV across the state. My mom said, "Don't turn on the TV!" I knew what she meant. I waited a few days before I looked up the newspaper articles on my phone. The stories were simply unbelievable!

Firefighter Captain Durand Joseph Murphy has been charged with Sexual Misconduct Exposure with the Objective to harm a minor. The stories were endless in the newspapers and twisted in ways I never could have imagined. The articles said that I offered Raven and her cousin alcohol and marijuana. I told Raven she had pretty eyes. I told Raven she needed to pinky promise me she would never tell anyone the story of me exposing myself to her. I told Raven May would be mad if she ever found out. I was "grooming" Raven to someday seduce her. I asked Raven to come into the bathroom. I "FLASHED" my genitals and said, "This is for your fantasies!" And here is the best one-- I told Raven that I was stronger than her and could RAPE her if I wanted to. If a man was ever labeled as a pedophile by an entire community and state, it was me! The words used: Genitals, Rape, Fantasies, Grooming, etc., all tagged me as guilty before I could defend myself in the courtroom. The stories went on and on. It was all over the TV, all over the newspapers. Locally and nationwide. I had been labeled a pedophile to what felt like the entire world. One punch in the face after another. Reading those articles felt like I was being stabbed repeatedly. My soul was crushed. My reputation was destroyed. I now had the image of a piece of shit pedophile. I finished reading them and just went and lay down in bed alone and afraid. My life felt like it had ended, and I was better off dead than alive.

The only thing I could tell myself to make it slightly better was, "God is my only judge."

I needed to have strength beyond what I ever could imagine to not put a bullet in my head. I had ZERO issues with lust, none. But here I was to everyone in the world, "Durand Joseph Murphy, also known as D.J., the pedophile fire captain." I was going to attack this horrible situation I was in with sobriety and God. I knew this situation was different. This stress was different. I recognized it was something very few people go through. The only thing I could think of that could have been worse is the loss of a child. Though I felt like I had lost all my children.

ONE STEP AT A TIME

The criminal investigation I was now under was terrible. But losing May was going to be the death of me. I needed a stress release, and I needed something now. I put my tennis shoes on, and I took off running. Running made me feel free. Even if it was only for a short amount of time, I felt free. Every day I ran farther and farther and farther. After my first run, that same day I started a journal. I had never written anything about my day, ever. I always thought Journals were for women. I soon realized that writing down on paper what transpired each day helped me cope with everyday life. I didn't just write down what happened. I wrote down all my thoughts. It was a second form of stress relief. Running and keeping a journal was extremely helpful for my well-being. However, there was only one thing that kept me alive. I prayed. I prayed nonstop. I surrendered my life to God. The more I prayed the more thankful I became. I was getting rid of pride through prayer and solitude. I was feeling strong spiritually. Each day my spiritual journey led me to find glimpses of joy in the trial of life.

Each day I would wake up and try to find solitude right away. Some days were harder than others. The articles printed by the newspapers didn't stop, and there were some very difficult days. I started to see what people were saying on Facebook and other social media platforms. I realized people believed what they read. Everyone wanted to judge me. People were absolutely evil. Comments such as, "He should be hung!", "We should go burn a cross in his yard!" "What a pedophile piece of shit that man is!" "Someone needs to KILL HIM!"

I only read the comments once. My reaction was sadness. I began to pray for my enemies. I began to pray for Raven. I began to pray for Raven's mother Karen. Praying for my enemies was one of the hardest things I did. I genuinely prayed for them. I knew I had to forgive everyone, and I set myself on a path of trying to realize forgiveness.

In my journal, I labeled at the top how many days May and my children had been gone. Each day felt like a week. After leaving the hotel and getting arrested, my communication with May was rare. She blocked me on her phone. Her entire family blocked me from their phones. I wanted to apologize to her family members. Not because of what I had done, but because I was a part of something that caused so much grief for their entire family. I was well-known in the community. When the story hit all the newspapers, their entire family had to deal with the drama. If nothing else, I just wanted to say sorry for the grief caused and that I never intended to hurt anyone. However, everyone had blocked me. May and her entire family were unreachable. They believed everything they had read, and I was dead to them.

MIDNIGHT GROCERY RUN

I will never forget the first night after it all hit the newspapers. I couldn't sleep, I got up; it was past midnight. I had very little food in the house. I had very few cleaning supplies. I needed batteries. At 1 a.m. I decided to head to the grocery store. It was in the middle of the night. I knew the grocery store would be empty of people, but I was still absolutely terrified to go in public now. The newspapers and TV had destroyed me. I loved going to the grocery store before all of this. Guess which grocery store I chose? The same one I met May at. I got to the store and had an eerie feeling. I just knew something was going to happen. I was walking fast, getting everything I needed. I get to the cleaning supply section, and I needed "lemon shine." I was struggling to find the product. I knew it was there, I kept looking. Next thing I know a tall man approached me. I turned to look at him. It was a past client I had and provided work for.

He said, "I thought that was you! Man, you are brave going into the public right now! Have you seen all the things people are saying about you on social media?"

At that time, I had not looked at any social media. I replied to him, "No sir, I have not looked."

He continued, "Oh man! People are saying they want you dead! That you should be hung! All kinds of crazy stuff!" I looked at him with the most disgusted look. I thought to myself, *How the fuck are you making this any better for me right now?*

I just looked at him and said, "Well there are two sides to every story."

After I said that he looked at me and said, "Well buddy, you better find yourself a DAMN good lawyer." I thought, *Wow! Really? No shit, man!* I kept my mouth restrained.

I responded, "Yes sir, I know." I think he was surprised that my demeanor was not super defensive. As he was walking away, he turned around and said, "Hey, D.J., I wish you the best."

And there it was, Something I realized over and over during the process: people immediately want to judge and persecute someone for something they read or see on the news. But when people were around me and talked to me, every one of them at the end thought, "Maybe there is a second side to this crazy story." As he walked away, I thought to myself, *Whatever happened to 'innocent until proven guilty'? Whatever happened to, we should not judge others?*

This entire experience ruined my faith in humanity for a long time. Most people immediately believe what they read in the newspapers. These people wanted me dead; they wanted me in jail, they wanted me burned alive. These are words I later read on social media. "Burn him alive!" "He should be in prison!" "He deserves no second chance!" "He needs to be killed!"

I got a glimpse of what Jesus must have felt like when he was being persecuted. This man, during a midnight grocery stop, made me feel worthless and beat me down for a few minutes. Then I reminded myself, *God is my only judge!*

The next day, my dad and stepmom stopped to see me. They both were amazing in not judging me at all. They knew the man I was and that I had a big heart, much like my dad. I needed to borrow money. They were the people I felt comfortable borrowing money from for attorney fees. Eventually, if I had to sell everything I owned, I knew they wouldn't hound me to pay them back. They also trusted me and knew when I had the money, I would pay them back. They let me borrow $10,000 cash, without hesitation. When I asked my dad to borrow the money, he responded, "Yes, absolutely. When do you need it?"

They never lectured me. They never asked when I was going to pay them back. They never judged.

They had my back the entire time. And time went on.

ANNIVERSARY GIFT

As the days passed, May unblocked me, just long enough to call me and remind me that every decision and action she was taking was in the best interest of our kids. Then she would hang up and block me again. She had said this so many times I began to wonder, *What is she going to do?*

The next day after May called, left a message, and hung up was August 1st. I had been charged with a felony. The world thought they knew who I was but didn't at all. And things felt like they couldn't get any worse. May and the kids had been gone for a few weeks. I was on suicide watch and, all at the same time praying more than I had ever prayed daily. I remember telling someone, "I feel like I'm as close to God as I have ever been, but the devil is on my shoulder."

I had a surreal feeling about life. This was a trial that felt like it would never end—a battle between Good and Evil. August 1st was a significant date. It was May's and my anniversary. That year, it would end up being the worst day of my entire life. I woke up and did my normal routine to stay sane. I prayed for an hour. I sat outside and wrote down my thoughts, and I went on a run. After the run, I so badly just wanted to call May and say, "Happy Anniversary. I am so sorry for all of this. I love you so much."

I tried multiple times; however, I was blocked. I was sitting in my living room midafternoon. Next thing I knew a Sheriff was pulling into my driveway. My initial thought was, *Did they find another charge and are here to arrest me again?* If so, I was not prepared. I would rather have it been that. Arrest me again! This would have been so much better than getting the papers delivered to my front door.

May had filed for divorce and I was being served divorce papers on our anniversary. I met the Sheriff at the door. It was a childhood friend I used to play football with. I said, "Hey man, what's up now?"

He said, "Durand Joseph Murphy?" in a questionable way. "Ya, man, you know who I am," I said.

The Sheriff continued, "I'm here to serve you, and I need you to sign this paper." I responded, "Serve me for what?"

He continued, "May Maria Murphy has filed divorce against you." I was in full-blown shock. I signed the papers as tears started to roll down my face. I was on the front porch and about collapsed. The Sheriff started to walk away, and I took a step down from the porch to sit down.

As the Sheriff walked away, he must have felt horrible for me, he turned around and said, "D.J." I looked up and said, "Ya?"

He said, "I'm sorry, man."

And he walked away, got in his vehicle, and drove off. I sat on that concrete porch step and cried for hours. May had not only filed for divorce, but I was also served the papers on our anniversary. The anniversary gift of a lifetime!

"D.J., I need you to remember that everything I am doing is for the best interest of the children," May repeated. It all made sense now. At this moment, I blacked out. I had been shocked so many times that I can't explain what happened to my mind after receiving this news. All I know is, the week that followed, I continued my routine. Pray, write, run. Only now, after I ran each day, I would break down and cry out the remaining stress. I was struggling. I missed the kids, and this might sound crazy, but through it all. I missed May more than anything I had ever lost in my life. As the days passed, I started to miss her more than ever, but my anger was building up. I started to ask myself, *How could she leave me like this? How could she believe a 15-year-old female over her husband? What is she thinking?*

Finding solitude was becoming a challenge. Joyful memories of the past helped. I would often try to recall anything possible to help find solitude. Joyful picture memories were becoming part of my daily routine.

CATHOLICISM

I would recall our wedding, the birth of our children, and other joyful moments of our marriage to find some type of joy. One memory had stuck with me for years and it was of May going through the process of becoming a Catholic. At the beginning of our relationship, May initially attended church with me and knew if we were to ever get married, she would need to be confirmed in the Catholic Church. She also knew if we were to ever get married in the Catholic Church this was a requirement as well. I never pushed it on her, May never did anything she didn't feel one hundred percent confident about. She wanted our children to be raised with structure with parents of the same religion. May wanted to raise her children in a church setting and she knew before ever talking to me on the phone via Skype, this was something I felt passionate about--that I was going to marry a Catholic woman with a strong faith. May could've chosen any other man or any other path in life. But she chose D.J.; she chose the Catholic faith, and she wanted both. Becoming Catholic is no easy task. The Catholic church has what is called the Seven Sacraments. They are as follows: The Sacraments of Penance (confession), the Holy Eucharist (body and blood of Jesus), Baptism, Marriage, Anointing of the Sick (being blessed before death), Holy orders (Bishop, Priest, Deacon), and finally Confirmation. These seven sacraments are the foundation of the Church. Becoming Catholic teaches you why they are all important, along with so many other things such as our heritage, traditions, etc. To become Catholic, you attend a program called Rite of Christian Initiation for Adults, or RCIA. It is a six-step process and requires a year of attending classes. In the end, the candidates are Confirmed in the Catholic Church. This Sacrament of Confirmation means the baptized person has been, "Sealed with the gift of the Holy Spirit," and is strengthened for service to the "Body of Christ." May went through this entire process. She enjoyed it. She learned a great deal. She understood why I carried this faith so strongly with me.

This vivid memory that hit me was the day she was officially presented to the entire church and became part of the Catholic religion. We both were so joyful. She was glowing that day. She had officially received not only the Sacrament of Confirmation, but she had also received the Holy Eucharist, The body and blood of Jesus Christ. I never forgot the joy that was on her face. My future wife had become part of the Catholic religion. She was joyful. I was joyful. We were so happy together. Our lives were growing together with Christ. We felt inseparable. This memory brought me solitude in the worst moments of my life. Even though my entire life was under attack, it was memories such as this that got me through those dark days. I will never forget when she was presented to the church. In the same church, we received the sacrament of marriage. In the same church, all our children received the sacrament of baptism. The same church we would grow our family in. I felt May was "The one!" The one for me chosen by God Himself. My "soul mate!"

CORRUPTION

I was interviewing Defense attorneys -- interviewing a few local attorneys and a few out of the city. I decided to hire an attorney from outside the city. Defense attorneys are expensive, this decision was not an easy one to make. I was on my way back from interviewing an attorney from outside the city when a local Defense attorney who I had already interviewed called me. It was Bertha Reynolds.

I answered, "This is D.J."

Bertha said, "Hey, D.J., it's Bertha Reynolds. I just wanted to call and check in on you. I wanted to see how you were doing and make sure I talked with you one last time before you made a final decision on who to hire as your defense attorney." I should have run away immediately.

I replied, "Hey, thank you for the call. What did you need to talk about?"

Bertha continued, "Well, you know I'm not supposed to say this, but would be wise to hire someone within the city limits. I wouldn't call myself a friend of Prosecutor Richard, but we have an upstanding respect for each other. It would benefit you to have someone with a good rapport with the prosecutor. I could even see these charges getting dropped or even a pretrial diversion program for you."

Here I was in the most tumultuous stage of my life and extremely vulnerable with this female attorney telling me there is a chance charges could just get dropped if I hired an attorney having "effective communication" with the prosecutor. She was a leach sucking the blood out of me. Sure enough, I hired her. It was $10,000 cash I handed her – her flat fee. This woman became the perfect example of why clients can't stand attorneys. The apology letter was bad. Hiring this woman was even worse. I had no idea I was hiring a corrupt attorney. An attorney inside the city limits. She was part of the vicious clan of mingling attorneys, prosecutors, and judges who met for lunch and worked out deals behind their clients' backs.

COYOTES

August 1st, both May and my anniversary had come and gone. I never got a phone call wishing me a happy anniversary. May never called. It was quite the opposite of that. She had me served. May had taken my kids from me, filed for divorce, and was taking Raven's side without ever hearing my side, the worst part of all of this. As if it could get any worse, our city printed divorce filings. So less than two weeks after I was charged with a criminal felony, the local newspaper printed, "May Maria Murphy filed divorce against Durand Joseph Murphy." By filing divorce and it being printed locally, it made me look as guilty as I could have been. It looked as if had told May I did everything the papers said and she filed for divorce shortly after. That was so far from the truth, and still, May had never heard my side of the story at this point.

The night after reading the divorce filing, I was disgruntled and couldn't fall asleep. It was around 2:00 a.m. and I gave up on trying to find rest. I got up and started walking around the house. My mind was going crazy. It was the closest I had felt to wanting to die. But suicide was not an option. I asked myself, *What are you going to do D.J.? You can't let the devil win!*

I was alone, by myself, in an empty house during my darkest days. I put on my running shoes. It was pitch-black outside, a full moon, but cloudy. I took off running through the country. No street-lights, no one in sight, and I could barely see a few feet in front of me. My fear of life circumstances had consumed me, I had no fear of the dark. As I took off running, I realized that at any other time in my life, I would be nervous. It was strange that I was unshaken. I ran harder and faster. I needed to feel something! The cornfields were all around me. I ran down an old paved black road with pitch-black surroundings. I began to run so fast I was in a sprint. Then suddenly I heard something coming towards me from the corn fields. I stopped and within a blink of an eye, a group of coyotes ran across the road directly in front of me. I jumped back, frightened! I thought to myself,

Okay! You can still be terrified!

I turned around and sprinted the entire way back to the house. This was a pivotal moment in my life. I had realized that if running in the dark and a group of coyotes could scare the shit out of me, that hell would be much worse! As I walked into the house, drenched in sweat, a sense of clarity and calmness came over my body. I knew I was going to survive this severe trial and I knew I could make it to the finish line!

LET ME SEE MY KIDS!

Another week goes by. By this point, I was desperately missing my children. May had unblocked me for a moment from her phone. I sent a text, "May, I miss the kids so much. I spoke with my attorney, and we are technically still married. I'm going to go pick them up from school today."

May lost her damn mind. She called me screaming. "I will never take you back if you go get the kids from school. You are not allowed to see your kids until all this is over. Do you understand?"

By this point, we were both losing our minds. I was not losing my mind because of the criminal charges. I was a dedicated family man. My family was the only thing that truly mattered to me. May had taken all that away.

I lashed back out, "May you fucking had me served on our anniversary! You fucking left and

239

took the kids and won't let me see them! You refuse to come to talk to me and listen to my side of the story! I am trying to stay calm, but you're making this impossible for me! Do you want me to just fucking kill myself!?"

She responded, "Boy, wouldn't that be nice!"

Then she hung up. I dropped the phone out of my hand. I will never forget that conversation. After I dropped the phone, I was pacing back and forth in our living room. My wife had just told me she wanted me dead.

Everyone knows the story in the Bible of Adam and Eve. God created Adam and realized it is not good for a man to live without a companion. So, God created Eve, to be Adam's companion. Men don't live well alone. Men need a partner. May was not just my wife. May was my entire life. She was my best friend. She and I had five children together. She took everything I loved so deeply and removed it from my life. She did all this without even listening to my side of the story. I was three weeks in of not seeing May or my kids. Not once. And what little I had talked to May, she was screaming at me or lecturing me. I was beginning to lose my mind. I didn't need a companion. I needed my wife. I needed my kids. I NEEDED MY LIFE! I felt psychotic! I started sending her emails after what she told me. She blocked me on her phone. I was going to find a way to communicate. If she was not going to talk to me in person, I was going to find another way into her life.

THE EMAILS

I began to email her, writing loving letters with no response. I would go in-depth about how much I loved her and receive nothing back. I thought, *How can she ignore me like this? I'm her husband!*

I would go crazy on the inside. I was going insane! When she refused to respond to the emails and refused to speak to me in person, I was beginning to feel hate for the woman I loved. Hate was something I had never experienced.

Everyone was telling me, "D.J., Don't take her back. She's making this so much worse for you!"

I heard those words so many times. I defended her every single time. I responded saying something like, "Yes, she's making it worse than it needs to be. Yes, she's stooping low. But this situation must be extremely hard on her. If May comes home, I will be standing with open arms." Though I was defending my wife, I would walk away from these conversations and think, *Should I ever take this woman back?*

These conversations were getting to me. They were festering in my soul. I became angry with May. This anger turned love emails into hate emails. I began to lash out at her. Though I was living through the hardest time of my life, these emails became my biggest regret. Instead of letting everything work itself out, I was going to make sure May knew all the feelings I was experiencing. The love I had for her and the kids and not seeing them truly made me crazy. True love is a "crazy thing."

When you love someone, they can do the most awful things and you still love them. My love for May was just that. It had nothing to do with how beautiful she was. Nor that she gave me five amazing children. I fell in love with May. True love never dies. True love never fades. True love is forever, like it or not. If anyone expects Jesus to forgive them for their sins, then you must forgive others for sinning against you. That goes for your enemies, let alone your spouse with whom you made a promised covenant with God. A promised covenant in marriage with God means no matter what, you will forgive them and hold tight to the covenant. I was holding on tight to the hope that May would come back home. I refused to give up on us. Neither of us had committed adultery. Neither of us had a valid reason to get divorced. Neither of us was perfect, and both of us were hurting badly.

DÉJÀ VU

The following days didn't get any better. After I hung up with May, saying I wanted to go get the kids, May made another decision. She had a sister-in-law who was a deputy prosecutor in our city. It was easy for May to get things accomplished and filed. The day after I said I was going to get the kids, it was like Deja vu. I was sitting in the living room. Same thing. I was sitting on the

242

same chair in the same room. A Sheriff pulls into the driveway. *Unbelievable!*, I thought this time. I met the Sheriff at the door. I didn't recognize this Sheriff. Before he got out of his vehicle, a second Sheriff pulled into the driveway. I thought, *What is going on?*

They both got out; I met them on the sidewalk outside, as one of them said. "Durand Joseph Murphy?"

I said, "Ya, guys, all of you know who I am by this point."

The other Sheriff spoke up like he was some type of drill sergeant, "Standard protocol Mr. Murphy!" I quietly thought, *Whatever, man!*

He continued, "We are here to issue you a protective order. We were ordered to read you the entire order." I couldn't believe this was happening.

Before they read the order, I said, "Hold on a minute, who filed this protective order?"

"Says here the warrant was requested by May Maria Murphy."

I thought again in my mind, *WOW! I have never done anything to harm May, and here I am getting served a protective order?* The Sheriff read the entire order that stated I was not allowed within so many feet of my own children or her. I signed, and they left.

JUST RUN

I didn't cry this time. I walked inside and said to my mom, "Am I in a fucking lifetime movie? What in the actual fuck is going on?"

Every single day I was living in this nightmare that wouldn't go away. The devil was not just attacking. He was beating me down. Instead of crying, I went on a second run that day. For the second run, I ran eight miles. I learned when you're under elevated levels of stress. Your body can do things you never thought were possible. I had already run six miles that morning. Now, another eight. Fourteen miles in one day. I thought running that far would ease the pain. As I was approaching my house from the second run, my entire body started breaking down. I got to my front yard, and I just collapsed into tears. I started punching the ground and eventually just fell over onto my back. I looked up, and there was a red cardinal flying above me. My mom had told me, "Where there is a cardinal nearby is an angel."

From that day forward, a dozen cardinals flew around my house every single day. When these cardinals showed up, things started to slowly get better. It was like I had survived the test, and help was on the way.

A month had gone by without seeing my wife or kids. There were ups and downs in my life like I

never could have imagined. Time was starting to heal my negative emotions. By the fourth week, I was getting better at finding solitude and trusting in God's path. My mom could see that I was doing better. The morning of day 33, before my run, she said, "D.J., you okay with me going back home to my hubby?"

I responded, "Absolutely, Mom! Thank you for all you have done! Go get some hubby time, and I'll check in with you daily."

Day 33 would end up being one of the biggest, most extraordinary days of my life. It started as every day did. Pray, run, find solitude. I had given all of my circumstances to God. I spoke aloud, "God, you take this. Everything is out of my control. I trust You!"

I cooked some eggs and sausage. I sat down and ate a good, high-protein breakfast. I was also starting to sleep through the night. Sleeping through the night was the biggest relief. I was starting to feel good again. No one was in my house. My mom and brother were starting to feel more confident in knowing that I was going to be okay.

EXTRAORDINARY DAY

I sat down in my living room and noticed the world felt still. I looked outside, and not a leaf was moving in the large tree in the front yard. Nothing was moving. The world was completely still. This feeling was similar to solitude, but something was different... I looked outside again, and the entire world fell still... God said, "Go outside!"

I replied quietly with a whisper, "Okay, I'll go outside."

I chose to go into my backyard. May's and my backyard was gorgeous. It was a farm setting with large barns, set on ten acres of rolling hills. I stepped outside and sat down on the steps from the deck, heading down into the grass. I crossed my hands, placed my head down, and started praying. "God, I'm your servant. I trust in you. This entire situation happened for a reason, and I know you are a good God", I said. I remained with my eyes closed, hands crossed, and I just listened. After a few moments, God said, "Look up!"

I looked up into the sky and saw five individual clouds. These clouds caught my attention because they were small to big and moving in unison. From left to right was the smallest cloud, with each cloud gradually getting bigger towards the right. These clouds were perfectly separated and didn't overlap with each other. I thought, *Okay! Maybe these are my five children, and God is saying your children are in my hands.*

I looked down and thanked God for this sign. God said, "Look up again!"

When I looked up the second time, there were two more clouds to the right. They were directly following the first five clouds that were still there. I thought, *How did I miss these two clouds the first time?* I thought, *Okay, I am the sixth cloud, and May is the seventh cloud.* This is my entire family dynamic, and God is telling me, "Your family is staying together."

I looked away again as I said, "God, thank you for showing me this sign above, and thank you for holding my family in the palm of Your hand and protecting us."

God continued, "Look up again!"

I complied. I saw a sight that, unless you witnessed it yourself, you wouldn't believe. To the right of May's cloud, in the distance, was the most perfect dragon-face cloud. It was so realistic I didn't question what I was seeing. God had my attention. The seven clouds remained perfectly still. As I was looking up in awe, the dragon began to open its mouth, and I thought, *What is taking place in my life right now?*

I was in disbelief at what I was witnessing. I had never experienced anything like this before. I thought, *This is not a dream! What I am seeing and witnessing is real! This is happening right in front of me.* The dragon opened its mouth, and flames of fire started exiting his mouth. I thought, *What in the world!?* The flames were heading directly toward the seventh cloud, representing May. I continued thoughts of disbelief, *No way is this happening right now!* The dragon's face was moving slowly toward May, and the flames were exiting the dragon's mouth, extending out farther and farther directly toward May. The flames were approaching May's cloud. I said aloud, "God, if that flame touches May, I will take it as a sign that I am to move on and let her go!" The flames got unnervingly close to May's cloud, and all of a sudden, the flames, in a very quick moment, were sucked back into the dragon's mouth. I thought to myself, *This can't be happening right now!*

But it was. The dragon closed its mouth, and the flames were gone. The dragon face was still moving towards my family. The first seven clouds remained in the original spot. The dragon's face changed direction, and proceeded to move up above my family. As the dragon's face moved, I saw that it was changing. For a moment, I thought it was just dissipating. Then it changed. The dragon's face turned into a large human-like face of a man. As it continued above my cloud family, it stopped. I noticed how large it was. The first seven clouds were not small by any means. However, this face was as large as the remaining sky. The face stopped in the center and appeared to be looking down upon the first seven clouds.

This experience was like no other I had ever witnessed. This sighting was like no other sighting. I had never seen anything remotely close to this. God had gotten my attention! God wanted me to know He was looking down upon my family! God's power was on full display. In an instant, all the clouds dissipated, and the sky was the most perfect blue sky you can imagine. I was in full disbelief at everything I had just witnessed.

I closed my eyes, crossed my hands, looked down, and immediately began to thank God for this experience and everything I had witnessed. God's grace is a friendship. That friendship is not just a one-way communication of human to God. God wants us to listen. God wants to give GRACE. I compare it to the relationship a child has with a loving father figure. I have never wanted my kids just to tell me all their worries. I wanted to communicate and have a relationship with my children. God feels the same way. If you take the time not just to pray and speak to God but to listen. God will speak to you! He is a loving God! He is a good God! Even during times of full turmoil in your life, God is loving, with open arms, and ready to bless you in ways you never thought possible.

SPIRITUAL GIFT

My eyes were closed, my hands were crossed, and I was thanking God for this unbelievable experience. God said, "Look up again!" I did. The sky was perfectly blue, and all of a sudden, I saw these things floating all around me. I compare it to when you stand up too fast, and you see something like stars. Only this was different. This was something else. It was not the same. To be completely honest, by now I thought, *D.J., you are crazy!*

I looked down and took some slow, deep breaths in and out. I looked back up, and what I saw moments before was still there. These tiny things were floating in the air, and they were all around me like little see-through dots. Hundreds of them. I thought, *Okay, this is real. What I am seeing is real, and God is showering something down upon me!*

I looked down again and said, "God, thank You for this moment. I am unsure of what I am seeing, but I know it is from You, and You are a good God!"

I looked back up. The little see-through dots were still there.

I was in full amazement. I was no longer in disbelief. I thought to myself, *THIS IS REAL!* I just gazed upon these objects all around me in every direction. The world had stopped. It felt as if time had stopped. I have no clue how long I sat there. I just watched all these objects swirling all around me. I began to ask myself, "What am I seeing?"

My natural instinct was to think, *Are these objects some type of guardian angels drawing all around me?* I received no definitive answer then. I was not ready yet for this knowledge. I was not ready to know what exactly it was that I was seeing. I believed in guardian angels. I believed in the Holy Spirit. I believed in the physical presence of a Godly spiritual world for our protection. The Word speaks of the Holy Spirit sending down His spirit upon us. Guardian angels? Holy Spirit? The Glory of God? It didn't matter. I knew it came from God, and I knew I was being blessed. And the best part was that it came directly after God had shown me in the clouds that my family was watched over. After some time, I went back inside and felt so much peace over my soul that day, but the day was not over!

BLESSINGS AND TEARS

Day 33 was not over. It had only begun. I started to journal everything I had witnessed. Less than an

hour later, my phone rang. It was May, and she said, "I'm going to let you see the kids today." I responded, "Thank you! When?"

May continued, "I have stipulations. I want your brother Matt there as additional supervision. You will get to see the kids for two hours from 5-7 p.m. My brother (Jack) will drop them off and pick them up. Do you agree?"

I had just witnessed the most incredible thing from God, and now May was letting me see the kids. I was full of joy. I responded, "YES, I agree!"

She hung up ,and I felt joyful. I hung up and called my brother and mom to show up before five. They both wanted to see the children as well and apparently Matt was my "supervision."

At five o'clock, May's brother pulled into the driveway. My kids ran to me. All of them! We hugged and kissed each other for a long time. They clung to me. They wouldn't let go! I was crying, they were crying, and yet through all those tears, we were so happy. I had my children in my arms. The same day, God, in the most unbelievable way, told me this would happen. It was mid-August—a beautiful sunny day. May and I had a big, inflatable water playhouse where you could hook water to climb a ladder and slide down into a little pool. I had set this up for the kids in the backyard, and I set it up going down this little hill so they could slide down the hill as well. It was a good twenty minutes before we stopped hugging. I looked at them and said, "You guys want to go have some fun?"

They all sprinted to the playhouse and were having so much fun. I sat and watched them as they would, one by one, come to give me another hug and kiss and another hug and kiss. I was full of joy! Real joy! Joy comes from God! I was drenched from all the wet hugs, getting eaten alive by mosquitos, and I had no cares whatsoever!

MY CHILDREN WERE WITH ME!

The two-hour mark was approaching. It was as if I blinked, and it had been two hours. I had to get the kids inside, fed, and dry clothes on. We went inside, dried off, and I fed them. The two hours were up. It was time for the kids to leave.

May's brother pulled into the driveway. He refused to talk, look, or even come close to me, instead staying close to his truck. He believed everything he read in the newspapers, and I was scum to him. It saddened me. He and I were previously close. I would tell him every day I loved him. He pulled in and stood next to his vehicle. The kids were flipping out. They were clinging to me and grabbing my shirt. They refused to let me go! The joy was gone. My kids were screaming and crying. They didn't want to leave their dad. My son was the worst. He was grabbing my shirt. He was a strong little guy, just big enough to run. He was holding my shirt very tight. When my brother tried to pull him away from me. Abraham gave him a look of death.

I said, "Matt, don't allow yourself to be the one who takes him away." Matt stepped back. May's younger brother Jack came up and grabbed Abraham. Abraham grabbed my collar as Jack pulled him away. Abraham gripped me so tight he stretched my shirt collar out. Abraham looked at Jack, and I will never forget that look. I let go! I was in full tears. Jack started carrying him away, and he was squirming, trying to get out of Jack's hands. Jack could barely hold him. Abraham was flipping out. Soon, Jack drove off. My kids were gone.

That day, I made a promise to all my kids. I said, "The time your daddy has missed from your lives, I will make it up times ten!" I had no clue how I was going to do that, but when I made that promise to my children. I knew I was going to keep the promise.

On day 33, I finally got to see my kids. Little did I know the day was far from over. I insisted that my mom and brother go home. I assured them that I was fine and just needed space and to be alone.

Later that night, my phone rang. I anxiously answered. It was May, "D.J., if I come to see you, can you stay calm?"

I replied, "Come see me? You have a protective order against me. You're not supposed to be around me?"

She continued, "This is my choice. I am allowed to come see you. You're not allowed to come to see me!"

I replied, "Okay! Yes, I will stay calm."

I later found out that May had violated the protective order. She was not to come to see me, as I was not to go see her. She knew this. She didn't care. She pulled around the back side of the house. I opened the back door and tried to hug her, but she was not going to let me touch her. I wanted to hold her so bad. She wouldn't let me. She said, "Let's go in the living room."

After 33 days of leaving me and zero communication, she was ready to hear my side of the story. She later told me that Wyatt (my crew leader who worked for me) had reached out to her, and she listened to what he knew about my side. Wyatt was the only person who somehow got through to May that Raven was far from innocent. The conversation with Wyatt was my saving grace for May to let me see the kids and come hear my side of the story.

May had so many questions. I answered all of them with full honesty. She argued. It was like she wanted so badly to take Raven's side of everything. I started to physically walk and show her step by step a reenactment of the entire story.

254

She refused to believe me. May was a mess. She was cussing. She was yelling. She was crying. I was begging her to take me back. During the 33 days, I moved our bed from our bedroom (also the laundry room) to the basement.

Before everything happened, May had a decorative sign made for me. The sign said: "Always & Forever." with our names below and our wedding date. Always & Forever was also what she wrote to me in her first Valentine's Day card. I mounted this sign in the basement above our bed. After hours of explanation, yelling, tears, etc. May had started to calm down.

I said, "Can I show you something?"

She agreed. I took her into the basement and said, "I know you will never again sleep in the room where everything happened, so I moved our bed down here and mounted the sign you made me."

I continued, "Can I hold you?"

She agreed. I held May for the first time in over a month. She cried on my shoulder. I cried with her. She had missed me, and I had missed her even more. That short time holding her filled my spirit. She had finally listened to my side of the story.

She had finally come back to her husband. She had finally cried on my shoulder, not someone else's. She stopped crying, she pulled back and looked up at me. Her eyes were saddened, but she still loved me. In the gentlest way in my entire life, I kissed her. We didn't stop. Her back was to the bed. She pulled me down onto the bed on top of her. I was unsure if making love at this time was the best decision. I didn't want to be aggressive in any way. She was going to have to initiate the removal of clothing.

I stopped kissing her and pulled my head back while looking her in the eyes and said, "I have missed you May. I love you so much."

She said in the most saddened voice, "Me too."

We kissed again, and she said, "I'm sorry, I just can't do this yet." I replied, "I understand, it's okay."

I lay down next to her, and she cried on my chest for 30 minutes. She was so sad. She tried so hard to move on with her life without me. She just couldn't do it.

She got up and said, "I have to go, I'm not supposed to be here."

We walked out to her car. I opened her car door, something I have done since we met. I always beat her to her side of the car and always opened her car door for her. I opened the car door, and she went to get in. She turned around and started kissing me again.

She said, "None of this means we are getting back together yet."

I responded and said, "I will be here when you're

ready, I love you and never want to live without you!" She got in her car and left.

STAY AWAY

The following day was extremely difficult. May had blocked me again from her phone and her life. I was confused. Later she would give me enough clues that I put the pieces of the puzzle together. Everyone in her life, you could say in her circle of communication, was telling her to never come home to me. I can only imagine the conversations. The newspapers described me as this family man that had committed this horrible act. Everyone she was involved with and everyone in her life hated me. To this day they still hate me. They have refused to ever listen to my side of the story. There was never an "innocent until proven guilty" for them. I was guilty. The papers and TV all said I was guilty. It was as public as you can imagine. I was a piece of shit husband and father labeled as a pedophile. May's family and others were all telling her just that. "STAY AWAY FROM D.J.!"

OUR FIRST CONCEPTION

Throughout those days I began to have so many thoughts and good memories of our time before this terrible event. I was trying to coax positive thoughts into my mind to get me by one day at a time. I was recalling the birth of each of our children. Those special moments she and I shared that no one could take away from us—our honeymoon in the Bahamas. I especially was recalling our sex life. Our sex life was so good. It was often what stripped away all worries and struggles in our marriage. We made love and we made babies. A few nights after, I was sitting alone and recalled when our oldest Demi was conceived. I was by myself and started laughing at how crazy May and I were in the beginning!

Shortly after May came home from Germany my family was heading to vacation at a lake in Wisconsin. I told May it was our family tradition to go to Wisconsin every year. Everyone in my family loved to fish. We would go stay in a cabin home on this beautiful lake in the summer and visit the Wisconsin Dells. May had withdrawn from her state college and was now registered at a local college so she could live with the man she had fallen in love with. The vacation was scheduled right before college courses were to begin. May didn't care about fishing, but she was excited to take a trip with my family.

May and I drove separately from the rest of the family. It was a long drive. Before we exited our home state, May unbuckled her seatbelt, and looked over at me with that look she would give. She then unbuckled my seat belt while driving on the highway. She grabbed my hand and placed it on herself. I looked over like any man would and thought, *Let's go!*

As I rubbed her, she was getting wet. I started to rub harder and faster. She was getting close to her climax, and she pulled my hand off. I was already fully erect. She started to strip my shorts off. I was driving on the interstate going 70 mph and couldn't believe what was happening. May didn't want to pull over at a rest area. She wanted the extra excitement while driving. She pulled my shorts off and grabbed me through my boxer briefs. She tried to take my briefs off, and it was a struggle. There was something blocking the easy pull-down. She laughed and said, "You're ready! You going to give it to me?!"

She got the briefs off and started sucking me. She would take her hand from the top all the way down with her mouth in unison. I thought to myself, *You just stopped your own climax! Don't make me go yet!* That was not her intention. She stopped and pulled her panties off. I knew where this was going. I pushed the driver seat all the way back and the steering wheel as far up and out of the way as possible.

The traffic was not heavy, and I hit cruise control. May climbed over and on top of me. She placed me inside her and started aggressively thrusting up and down while screaming and moaning in a high-pitched tone, "Ahhhh Ahhhh Ahhhhhhhh!"

On the road, before exiting our home state, she had to cum, and I was going to let her. My left hand on the wheel, my head off to the side to watch the road, and May in my peripheral vision, aggressively attacking me. She grabbed my right hand. She would always say, "I love your hands!"

She placed it in her midsection. She arched her back and within seconds she finished. She jerked my hand off and continued only now she was rocking slowly. She started sucking my neck and ear. She knew I loved that feeling. Then she started to go up slowly with her hips, then down quickly. She did this over and over. She whispered in my ear, "Cum inside me, I want it all!"

I was convinced that May not only wanted pleasure but also wanted a baby with the man she was addicted to. Seconds later, she received me. From this point forward, every single state we have ever passed through became our thing. We must have sex everywhere, and in every state, and we did. Our sex was amazing, and I was the most unselfish husband in bed. She always finished as many times as she would like before I did. I never prioritized myself. May came first.

As soon as we got to the lake I said, "Come fishing with me!" We took off in a little boat and headed to one of my favorite spots. It was dusk and the surroundings were amazing. Lake, trees, flowers, and a stunning sunset. May wouldn't put the leach or worm on her hook. That was okay, I did it for her. We sat in the boat, and it was so peaceful—just the two of us in this big world. We were excellent with that. We adored each other, we were addicted to each other, we were in love. The fish were not biting, the sun was setting, and we were in a secluded area tucked in a little cove.

May got bored. She said, "Reel in."

I reeled my line in and said, "You ready to head back?" "Not yet, baby," She replied. She had this sundress on. She said, "Come take these panties off, I'm hot!"

"Yes, ma'am!" I replied. I got on my knees and slid her thong off. She leaned back with both arms behind her and spread her legs. I started slowly licking her from her perineum to her clitoris. Long. Slow licks while looking up at her. I enjoyed it more than her. I could taste the salt from her sweat, the natural taste of the wetness I was making her body create. She pulled my face up and stood up as she bent over on the side of the boat. I came up behind her. I reached around and began slowly massaging her.

She said, "Quit teasing me and give it to me!" I did.

I went inside her, enjoying the moment. She wanted it hard as she said, "Harder! Harder!"

After about a minute, I hugged her backside and reached my hand around. May didn't like to touch herself. She always said, "Your hands are too magical for me to touch myself."

I reached around and eagerly grasped her with my entire hand. She was getting close to the climax.

261

I took my index and ring finger and spread her lips out while I took my middle finger and started to vibrate her clit aggressively. Seconds later, in the highest pitch scream that echoed across the entire lake. She finished and said, "Maybe a little too loud?"

I replied, "No baby, scream as loud as you like."

She responded, "You spoil me. I am the luckiest woman alive!"

I said, "I love you, May. More than anything."

And she would always say, in response, "I love you more, baby, way more." She continued. Now finish yourself. I want all of it inside me."

I was ready. It only took a few seconds. After I finished, she said, "Stay inside me for a second, it still feels so good. I love your dick."

I did. I stayed inside her, and kind of stood up a little. I looked around, and my next thought was *May just got pregnant.* How I knew, I don't know, but that next April, exactly 9 months later, May gave birth to our first child. Demi was conceived during a beautiful sunset tucked in a cove on a beautiful lake.

A little over a month after the vacation, my alarm went off. I needed to get up and get dressed for work. I always hit snooze a few times. After I hit snooze the first time, I saw May get up and walk away. She said, "I'll be right back, baby."

She walked down the stairs, and I was back to sleep.

Before the snooze went off again, she came back into the room. She said, "Hey baby?"

I could tell something was up because she would always come snuggle with me and beg me not to go to work. She would often say, "PLEASE, PLEASE, PLEASE call in sick, PLEASE don't leave me!"

I never missed work, but she tried often. This time, she was standing up and not coming back to bed to cuddle. "Hey, baby!?" She said again. I have never been a morning person in my entire life. My brain turned on very quickly. I turned around and saw her standing up.

I said, "Ya, baby, what are you doing standing up? Come cuddle!" We loved to cuddle. I didn't miss work, but I pushed the edge of being late after meeting May.

She continued, "I have something to tell you!" May had this early morning excitement I had never seen. Her eyes were glistening. Her cheeks were rosy red. She was standing with her legs crossed with one of my fire department shirts on, so sexy!

"What's up, babe? "I spoke.

"Guess what?" She said. The anticipation was killing me. *What is she up to!* I thought in my head. "May, what?" I repeated. She pulls her hands out from behind her back and had a white stick-looking thing I had never seen before.

"What's that?" I spoke. She just looked at me with the biggest smile. Then it hit me, *NO WAY*! She started to shake her head yes and cry joyfully, she was not sad at all. Neither was I. I jumped up and picked her up as she straddled me. We kissed probably a hundred times.

"We're having a baby!!!!!" I said in the happiest voice. "YES!" May replied. I set her down.

I ran to the window upstairs, opened it, and yelled outside to the world, "WE'RE HAVING A BABY!"

I had never been this happy in my life, and neither had she. Though we were not married, it felt like we were. May and I would have gone to the courthouse days after she got back from Germany if we both didn't want a big wedding. It felt like we were already married. It was late September. May and I had just experienced, for the first time, together, a positive pregnancy test. There were many more to come, but this one was unforgettable. We had the maximum amount of love possible for each other. We had no doubts that we wanted to live the rest of our lives together. This was what we wanted. Each other and lots of babies. I was like a big kid as I said after screaming out the window, "Can I tell everyone?"

May said, "Are you crazy? No! We need to wait a minute!"

I replied, "Okay! Fine! Give me a kiss. I love you. I have to get dressed and get to work!" Off I went. We texted a million different baby names all day. This was one of the most memorable days of our lives.

LET GO, LET GOD

All these memories would bring me hope each day after Day 33 had come and gone. My kids were missing their dad more and more. I found out later Abraham was an absolute mess without his daddy. I thought after our moment together on Day 33 that things were going to change. That May was going to unblock me, and we would start communicating again. I was wrong. I was blocked. I didn't exist for a week. The mixed emotions were frightening, not knowing what her next move was going to be. I had

gone 33 days without seeing May. Thirty-three days without seeing my kids. Those 33 days felt like death. I had lived alone in my life before meeting May. But loneliness was on an entirely different level when I lost the person I loved most, who I was used to seeing, touching, and talking to every day for ten years. Add five missing children to my suffering, and it was the closest thing to experiencing hell on earth. And then all of a sudden, I was allowed to see all of them in one day, and bam "gone again." It was like surviving a trial, then thinking the trial is over, and then the darkness comes right back. Through all the darkness,

I never lost hope. My hope could be described as stronger now that May knew my side of the story. She had finally listened to me.

In life, when the person you love most on earth decides to make decisions, and you're no longer part of the picture, your mind wanders. When those thoughts are negative, you become consumed with emotions that lead to depression. By Day 40, I was starting to realize something. Guessing what May was doing or the next action she may or may not take was eating my soul alive. I couldn't change her mind or the steps she was going to take. The only person I can control is myself. If she decided to leave me, I was going to have to let her go. The thought, *There's no way I could live without her* was false. I could find happiness and peace without her. It was just going to take time, a lot of time. Leaving me was up to her. I eventually gave the entire situation to God and said, "Take this painful situation away from me and into Your hands."

The key is trusting this thought and believing that no matter the outcome, God knows what is best for you. That thought of trust in God's path became my life. I had to "Let go and let God!" Each day, through all the heartbreak, I got a little better at this.

AN AWFUL FAMILY GATHERING

After another week, my phone rang again. The same scenario repeated. May was letting me see the children again. This time, I got to see them for much longer. It was a Saturday. May was back to being a mess. I was truly starting to wonder if she was ever going to come back to me. She called, and was so rude, "Hey, you want to see your kids?"

She said this in the meanest voice you can imagine. It was as if she was accusing me of not wanting to see my kids when she was the one who filed the protective order. I replied, "Yes! Please! I'm going crazy not seeing my children."

She responded, "Fine, they will be dropped off at noon. Your brother Matt must be there the entire time. You're not to leave the house with them. They will be there until after you're done with dinner. Understand?" I thought, *My goodness, why is she so rude?*

I responded, "Yes, I understand."

This day was awful. A lot of people came to see the kids that day because everyone on my side was missing them so much. My dad and step-mom, along with my half-sisters and half-brother, came. My Mom and my brother, Matt, also came. They all missed the kids and wanted to see them. I never even asked May what she was going to be doing, but I soon found out. It started the tears again. My kids missed their daddy terribly.

Things calmed down, and then all hell broke loose. My younger brother and a few of my kids were in the basement playing. My little brother had accidentally dropped my 6-year-old, Scarlette, on the concrete floor in the basement on her head. It was bad. Scarlette was screaming uncontrollably. She had a bad concussion. I had to call May. May was with her friends at a winery, getting wasted.

She was so drunk she couldn't speak a sentence without slurring. From the time I met May, when she drank any alcohol, it was typically a horrible experience. May and alcohol didn't mix well. May was now drunk. I had a child with a concussion, and she told me.

"Don't leave the house!" May had manipulated my mind so badly that even during an emergency, I was terrified of the decision I should make. She still had this protective order against me. You can imagine how the conversation went. As she was slurring half her words, she said,

"Take her to the fucking hospital! I leave town for one fucking day, and this is what happens?" I replied, "Leave town? What are you doing, May?"

"None of your fucking business, you piece of shit!" She responded. Then she hung up. May made me feel like the worst person in the world. And she was still my wife, drunk without me, and I was the only person who saved her half the time when she drank from making regrettable drunk decisions. So, needless to say, my anxiety was through the roof.

Moments later, she called again, "Never mind! My brother is picking her up and taking her to the hospital! You're not to take her!"

This accident was all my fault. My family could hear her screaming at me on the phone. All the kids ended up leaving earlier than I was initially told. I was being punished. I was being punished repeatedly. May didn't see it this way. The wedding vows of "in good times and bad" never existed with May. Things were bad, and she left me. I felt alone in a desert, fighting for my life with every inch of energy I could gather each day. I truly started to wonder if May had some type of undiagnosed medical condition, but every time I had this thought at this stage of our marriage, I wrote it off and told myself, *She's just in shock!* This time it was not shock. This felt like uncontrolled manic behavior, as she was making erratic decisions.

The most heartbreaking thing happened that same day, a story I wouldn't be told until later when the kids were taken away from me again and taken back to May's mom's house. Our son Abraham, who was barely old enough to run, took off running down the road after they got back to May's mom's house. When they parked, he jumped out of the car and started sprinting as fast as his little legs could go. Up the driveway to the road and down the road before someone caught him. He was screaming, saying, "I'm running home to my dad! Let me go! I'm running back to my dad!"

As tears drenched his face, all Abraham wanted was his dad, and he was willing to run all the way home to me.

LET HER GO

As time continued to pass, as hard as it was, I began to tell myself, "D.J., you have to give up on her man!"

May was awful to me every single day for almost two months. She triggered a mix of all emotions imaginable. I was simply going crazy without my family. I was under criminal investigation. I lost my wife. My wife took my kids. I had no money. I felt like everything in the world was against me. It had been a month and a half since I turned myself in. My attorney was not doing anything. All my guy friends cut themselves out of my life. Every morning I woke up was terrifying. In 45 days, I had one good day. The rest was chaos. It was chaos for May, too. I often wonder how much easier it would have been if she had listened to her husband, taken his word over a 15-year-old female, and supported me. If she would have embraced me and allowed me to embrace her. Instead, she built an unimaginable anger toward me, and it felt like to me she was taking everyone's side except her husband's.

I have never been a hateful person. My dad would always say to my brother and me, "Boys, we don't say the word hate!" He meant it. It stuck with me. I thought a lot about this as a kid. This was not advice from my dad. This was a demand. As I grew in age, I not only tried not to say the word hate, but I also tried not to hate anyone. If my dad didn't want us to not say the word hate, he doesn't want us to hate anyone either. What my dad was really saying was, "Forgive Everyone!"

Forgiveness is the key to keeping hate out of your heart and mind.

May's actions, words, and decisions were causing me to hate Raven. Even after I was arrested based upon a story from one person, I didn't "hate" Raven. I had a strong dislike for her, but I didn't hate her. I may have hated the situation. However, I didn't hate Raven. I viewed her as a teenager making irrational decisions. I knew she was craving attention. I knew she wanted to prove to May that none of this was her fault. I also knew and thought often *Raven, knows the entire truth.*

However, as time passed, May was losing her mind and treating her husband as if I had just raped this female. And I had never even touched Raven. If I had not gone four days without sleep, I wouldn't have even said anything mean when she caught me off guard in my bedroom. That type of mean reaction was not the type of person I was. Did I feel bad for Raven? Yes, but only because she had been molested by her grandfather. Which was primarily what the apology letter was about. I did feel guilty because Raven blamed me for those thoughts coming back to her mind. In all reality, looking back, those thoughts of her being molested had never left her mind since the day it happened. I had become the excuse for her to "open up" about it to her mother since she had never spoken a word about it to her. I started to question my mind, *Why did she never tell her mom?*

271

Could it be that this grandfather who molested her was her mother's dad? Is that why she had never told her mom? If any of my girls were touched by anyone inappropriately, I have told them numerous times, "Girls, if you're ever in an uncomfortable situation that you know is wrong, call me or mommy immediately, and we will get you out of that situation."

Raven had gone years without telling her mom about a horrifying memory. It led me to do some research. I needed to get down to the bottom of this. I couldn't stop asking myself, *Why was Raven and her mother taking this situation to extreme levels?*

HYPOTHESIS

I started my research by looking up the biological father of Raven. As Raven had told me, he was in prison in Texas. However, why was he in prison? What led to him being thrown in prison? Was Karen involved in any of this? I had help with this research. I didn't do it all on my own. Even finding the name of this biological father was hard. I came to two separate opinions after the research.

First scenario: Karen lived in Texas. One night she goes out to a bar and meets this guy. This guy felt like a stalker and wouldn't leave Karen alone. As the night continued, Karen decides to go to another bar with her friends while saying, "Hey girls, how about we get out of here? This weirdo won't leave me alone."

They go to another bar and continue having drinks. The creeper guy followed her to the next bar.

Karen didn't notice it as she was occupied having fun and carrying on with her friends. This man waits for her to make a mistake and walk away from her group of friends. Karen goes into a single-person bathroom alone. However, she forgets to lock the door. This horrible excuse of a man follows her in there and does awful things to her. Karen is left alone, beaten, and sexually abused in the bathroom. The man escapes out of the bar, and eventually, Karen's friends find her in the bathroom. They take her to the emergency room to be helped. Karen helps authorities find the man and presses charges. She has him arrested for first-degree rape. The case concludes, and this man is eventually set free under one requirement. He had to register as a sex offender. The man refuses to register, and eventually, the Sheriff's Department shows up at his house to arrest him. He not only resists arrest but also shoots a Sheriff's deputy and then gets sent to prison for a long time. The story gets worse for Karen. She becomes pregnant and she decides to keep the baby. That baby was Raven.

Second scenario: Karen lives in Texas. She goes out to a bar and takes a liking to this guy there. The man is buying her drinks and having a fun time. Karen loves the free drinks and is flirting and carrying on. The man is saying things like, "You're funny!" "I like you!"

As the night carries on, Karen has one too many shots. She starts to think about a one-night stand with this guy but wants to stop herself. She has done this in the past and felt shame afterward. By the end of the night, Karen is wasted and unclear of her words and decisions. The man asks, "Want to come back to my place?"

This man sees how drunk she is, but the girl was flirting before she was this drunk. He thinks, "It's not like I'm taking advantage of her. She was giving signs before she was intoxicated."

What the man doesn't realize is Karen has already blacked out. Karen's last active memory would be the last shot she downed before leaving the bar. Unknowingly, from the alcohol, Karen decides to let this guy take her back to his house. They go back to his house, and by then, Karen is not in control of her decisions. Karen sleeps with this man and has no idea.

The next morning, Karen wakes up naked in another man's bed in a strange house. She feels violated and afraid. She blames herself for getting so drunk, but she remembers how she ended up in a man's bed naked. She immediately blames this man. As she starts to blame him, she convinces herself with the thought, *This man took advantage of me! This man has no clue about the type of person he had just taken back to his house.*

274

Karen was vindictive and mentally unstable from her childhood. Karen decides to go to the authorities and blame this man for his actions, not taking any accountability for her actions that led to the ultimate outcome. Karen had just accused this man because she refused to admit to herself her own guilt! A few days later, this man gets a knock on his door from a detective who says, "Sir, we need you to come in for questioning."

The man asks, "Why?"

The detective continues, "You're under investigation, come with us."

The man flips out and says, "I didn't do anything wrong! She encouraged more drinks at the bar. She consented to everything that night!"

During the investigation, he finds out that Karen checked herself into the Emergency Room the next day, and sure enough, his DNA was found inside Karen. It was Karen's word against his. Guess who lost?

He may not have been right to give Karen so many drinks, but Karen didn't stop herself. The man is later arrested and charged with "second-degree rape." This man's life just ended. He lost his job, and his reputation, and now is faced with prison time. He decides to take a guilty plea to stay out of jail. However, that includes registering as a sex offender because Karen was only 19. She was under the age to drink alcohol. The judge says, "How she got into the bar that night is irrelevant. Sir, you should have known better!"

This man is pissed off at the world when eventually, the Sheriff's department comes to arrest him for neglecting to register himself as a sex offender. He grabs a gun, shoots a Sheriff, and has been in prison during the entire course of Raven's life. All Raven knows is her dad sexually abused her mom and is in prison. Raven grows up being told this story every time she asks, "Will I ever get to meet my real dad?"

This entire situation gave Raven a horrible depiction of her father and what sex is. As for Karen?

Karen became Crazy Karen.

Now, years later, they are in a situation where Raven is accusing a man of a crime beyond anything that took place, and who does Raven go to for advice? Her mother! Does Raven tell the whole story? No way! She was 15 years old, and as with any 15-year-old, Raven was going to spin the story so everyone thinks she is innocent. Meanwhile, subconsciously, Raven has been craving attention from her mother her entire life and never got the attention she deserved. Why? Because Karen looked at Raven as the bastard child she never wanted. Karen tells herself, "I did the right thing by not aborting the baby," but every time I look at Raven, I have that horrible flashback. Karen feels guilty and is ashamed of the way she treats Raven. So, what does Karen do? Karen starts fostering kids and bringing them into her home so she can make up for all her mistakes. Karen thinks, "I'm doing the right thing!"

ILL THOUGHTS

Meanwhile, I saw my entire life end rapidly over a situation that was less than three seconds. I never touched her, was caught off guard, and it happened in the bedroom of my house! I lost everything. The only positive aspect of the situation was that my charge didn't require me to register as a sex offender. When you're accused of this crime, the charges include stipulations such as recommended jail time, probationary periods, registering as a sex offender, etc. Here I was facing a Level Six felony that I didn't deserve and not just fighting for a clear background. I was now fighting for my family. I was fighting for my career. And more importantly, I was deeply in love with my wife. I was fighting for May. By nature, I grew to hate Raven. I wish I could say it another way. The reality is I thought often, *I hate this female!* She had taken my entire life away from me.

However, when I had those thoughts, I remember what my dad always told me. "Boys, we don't say we hate anyone! I thought, *I can't allow myself to continue hating Raven.* God says, pray for your enemies! I did. Every single day, I forced myself to pray for Karen and Raven. Though the evil in me wanted to never see them again and never pray for them. I recognized that if I held this hatred in, it would kill me. So, I prayed. I dedicated specific prayers just for them. I tried very hard not to hate them. Time, along with prayer, healed my "ill thoughts" towards them.

PRETRIAL

My first court date for the criminal charges came. I had no idea what to expect. My attorney, Bertha, called me the day before, "Hey, D.J. your first court date has been delayed. I will be in touch to have you come in and talk soon!" She said this with excitement.

A delay in court is called a "continuance." Bad attorneys love continuation. It buys them time to be lazy with a specific case. And for good attorneys, it buys them time to gather more information and get ready for court.

Bertha said, "This is good. I'm sure you're not ready to deal with all this yet, considering all the publicity!"

My response was, "I guess."

I didn't want this case to carry on for long. I had the thought, *If I get this criminal shit out of the way, maybe May will come home.* Almost two months had come and gone, and I had yet to see my first day in court.

It finally happened. My first official court date was coming. It was called a "pre-trial conference." In my opinion, this means absolutely nothing but a bunch of bullshit.

Bertha emailed and said, "Hey, I have a bunch of cases I'm working on. Your pre-trial is coming up. It really is nothing at this stage. Do you mind just showing up to make a presence in court, and you and I will meet later?"

I responded, "Bertha, I haven't even told you my side of the story yet. I think it's important we meet sooner than later."

Bertha continued, "I understand. Are you okay with my request?"

What Bertha didn't tell me before hiring her was that not only was she a lazy and worthless attorney who was friends with the prosecutor. She only communicated through email. If I called the office, the response was the same every time, "Sir, I'm sorry she's not in right now, she's in court."

Regarding email, I am 100% certain every message sent in reply was from her paralegal. Contacting Bertha face-to-face was a challenge. Getting Bertha on the phone was almost impossible. All my communication was with the paralegal. I later found out that not only did I hire a defense attorney who was friends with the prosecutor. I hired a drunk who got a DUI from a hit-and-run. Of course, her charges were all dropped. She was slapped on the wrist, kept her job, and carried on with her life. Eventually, I couldn't stand this woman. I often thought, *Hey dad, it is getting more challenging every day to not hate anyone!*

YOU FIND OUT WHO YOUR FRIENDS ARE

Throughout these first fifty or so days, I discovered realities of life that are highly disheartening. When people say to you, "You can't trust anyone nowadays!" It is so true. When people say, "When bad times come, you find out who your real friends are!" It is so true. And when the guys would always say, "Women are all crazy!" This was starting to feel true.

Women run the world in today's age. Men should not label women as "all crazy!" Men are ridiculous too. You know the song! "God is great! Beer is good! And people are CRAZY!" Well said, Billy Currington! I was questioning if I was crazy and thought everyone around me was crazy. I will repeat in my own words, *You find out who your friends are when shit hits the fan!* Shit had hit the fan in my life, and my only friends were family and a few select others.

Among my childhood best friends, my career firefighting so-called "brothers," my church "brothers in Christ," all but a few had abandoned me. The moment the newspapers hit, everyone disappeared. The most disappointing one? My childhood best friend that I loved deeply. Remember Max from my wedding? Max and I did everything together as kids. Poking ourselves with needles and becoming "blood brothers." Boxing our faces off just because we were boys. Wrecking a moped because we were trying to be Evel Knievel, and I landed on my nut sack crying for my mommy while he was laughing his ass off. Max and I were always tight. Our parents were best friends. In a way, we were born together.

Before everything went down in my life, I even helped Max get into the fire department. I would have done anything for this man, and I did. I spray-painted all the trim in his house professionally for free. Not to mention the guy who called him and said, "The Fire department is hiring. I know you've tried in the past to get on. Now is the time!"

Guess what? He got hired! Of all the people who abandoned me, Max was the one who broke my heart the most. He was not the only one. I would love to go through every single person who turned their back on me. Max and my other best friend, also employed at the fire station, loved to write children's books. Those two guys crushed me. I loved them. After the newspapers hit, they were never heard from. I will repeat as I said earlier in the story. I was alone and afraid.

ST. MICHAEL THE ARCHANGEL

My phone rang late one night. Having a phone at this time felt immaterial. No one ever called me. No one ever texted. It was rare. Especially at night. I jumped up hoping it was May and that she was not going to scream at me again. It was not May. It was a guy from church. An older gentleman. His name was Steve.

Steve said, "I know I have only been texting. I wanted to call and let you know that I have been thinking about you and praying for you every day." The conversation led to me vent the entire story. Damn, that felt good that night to get it all off my chest again. It had been a month since I got everything off my chest.

His response? Same as everyone else. "WOW!"

He said, "I don't have much advice. I'm sure anyone who has given advice didn't help much in this situation." He was right. Any advice I got never seemed to help, given the circumstances. No one had been in my shoes; How do you even give advice when you have never experienced anything close to this situation I was in?

Steve continued, "I do have one bit of advice that helped me in the past, and I know will help you now!"

"Go on," I said.

Steve replied, "I started praying the St. Michael prayer during a really hard time in my life, and it dramatically helped my situation. That is the only advice I have for you!"

What Steve didn't know was that I took the advice. I started saying this prayer every single day. I started seeing things change. To this day, I pray this prayer every single night with my children. Especially my son Abraham, who refuses to go to sleep until he prays with dad. This prayer began to change my circumstances. It carried a power that infused my life and helped me through.

"Saint Michael, The Archangel. Defend us in battle. Be our protection against the wickedness and snares of the devil. And do you thou, prince of the heavenly host, by the POWER of God thrust into hell Satan and all the evil spirits that prowl about the world seeking the ruin of souls! Amen!"

THE BUTTERFLY

From the moment I started to say this prayer, everything changed. I started to experience more situations, much like the clouds in the sky on Day 33. Cardinals were flying up and landing right next to me. Blue jays and butterflies were all over the place, getting my attention. On day 57, the most amazing thing happened. May and I had a huge property, and I was still mowing the lawn often. I was mowing more than ever. I had nothing else to do. I started mowing three acres of the property when this huge butterfly landed on my lap. My sweet cousin, Lillian, had told me, "Where there is a butterfly, there is an angel, D.J.!"

I had a big zero-turn mower that was loud. I couldn't believe this butterfly landed on me. I thought,

I'm going to see how long this butterfly stays on my lap!

I mowed for an hour and a half, and this butterfly never moved. I was about done, and I pulled up to the barn. I wanted to look at this butterfly a little more closely. It was a huge orange butterfly with black dots. Both its wings were extended, and it was just sitting there. I thought for sure once I stopped the mower, it would fly away. It didn't. I looked at this butterfly for a while and thought, *Did this butterfly die when it landed on me? No way has it stayed right here on my lap this whole time.*

I was looking at it for so long that I started to count the black dots on its beautiful orange wings. I started on the left wing. Eleven perfect black dots. I thought, *Huh! My lucky number is 11!* I started counting the black dots on the right wing. Twelve perfect black dots. Now I thought, *NO WAY!*

I counted again, still twelve. May's lucky number was twelve. *Did this butterfly stay on my lap for over an hour and a half until I counted the dots?* Sure enough! Less than an hour later, my phone rang. It was May who said, "Hey, D.J., I'm coming to see you tonight after I get the kids in bed. I am trusting you to tell NO ONE! See you at 10 p.m.."

I responded, "I won't tell a soul!" I teared up. May didn't give any other details. Was she coming over to figure things out? Or was she coming over to start making divorce plans? She gave no indication either way. But this butterfly was my sign that it surely had to be good! Simultaneously, my favorite uncle (my mom's brother Danny) pulled in around the back where I was sitting on my mower. I wiped my tears, took some deep breaths, and was good. This uncle is on a trip. Through my younger days, he was the uncle I partied with, knowing I was in a safe spot to party and wouldn't get in trouble. He was the uncle who took me to all kinds of places when I was a kid because he said, "I always pick up chicks when D.J. is with me!"

He got out and saw my red eyes from crying as he said, "You back here chiefin' out or what!?" That meant smoking weed.

I replied, "Fuck no man! I'm under criminal investigation, with Sheriffs driving by my house five times a day. They're begging to catch me doing something else so they can plaster me all over the newspapers again! I tend to cry a lot nowadays!"

Danny replied, "Well, I got you a 44-ounce Diet Mountain Dew for you, my nephew!" For whatever reason, Diet Mountain Dew tasted wonderful during these horrible days. We talked for hours. Uncle

Danny was convinced I should take the criminal case all the way to jury trial and then sue EVERYONE!

He said, "My nephew, you're going to be rich from all this. Just hold tight and get by!" Uncle Danny always found a way to make me smile in life's turmoil.

CLEAN UP!

It was about five o'clock when Uncle Danny left. May liked a clean house. The yard was freshly cut. I started to clean the house. I detail-cleaned the entire house, thinking, *May will be happy!*

Through everything May had said to me, I was still and always will be in love with this woman. After 57 days, all I could think about was getting May home with my children following behind her like little ducklings. I also knew I had always not been nice with my reactions to her decisions. May made my mind spin constantly. And I never could stop wondering what May was doing without me by her side. I became even more crazy, missing my kids. And to top it off, I only had a couple of people who checked on me each day. My mom, my brother, and occasionally someone else would pop in or call to let me know they were praying for me.

I finished cleaning and wondered, "What's next?" I thought, *Well, if things go well with May, I better go clean up and shave!* I cleaned up and was ready for May. Mentally, I was fighting for stability. I'm not sure how anyone in my situation would say that they would be mentally stable. Pray, run, cry, journal, find solitude. The butterfly gave me solitude that day, and I needed it for the conversation coming with May. Leave it to a butterfly to bring peace! At times, May would call and say, "I would consider coming to talk to you, but you can't stay calm, and I don't trust you!"

Then she would hang up. Every time she made those types of phone calls, my first thought was always, "Fuck no, I'm not calm!"

How could any man under a criminal investigation, while losing everything he loved, stay calm? I always wanted to reply, in the most smart-ass voice, "Ya May! Everything is fine over here! Staying calm is easy!"

THE ANTICIPATION

May texted, "Bobby (her stepdad, who was like her dad) is still awake in the living room. I need to wait for him to go to bed so I don't get harassed about where I'm going. I will be there soon."

She knew it was 10 o'clock and I was waiting for her. At 10:30, she shows up. I was standing on the back porch where I knew she would pull up. She gets out and walks up. She puts her hands out with her palms facing out, and without saying a word, I knew she just wanted to be held. I held May so tight. She started crying her eyes out. She started to vent, "Why did this have to happen? Why did you do this? Why? I don't understand!"

I grabbed her face while looking her in the eye and said, "May, I am so sorry for everything. I can't live my life without you!"

May responded, "Before we go any further, I need to hear the story again."

May had made up her mind that she wanted to see if my story from Day 33 and my story now on Day 57 matched up perfectly. Was I lying? Was I telling the truth? We went inside, and she asked, "Where did

you say she was when you stepped into our bedroom?"

I said, "I'll tell you what, you stand right here in the kitchen like you're about to step into our bedroom. You know, where I dry off every day. I want you to stand right here while looking into our bedroom, and I'm going to go stand where she was. You tell me if you can see me. I DID NOT APPROACH THAT GIRL!"

She agreed, and sure enough, she couldn't see me. Her next question, "But she said she was folding laundry! If she was folding laundry, she wouldn't have been standing there!"

My response was, "May, she was lying. When in almost two years did you ever see her folding laundry?"

May replied, "I never once saw her fold laundry." I replied, "Exactly!"

May continued, "Why in the fuck did you let her cut the hair on the back of your head? That is not her job. It's mine!"

I spoke gently, "May, I am so sorry I let her do that, I have no excuse, I fucked that part up." Surprisingly, May was okay with this response.

May continued with so many questions. "Why did you tell her she had pretty eyes?"

I responded, "May, I didn't tell her that directly. I was trying to help her with confidence when kids at school were mean to her. I didn't walk up to her and say, 'Oh! Your eyes are so pretty!' That conversation was nothing like that!"

May continued with all the questions. Eventually, I answered every single question while looking her directly in the face with each answer. When she was done with all the questions, she said, "If I get rid of this protective order, do you promise not to show up at my mom's house?"

I replied, "May, I will never show up at your mom's house before the protective order is lifted.

Honestly I never want to go to that house again. Your family abandoned me like everyone else!"

May didn't like that response, so she spoke again, "So you're never going to go to my mom's house again?"

I continued, "No May, that is not how I meant it. You know I am a very forgiving person. I'm just saying that I will only go there if you want me to be with you, and they say it's okay!"

May said, "Okay." And when she said okay after this last question, she looked up at me, and I got the look. The look she had given me thousands of times in the past. I knew this look.

IT HAPPENED

We started kissing, and I remember us both stopping for a second to take a breath at the exact same time. It was like our hearts took a breath together. I picked her up, still fully clothed. She had these jeans on that she knew I loved. I picked her up, and she started licking my ear and neck as I carried her downstairs to the basement to make love on our bed. I wanted her to see the sign she had made for me, "Forever and Always!" I laid her down. She knew what was coming. Her jeans were tight. I ripped them off! While I was ripping off her jeans, she removed everything else. It was like a movie scene of two people who couldn't get undressed fast enough. She had no underwear on. She knew before she came over what she wanted. I went down on her. She was screaming and she pulled my face in as she came into my mouth. I swallowed everything I could get my tongue on. Two months, no sex, and I withheld any self-pleasurable acts. I waited for May even when things were bad. I was dreaming of this moment. She said, "I want you inside me! I have missed you!"

I stood up and pulled her to the edge of the bed. Right before I went inside her, she looked over at the sign and said as a question to me, "Forever and Always?"

These words coming out of her mouth were like heaven coming down to earth and whispering in my mind. I said, "Heaven only with you May!"

She looked down and said, "Have you grown?

You look huge!" I laughed and said, "No May, you forgot!"

She said, "Put that big dick inside me and make love to your wife. I want it hard! The slow stuff can be later."

I was a man without sex for over two months, I didn't hesitate. At first, I grabbed her hips and pulled her in hard and fast repeatedly. She was screaming so loud it was echoing off the walls. She only let that last for a few minutes and said, "Give me that magic thumb!"

Her legs fell, her back arched, I took my thumb and started to rub her clit just how she liked. It was seconds later, and it sounded like a volcano erupting out of her vagina. In ten years, she had never come that much at one time. When the noise stopped, I stopped. We looked at each other and started laughing as she said, "You think you're the only one that has been deprived?"

I said, "Can I taste it?"

She responded, "You're crazy, go ahead!"

I sucked her dry. It was like I was dying of thirst. Her fluids hydrated me, and I didn't stop. I ate her out for another 10 minutes. She came again, which was her third time. I was going wild with my mouth. My jaw felt like it was going to fall off. She was about to cum a fourth time and said, "I want to be on top, come here!" I jumped on the bed while spinning my body so I was face up. She got on top and just started going crazy.

May and I didn't masturbate throughout our marriage. We always saved ourselves for each other. She was taking all her sexual deprivation and her stress out all at once. She came three more times as she thrust and jerked her body up and down over and over. After the sixth time, she said, "It's your turn."

She knew I always waited for her. She continued, "How do you want it?"

"I want on top so I can kiss you while I cum." I spoke. She laid down on her back. In the past, whenever she would say, "It's your turn," I would always try to get one more out of her. I did. She came for the seventh time. As she was having her seventh orgasm, I simultaneously went down and kissed her while I came inside her. We were both drenched in sticky sweat. She bit down on my lip hard while at the same time digging her nails into my neck. Her seventh orgasm was as good as the first. After that, it was like she passed out for a split second. I thought my neck was going to start bleeding, she dug her nails in so hard. I also felt like she was going to bite through my lip.

She released her nails and bite at the same time, and I released my orgasm inside her. This orgasm was one of the best of my life. She always liked to call me "D.", Short for D.J. She said in the softest voice, "I love you, D". I tried so hard to stop loving you. It is impossible to stop loving you. Forever and Always."

After 57 days of tears, you would think I was out of tears, but I was not. She started to wipe them away and said, "It's going to be okay. I'm here now." It was like she knew what being away from me did to me. It fucked me up, bad!

As I slowed the tears down, I said, "Are you hungry?" I was ready to make her some food. She said, "I haven't eaten anything in two months. All I've had is wine and frozen cokes." I responded, "Frozen cokes? Since when do you drink frozen cokes?"

She replied, "Since I left you, I'm not really sure! But no, I can't eat right now. I need to get back home before someone notices I'm gone."

I said, "Okay." I knew she still had a protective order. She was a little paranoid, knowing she was not supposed to be at our house with me. I walked her out to her car. We looked up at the sky. It was the clearest night. Every star in the sky looked like it was glistening.

May turned to kiss me and hug me before she left as she said, "I don't want to leave." At those words I knew I had my wife back, I had my May back, I had my children back.

I kissed her and said, "Cancel the protective order, please. It has been long enough."

She said, "I will. Just give me a few days to figure everything out. I'll need your help getting all the kids' stuff back over here to the house."

I took the biggest gasp of my life and said, "Okay."

May got in her car and drove off. I sat down on the concrete step, looked up to heaven, and said, "THANK YOU!"

PONDERING

After saying thank you to the heavens, I had a lot of thoughts. The entire time May was gone, every single person that I spoke to said the same thing, "D.J., she is not staying gone; she will come home!"

At heart, I believed this as well. However, my mind was a mess during the process. But this was not the only thing I couldn't stop pondering. For 57 days, May was an absolute mess. When I say a mess, no one could hold a conversation with her without thinking afterward, *Woah, May is mad!* Or, *Oh my God, who did I just talk to?*

Everyone thought that May was not her normal self. Everyone thought this. Everyone. People would call me after talking to her and say, "Well, I tried to talk sense into her, but she is gone D.J., I am sorry, I tried."

I consistently thought the entire time that she was in shock! She was so far from her normal self. I wondered, Is this shock? Or is this something else? This behavior was beyond explanation. This was my reality at the time. I didn't care what was going on with her. I just wanted May, no matter what.

My personality is overly optimistic. I was always a glass-half-full kind of guy. No matter how May treated me, spoke to me, fought with me, or anything else, I never for more than an hour thought anything other than, *I will never divorce this woman*. Or *Things will get better.*

This was before being arrested. After getting arrested, my optimism was not as persistent. May leaving me and taking the kids with her along with the criminal investigation brought more clarity to my thinking than ever before. A "reality-based" person knows they are genuine and would say they are not optimistic. A pessimist knows they are a pessimist and are always looking at things with the "worst possible conclusions." Life had grabbed me, and I lost everything I loved virtually overnight, but I have never looked at things pessimistically. I had never been much of a realist, either. For me before this crisis, I was always optimistic.

May and I would have horrible fights. They were so bad I would say awful things out of anger. She would too. But after I calmed down, I was right back to being optimistic. I have concluded that for a married couple that never fights, there is something wrong. Maybe they don't really love each other. Maybe they are not attracted to each other. Maybe there's no sex life. If a couple fights, at least a little, I am convinced that they love each other. That said, they know they can live without one another. A couple that fights too much is a couple that doesn't feel like they could live without the other. They fight hard to change the other person's opinion or overall attitude, feelings, and thoughts. They fight hard because they want that person to think and feel exactly like they do-- because they know they are going to live the rest of their lives with that person. So, they think, *I am going to fight hard to make them think like me in this situation, so when something like this comes up again, we are on the same page.*"

The reality? The couple that "can't live without each other" needs the most counseling. Because if that couple can find a way not to fight, they can accomplish anything together as a team. I don't have to say where May and I fit into this category. We recognized that we needed counseling, and we needed counseling often. Someone else PLEASE tell us how to never fight again.

Someone, PLEASE help us to respect the other person's opinion and understand it is okay to "agree to disagree!" I might be completely wrong about all of this. I just know one thing. The thought of living without May HAUNTS ME! I would call her a lucky woman. Finding a man who commits his entire soul to one woman is a rare find. So, what if we fight hard? We love harder! And we make love EVEN HARDER! But what if I'm completely wrong?

After day 57, May had work to do. You can't just snap your fingers and withdraw from a protective order, and May couldn't move back in until it was removed. By law, I could have filed charges against her for violating her stupid-ass protective order. May could have pushed the issue against me as well. The only difference between her and me in our violations of the protective order was I was smart and devious about violating it. May was just flat-out clueless. If I had not loved her so much, I would have called the Sheriff's Department as soon as she arrived at my house any of the three times. Well, actually, four times. May had broken into the house one day and crawled through a window to see I had a camera set up facing directly towards that window. I thought it was funny, to be honest, and I'm not sure what she even got that day. I'm sure you're curious and wondering, *How did I violate the protective order?*

MY CALCULATED RUNNING PATH

May had to hire a new babysitter after Raven was done. She would drop the kids off at the babysitter before heading to work or pick them up after work. Kinda funny how that all worked out. This babysitter was my third cousin. I'm not sure May even knew that when she hired her. My cousin, Veronica, was a cool chick. She had the same genetics as I did. Very outgoing, talkative, and good with kids. Veronica lived a few miles from my house off a busy highway. May had to drive down this busy highway past our house to get to Veronica's house. So, you know what I did! The first week of the protective order I found out who was watching my kids. I found out she lived past May and my home. And I just so happened to take off running at the same time every single day would be running down this highway, by coincidence, at the same time May was driving down this highway to drop the kids off. If May would have ever called it in, I was just going to play dumb and say, "I have a routine, and I run down that road at the same time every single day!"

Would it have worked? I don't know, but I was willing to test it just so I could see May, even just for a glimpse each day. I thought, *May has caused enough extra damage, surely she won't have me arrested for running on a highway at the same time she drove by just so she would have to see me every day.*

Later May told me, "Ya, it worked, I had a horny and hatred feeling at the same time every day!" I told her later, "That is exactly what I was going for!"

SO CLOSE

Days 57-61 were the easiest days I had experienced during the crisis. I was convinced May was coming home. What caught me off guard was that she blocked me again. I still don't know why she blocked me then. Day 62 is among the top ten best days of my life. It would be the top five, but I have five children that I watched come out of the most beautiful woman, and of course, you probably know me by now. The best day of my life will always be the day I married May. So, let's call this the seventh best day of my life. May called, "Hey, the protective order is getting removed tomorrow.

My family is fucking pissed, so don't say anything to anyone yet. The kids and I are coming home tomorrow. Will you help me move all their stuff home tomorrow while my parents are at work?"

I responded, "May what you just said is the best news of my life besides the day you told me YES, I will marry you!"

May was still a little worried about everything, from what I could tell. I was getting my family back, I was ecstatic. What May didn't tell me was she was going to give me a surprise visit that same night on day 62. I was in my living room watching TV late at night. I was too excited to sleep. Around 11:00 p.m., May's car pulls into the driveway, and she drives around back again. I was like a little kid! I ran full sprint through the house, out the back door, and she saw me coming. I leaped down all the steps and met her as she was closing the door to her car. She had the biggest smile I had ever seen besides the day she said, "I do!" We just started kissing and holding each other. There were no words spoken for like five minutes, it was nothing but pure love and a passionate feeling with the mutual thought unspoken! I had this chair set up in the middle of the backyard. I set it up there because I would soak in the sun and do a little writing in my journal. I saw the lawn chair and said, "Let's go cuddle in the lawn chair under this beautiful sky."

The cuddling didn't last long. Next thing I knew we were naked outside making passionate love in the middle of our yard on this lawn chair. May and I had broken every single bed we ever owned. This lawn chair was no different. May started out on top. She had a little summer dress on and surprised me with no panties. She tried to dry hump me for a second until I took my hand and started rubbing her. She was dripping wet before I even touched her. She came once right away before any sex took place. I took my middle finger and slowly slid it up inside her after she came. As I gently pulled it out, simultaneously, I took that same finger and put it deep inside my mouth and let her watch me lick her taste off my finger while at the same time, she said, "I want the real thing!"

I was sitting, not laying back with her on top. We grasped each other like that for ten minutes and made continuous love with no orgasms. Holding each other tight as I licked both her breasts and gently dug my nails into her back.

I always liked to leave a hidden mark for her to remember for the days to come. My spot was always on the underside of her breast. Hidden enough that no one would see except her as she would get dressed in the mornings. Often, she would like the hickey so much in the morning I would wake up to her sucking me as a thank you for what I did for her the previous night. We made love. This night was passionate love. After about ten minutes, I lifted her up and gently laid her down on the lawn chair. I slowly continued. She had only that one orgasm, which was triggered with my hand before we started. We were slowly working her into the second orgasm. After another ten minutes, she started shaking like she had a cold chill. She said, "Oh my God! You're making my entire body quiver!"

Right when she said that, I leaned over on my left side, her right side. This was always her favorite position because I could simultaneously use my right hand. I took my index and middle finger and turned them into a vibrator on her clit as I slowly went in and out. And twenty minutes later, after her first orgasm, May let out this noise from every part of her body. I had never heard this intense noise come out of May. We had every type of sex five to six days a week. This noise I will never forget. The only way I can even describe it is to imagine you're a woman in the highest stressful situation of your life and that stress comes out of your vagina. It was so loud it echoed off the barn siding.

May said, "I'm not even embarrassed by it. The things you can do to me is why I'm here right now." When she said this, she sounded so serious.

She then said, "D.J., you should pat yourself on the back. What just happened to me is unexplainable and might never happen again like that. That was another level."

She then said, "I'll be honest, I'm done. That cured me. How do you want to cum inside your wife?" I responded, "Will you get back on top like we just were a few minutes ago?"

Without hesitation, she said, "I will do whatever you want."

Again, in a profoundly serious voice. She got on top and, at first, started going hard. I said, "No baby, I want it slow like we just did a moment ago."

She went slow, even slower than the last time. Slow up and slow down. to the top of the head of my erection and all the way down. She was enjoying just that feeling as much as I was. She grabbed my face and started French kissing me. She knew that would be the end. It felt like I came twice at one time. My orgasm was like a woman's. It lasted what felt like ten seconds. I almost passed out. I fell back on the lawn chair and said, "Oh my God, I just about went out!"

She fell on top of me as she collapsed. It was well past midnight at this point. We lay there naked, both feeling and thinking the same thing, "I love this person more than anything."

We both, at moments throughout those 62 days, had tried so hard to stop loving each other, but that was simply impossible. We tried, and we failed. We were back together. Back making love. Back raising our children together. Before she left that night, we kissed each other, standing up for another thirty minutes. It felt like we were kids. The repeated comments were, "I don't want to leave, please don't leave, I love you so much, I love you, too, baby, I can't wait to see you tomorrow," Etc., etc.

We went on like this for thirty minutes. That night on her way home, she called me, "Hey, I was just praying to God and saying thank you for bringing me back to my husband and the biggest shooting star you could ever imagine shot across the sky at the same time!"

We had each other again in this world that can be so evil. The stress was not even close to over. The hell on earth had just started, but at least we had each other.

THE END OF LONELINESS

I ended up going 63 days of waking up in a lonely house. Sixty-three days that probably took ten years off my life. Those sixty-three days of me not waking up next to May and kissing her. Sixty-three days of not saying good morning to my children. Sixty-three days of not hugging and kissing my children before I left for work or before they went to school. Those 63 days were pure hell on earth. I had the most unbelievable experiences, but the loneliness was unbearable. God is always with us in our life. During those 63 days, God sent dozens of angels to watch over me. Day 33 God gave me the ability to see something physical in the spiritual realm that I knew was there for my protection. Day 57 God brought May's soul back and reconnected it with mine. Day 62 All of May's stress was relieved from those two months. And on day 63, I had never been happier to help someone move my kids' stuff back to my house!

COUNSELOR CAM

Before day 63 came, I started to reflect on the people who helped me get to this point. 63 days of survival came with a small group of incredible people, and each one played a significant role.

My family and a few select friends. But there was this one woman who picked me up as I was falling. A few days after getting arrested, I reached out to a bunch of counselors. Of all the reviews I read, there was one counselor I wanted to meet above all the others. Her name was Dr. Cameron, and she liked to be called Cam. She was booked up for months. Initially, the office told me it would be three months before I could get in. I said, "Please tell the counselor my name is D.J. Murphy. I really need to see her as soon as possible."

Dr. Cam fit me in somehow. I arrived at her office and had a seat after filling out the paperwork. Cam opened the door and said my name. I had never met this woman and didn't know what she looked like. She carried herself with confidence and a sense of serenity.

We sat down, and she said, "Nice to meet you, D.J. My name is Cam. What would you say is the primary purpose of your visit?"

I responded, "I am in the middle of a very traumatic stage in life. I feel like I'm losing everything and everyone I love, and it has all happened so fast."

Her only response possible was, "Explain."

I explained the entire story and everything that I was going through as honestly as I could, with no sugarcoating. I typically never looked forward to telling someone the story because, for someone to fully understand, I had to tell the entire story. The short version never worked. Her response was the same as every single person I had told the story to, "Wow!"

No one else surprised me with their response except Cam. This lady was a counselor who heard every story you could imagine throughout her career. For her to say, "Wow!" meant that my story really was incredible. She proceeded to ask me questions such as, "What are you doing to relieve stress? What are you doing to stay positive? Are you relieving stress in some way and trying to stay positive?"

Her initial reaction was to make sure I didn't fall into a deep depression. I think she knew and understood that I was depressed. How could I not be? But there are levels of depression. As you fall deeper and deeper into depression, the world gets darker and darker along with your thoughts. Cam strongly encouraged me to continue running but especially to continue writing in my journal. Cam encouraged me not to worry about the situation.

We pulled in, and May was anxious. She started directing me on what to get and load into the UHAUL. We were about half done when all of a sudden, a Sheriff came flying into the driveway.

This story is as dramatic as it sounds. I started to walk out to the Sheriff, and May stopped me and said, "Let me take care of this."

Turns out her stepdad, Bobby, got a phone call from her uncle, who lived a few doors down. May's uncle called Bobby and said, "D.J. is at your house loading the kids' stuff into the UHAUL!"

Bobby called 911 and said, "D.J. Murphy is TRESPASSING ON MY PROPERTY!"

Not dramatic at all. May told the Sheriff, "No, he is not trespassing. My stepdad is wrong, the protective order has been removed."

The Sheriff said, "Can I talk to D.J.?"

The Sheriff continued and said, "Sweetie, you can keep loading your children's items so you two can get out of here."

I heard the Sheriff yell, "D.J. come over here, man!" I worked in the fire department for eleven years. I knew all these guys from vehicle wrecks, and I was usually on the Squad/Rescue truck, so we all knew each other.

I went over there and said, "What's up, man?"

He said, "You tell me, man! Jesus, what have you got yourself into!?"

I responded, "Look, man, I'm just helping my wife get our children's stuff back home. That is it!" He said, "I can tell that, but WHAT THE

FUCK DID YOU GET YOURSELF INTO!?"

I replied, "Buddy, if you only knew the truth, it would blow your mind what I have been through."

He continued, "You know that most of us Sheriff and local detectives think the entire situation is bullshit, and if any other criminal detective on the force would have done that interview, it would have gone much differently, and you wouldn't have ever been charged. That guy was out to get you or something! What did you do? Fuck his wife?"

I chuckled and said, "No, man, I have no clue what I did to that man. But you are the second Sheriff that has pretty much said the same thing."

The Sheriff continued, "This is all off the record, but I want to say what anyone was saying about me and to make sure I didn't allow my thoughts to wander off into the unknown."

I remember Dr. Cam saying, "D.J., you can't control other people's actions or decisions. People are going to say and do whatever they think is right. Even if what they are doing is wrong, you can't change them. They have to change themselves."

Cam was soft-spoken and a woman of few words. But when she spoke, I knew I needed to listen. She continued to fit me in every week. I saw her every week until May came home. I should have kept going. Over that time, I concluded that Cam was the best listener I had ever been around. She also chose her words extremely carefully. She was simply amazing as a counselor and so helpful in helping me control my thoughts. It also felt like she had my back. At one point, she said, "D.J., I have been around a lot of liars. Your version of the story is not a lie. I believe you!"

I don't know why before falling asleep on Day 62, Dr. Cam's image came to mind. Cam had once said, "D.J., I might be wrong because I have been wrong before, but I think May is going to come back to you eventually." She was right!

SHERIFFS AGAIN

Day 63 started so well and quickly became a mess! May called, "The protective order is terminated, I'm on my way to the house. We are going to go pick up a UHAUL and do this all in one quick trip."

"I can't wait to see you, May," I said.

She showed up and said, "We don't have time to mess around. As much as I would love to go inside with you and relieve some more stress, we need to get this shit done. We will celebrate when the work is finished!"

"Sounds good, babe," I replied. We drove over, picked up the UHAUL, and May followed me in our truck. Her parents lived on the same country road, on opposite ends of the county. The weird part about this was when May moved in with me into another house. Her parents also lived in a separate house, and those two houses were on the same road in another part of the county. Until May and I moved a third time, we had almost always lived on the same road as her parents, though that was never planned.

We pulled in, and May was anxious. She started directing me on what to load into the UHAUL. We were about half done, and suddenly, a Sheriff's car came flying in the driveway. This story is as dramatic as it sounds. I started to walk out to the Sheriff, and May stopped me and said, "Let me take care of this." It turns out that her stepdad, Bobby, got a phone call from her uncle, who lived a few doors down. Apparently, May's uncle called Bobby and said, "D.J. is at your house loading the kids' stuff into the UHAUL!" Bobby called 911 and said, "D.J. Murphy is TRESPASSING ON MY PROPERTY!" Not dramatic at all.

May tells the Sheriff, "No, he is not trespassing. My stepdad is wrong, the protective order has been removed." The Sheriff said, "Can I talk to D.J.?" May said, "Yes." The Sheriff continued and said, "Sweetie,

you can keep loading your children's items so you two can get out of here." I heard the Sheriff yell, "D.J. come over here, man!" I worked in the fire department for 11 years. I knew all these guys from vehicle wrecks, and I was usually on the Squad/Rescue truck, so we all knew each other. I went over and said, "What's up, man?" He said,

"You tell me, man! Jesus, what have you got yourself into!?"

I responded, "Look, man, I'm just helping my wife get our children's stuff back home. That is it!"

He said, "I can tell that, but "WHAT THE FUCK DID YOU GET YOURSELF INTO!?"

I replied, "Buddy, if you only knew the truth, it would blow your mind what I have been through."

He continued, "You know that most of us Sheriff and local detectives think the entire situation is bullshit, and if any other criminal detective on the force would have done that interview, it would have gone much differently, and you would not have ever been charged. That guy was out to get you or something! What did you do? Fuck his wife?"

I chuckled and said, "No, man, I have no clue what I did to that man. But you are the second Sheriff that has pretty much said the exact same thing."

The Sheriff continued, "This is all off the record, but I want to say that there are a lot of guys that are praying for you and hope you come out of this decently." I replied, "Thanks, man. I miss all you guys."

He said a few last words that stuck with me forever, "There are a lot of guys that are praying for you and hope you come out of this decently."

I replied, "Thanks, man."

He said, "Look, man, why don't you walk down to that gas station and hang out and wait until your wife is done loading the UHAUL. I'll deal with whoever this stepdad is who seems to hate you for no reason. And one more thing, no one in the department likes that bastard that charged you. He's a young, arrogant prick who has something up his sleeve for you. He's over the line in what he's doing to you, and unfortunately, you must deal with it. Now get out of here before this Bobby guy gets here."

I took off walking down the road. It was about a half-mile walk to the gas station. I got there and sat there for an hour, waiting for May to finish packing the UHAUL. I had been sitting there for about ten minutes, and May's uncle and stepdad, Bobby, decided to drive down to the gas station. I was sitting on the bench outside. They knew I could do no sort of fighting or anything due to the current criminal charges I was already dealing with. I'm not certain May's uncle wanted anything to do with this, though he was the one driving the truck that pulled into the gas station.

He probably regretted even calling Bobby at all. Bobby was dramatic when anything in his life didn't go perfectly. He and May had some similarities in this regard. The difference? May was a female. This guy acted like a female in this situation. They pulled into the gas station and drove oh so slowly past me with the window down. Bobby's upper half of his body was sticking half out the truck window on the passenger side closest to me from where I was sitting. May's uncle was driving. As they slowly drove by me, they didn't say a word. Not a peep. It was the lamest version of intimidation I had ever witnessed. Shortly after the Sheriff noticed they were heading that way, he followed them over to make sure they didn't shoot me or do something crazy. All I could think at the time was, *I'm the crazy one?*

The Sheriff pulls in as they are pulling out. The Sheriff pulled up next to me and said, "Did they say anything? Because I told them to leave you alone!"

I replied, "No, they didn't."

The Sheriff continued, "I told them that if they were not going to let you help load all this furniture, they needed to be the ones to help that lady of yours."

I responded, "I bet they didn't start helping, did they?"

The Sheriff's last words to me were, "Nope, and it kinda pissed me off that they were making her do all that by herself. Take care, D.J.. They're going to leave you alone. I wish you the best."

"Thank you!" I said.

At that, the Sheriff drove off, and I waited another thirty minutes for May to get done. Absurdly she had to load the entire UHAUL by herself. May finished and picked me up. We drove the

UHAUL home and unloaded her and the kids' stuff. My family was home!

My kids had never been so happy! Especially Abraham. A father and son bond is unlike any other. That bond is ten times for a boy when all he has for siblings are sisters. Abraham started making comments like, "I don't ever want to be away from Daddy again!" And, "Daddy, I never want you to go to work ever again!"

"Mommy, don't ever make me go back to that house without Daddy ever again!" A 3-year-old should never be worrying about things like this. It got to May. We had no idea how we were going to survive the following months, but I made a promise to all my kids, "Daddy will make up all the time missed with you, times ten!"

I was determined to spend as much time with the kids as possible. It was the beginning of October.

May and I were back together. However, the hell never stopped. YOU CALL THIS FAMILY?

May's family didn't help the cause. Come to think of it, May's family made the situation so much harder on our marriage. Most of them hated me, and it continued for years to come. This had a dramatic effect on May and a dramatic effect on our marriage. May felt like she had just given up her entire family for me. She did, and it should never have been like this. Her family should have acted like family. Thou Shall Not Judge! Clearly, they were never taught this. They didn't just judge

313

me. They judged us. They judged our lives together. They even judged each other. They hated our marriage, and they especially hated me. May and I thought eventually they would get over it. They never did. It was never the same after that. May's mom did an awful job raising her children not to judge others. She's always quick to speak about Jesus, though, and how one should act! She needed to look under her roof many years ago when she was raising her children. They talk behind each other's backs. They can't stand each other half the time. And May's mom just says, "May, I'm just trying to keep the peace here, okay?"

Years later, one of my daughters said, "Dad can I tell you a secret that you will never tell anyone?" She was young when she said this.

"Ya, baby, what is up?" "You promise!?" She spoke.

"Yes, baby, what is up?" She continued,

"All of us but Demi (our oldest daughter) act like Grandma Jane is our favorite, but she's not. Not even close." I secretly thought, *Oh shit, I didn't expect this statement*!

I replied, "Well, baby, kids your age like grandmas differently, depending on the day."

This daughter continued, "NO DAD! I'm serious. She's not and won't ever be anything close to our favorite!"

I thought to myself, "WOW! Alrighty then!"

I replied again and said, "You should love everyone, okay?"

She finished, "Okay, dad! But this won't change." Come to think of it, I have gone above and beyond to show this woman respect, love, and help care in any way I can since I met her. Yet, when shit hits the fan, I become her worst enemy! My baby girl was right. She and the others besides Demi saw through May's mom. I did, too, after all this drama. Jane was the type to have heart-to-heart conversations with me about how proud she was that May and I survived and kept our marriage strong, then turn around and tell May to divorce me if that would make her happy!

Before this situation, I loved May's family. I never judged any of them. I told both her brothers, her mom, her stepdad, her uncles and aunts, her grandmas, ALL of them that I loved them. From the time I knew I was going to marry May, I knew I was marrying into her family. I embraced all of them. I spent the holidays with them. I went on trips with them. I had hobbies with them. My door was never locked, they could pop in and out of our house at any time, and they did without knocking. I started to tell them all whenever we would leave events, "Love you!"

They initially looked at me like, "Who is this guy?" All these words of love almost bothered them. I never stopped saying it, and I still, to this day, love them so much, even through all their judgments. I want them in my life. I am extremely forgiving, God just made me that way. Even May's step-

315

dad, Bobby, I respected and loved after he called 911 on me. Even though May's mom never once called me during my life turmoil, and I had considered her like a second mom, I still respected and loved her the best I could. Life is short. We all need to love a little more, judge a little less, and FORGIVE! The problem is, they don't even know what they are forgiving me for. They all still believe what the news wrote and spoke.

LOVE YOU MAN!

I never forgot a moment that occurred right before everything happened with May's oldest brother Richard. Richard was a hard nut to crack. I don't think he ever really liked me much. Not sure why, I just always felt like he didn't care for me much. He probably envisioned May's husband as some rich fuck with porn stuffed underneath his bed. For him, this would have been better! May wouldn't have to worry about money this way. Richard prioritizes money in his life above most other things. I never judged him for being this way. I just wanted to have a good relationship with him and show him I loved him, which I did.

Just before everything happened, May and I had a big party at the house. It was for our youngest daughter's baptism. Baptisms for all my children were one of the biggest days of my life. My child became a "Child of God!" It was always a big deal to me. After baptisms, I would host a celebration party! It was our first big party at the new farm-

316

house that I had just finished remodeling. Though it was a much smaller house that her brother Richard thought was too small for five kids, after seeing the remodeling and the property, he started to see my long-term vision of the house and property. We were outside playing KanJam. I loved this game. Richard and I had different partners, so we were standing next to each other. We had the best conversations we had ever had in ten years of knowing each other. We were both surprised at how well we got along and how easily our conversation flowed that day. May's younger brother and I always clicked, and I think that may have bothered Richard. For ten years, I would occasionally say to Richard as we were leaving a family function or party and say, "Love you, bro!"

I am a hugger; I am a lover. I always expressed these feelings. The opposite of Richard. At the end of this party, Richard was about to leave, and I hugged him and said, "Love you, man!"

For the first time in ten years of me saying this, Richard replied, "Love you too, bro!" It shocked me! I was joyful that day for not only the baptism but Richard's words. It was a glorious unfolding day!

LOVE EVERYONE

I treasured these moments in life! I tried to live with love. I tried to love everyone. I tried to make everyone happy and feel welcome. That included everyone. Even my enemies, I would talk to and be respectful. I didn't have too many enemies I knew about before everything happened, but I would talk to and respect the few I had. Living your life loving others makes life better. It brings joy in unexpected times. But no matter how nice you are. No matter how much you respect people. No matter how much you love others. When the shit hits the fan, you can quickly become enemy #1. I was everyone's enemy except for a select few after I was arrested. Everyone was quick to judge. Everyone believed everything that was written and broadcast. Everyone hated me. I went from everyone loving me or thinking, *He's a good family man!* to *He's a horrible person that everyone despise!*. Though the years have passed, this situation seems like it will never leave me. Yet, I still pray for them. I still try to love everyone. I still show respect. I never changed who I was, a loving person. Unfortunately, it only takes one person to ruin your life, or at least attempt to ruin your life.

ONE WITNESS

One of my favorite Old Testament books in the Bible is Deuteronomy, written by the great man Moses himself, relaying messages directly from God! God's words given to Moses were carefully placed within the Bible so perfectly! Moses was speaking to the Israelites and giving them orders from God about true and false profits. He was giving them direct orders from God, such as not worshiping false gods, don't ever engage in witchcraft such as speaking to psychics or mediums, and God gave plenty of other advice including the Ten Commandments. Moses went on to speak about concerns for JUSTICE! This one bible verse caught my attention, and it is the most relevant bible verse to my story that put me through hell on earth. Deuteronomy Chapter 19, verse 15: "You must not convict anyone of a crime on the testimony of only ONE witness!" My life was destroyed based on the testimony of one witness who knows her truth, and the stories printed were so far from the truth and the full story.

HOPE

All this said, I dug myself out of the grave everyone put me in. I kept my head above water. I prayed hard and gave tremendous effort to keep myself sane and my family together. And through it all, I continued to love others and pray for my enemies. I viewed this trial in life as a blessing. God wanted more from me. God had special plans for me. God knew I was strong enough to withstand the awful attacks of the devil. I survived all of them. Little did I know there was so much more to come. The tragedies in my life and the trials were only beginning. I would often say, "God! Why is this happening to me?"

I didn't understand then, but I do now! I can write and tell my story. A story many thought I would never make out of alive and well. I am alive! I am well! I have spiritual strength I never thought I could obtain. The saying goes, "All good things come to an end!" I always thought, *Those people haven't met May and me!* Was our love to always remain good? We had five children relying on mommy and daddy to make it! I can say for myself that I will always love May and I will never stop praying for her! Finally, I will never give up on this beautiful word called HOPE!